The
BELL TOLLS
for NO ONE

T0272988

The BELL TOLLS for NO ONE

STORIES BY
CHARLES BUKOWSKI
EDITED WITH AN INTRODUCTION BY DAVID STEPHEN CALONNE

City Lights Books | San Francisco

Library of Congress Cataloging-in-Publication Data
Bukowski, Charles.
 [Short stories. Selections]
 Bell tolls for no one : stories / by Charles Bukowski ; edited
with an introduction by David Stephen Calonne.
    pages ; cm
 ISBN 978-0-87286-682-9 (paperback)
 ISBN 978-0-87286-684-3 (e-book)
 I. Title.

 PS3552.U4A6 2015
 813'.54—dc23

                        2015014714

City Lights Books are published at the City Lights Bookstore
261 Columbus Avenue, San Francisco, CA 94133
www.citylights.com

INTRODUCTION
Charles Bukowski's Graphic and Pulp Fiction
David Stephen Calonne

Charles Bukowski was devoted to "graphic fiction" from the beginning of his career: one of his earliest works, "The Reason Behind Reason," published in 1946 in *Matrix*, is adorned with a lively drawing depicting the anti-hero Chelaski with legs flying, arms outstretched comically attempting to catch a flying baseball.[1] During his years crisscrossing America between 1942 and 1947—a period in which he sometimes had to pawn his typewriter due to lack of funds—Bukowski also submitted to Whit Burnett, editor of the celebrated *Story* magazine, a series of hand-printed, illustrated short stories, including "A Kind, Understanding Face," demonstrating that he often conceptualized text and image together in a complementary relationship. He wrote Burnett from Los Angeles in November 1948: "I thought the drawings came out especially well in this one and I hope you do not lose it."[2] Burnett urged Bukowski to collect his drawings in book form and also repeatedly asked him to consider writing a novel. On October 9, 1946, from Philadelphia, Bukowski also composed an illustrated letter to Caresse Crosby, publisher of *Portfolio*. Already he had developed the clean line style of his charming, minimalist, Thurberesque drawings which could not but ingratiate him to prospective famous editors such as Crosby and Burnett. Here a stunned man with a bottle and lines for eyes drinks, smokes, and lies in bed with bare lightbulb, curtain with a drawstring, bottles on the floor. Later he would add sun, flying birds, companionable dogs. Psychologically, it is clear that these gently humorous drawings were one of the ways he had developed to deal with his considerable childhood wounds: his physical abuse by his father, the eruption of *acne vulgaris*, his status as misfit German-American. Here was a medium in which he could play and entertain, qualities he also strove for in his writing.

The autobiographical "A Kind, Understanding Face"

(1948) begins with an epigraph describing a crippled spider being dismembered alive by ants and sets the theme for many later stories: Nature red in tooth and claw. The protagonist, Ralph, like the young Bukowski, avoids the draft, has journalistic ambitions, and wanders the country from Miami to New York to Atlanta. Though Ralph is in some respects a stand-in for the author, in the story his father and then his mother are deceased, while Bukowski's mother Katherine died in 1956 and his father Henry in 1958. The tale presents a series of odd, disjunctive events, concluding with three mysterious quotations, appended without citations: one from Rabelais's *Gargantua and Pantagruel*, Book Five, Chapter 30, "Our Visit to Satinland"; another from George Santayana's "Ultimate Religion" (1933); and finally a reference to René Warcollier (1881–1962), the French chemical engineer who developed a method of making precious stones synthetically and who also published *Experiments in Telepathy* (1938).[3] Given that there is a reference to copulating and defecating in public, it's possible that Bukowski by this time had also encountered the writings of Diogenes the Cynic (ca. 412 CE–323 CE). Just as the narrative itself is weirdly dissociative, these three allusions left in the suicide note of young Ralph seem a kind of fragmentary riddle or hidden message which the reader is meant to assemble and decode: What, if any, is the connection between Diogenes, that odd manticore, the lofty language of Santayana, and the making of jewels from fish scales? One recalls Vladimir Nabokov: "Human life is but a series of footnotes to a vast obscure unfinished masterpiece." The range of these rather recherché allusions indicates the depth of Bukowski's reading, and placing them one after another may suggest the absurdity of the quest for meaning as well as the indecipherability of an obscure unfinished life.

From the beginning of his career, Bukowski depicted the terrible human encounter with the Other: insects (here spiders and ants) in particular pullulate through many of his early poems and stories. His work also shows the influence of Robinson Jeffers's hawks and herons as well as D.H. Lawrence, whose *Birds, Beasts and Flowers* can be heard echoing in the title of Bukowski's first book of poems, *Flower, Fist and Bestial Wail*. Mockingbirds, wild horses, and dogs appear in three other poetry titles. In the stories in this volume, there is a frightening encounter with a hog, while another tale set in Bolivia depicts a man, a woman, and a monkey engaging in a bizarre psychological battle, a theme Bukowski would return in his late story "The Invader" (1986).[4] And in "The Bell Tolls for No One," the narrative draws to a close on an awesome note: "Then in front of me there was an animal. It looked like a large dog, a wild dog. The moon was to my back and it shone into the beast's eyes. The eyes were red like burning coal."

In the same issue of *Matrix* as "The Reason Behind Reason," Bukowski's poem "Soft and Fat Like Summer Roses" appeared, recounting a love triangle involving a waitress, her husband, and her Greek lover; this suggests Bukowski most likely had read James M. Cain's *The Postman Always Rings Twice* (1934), in which the plot is very similar, though the restaurant owner is Greek and the other man steals his wife. Cain famously shaped the style of Albert Camus's *L'Etranger*—the French existentialists owed a debt to the cool, tough American private eyes—and Bukowski also acknowledged Cain's style as a significant influence on his own work.[5] Like Cain, Bukowski often takes a detached, clinical view of crime, and Los Angeles *noir* would be the style of his many "hardboiled" crime stories, culminating in his homage to the genre, his final novel, *Pulp* (1994).[6] When Irene in one of our tales tells the Bukowski-character that he is the "greatest thing since Hemingway," he responds: "I'm closer to Thurber mixed with Mickey Spillane": the hero of *Pulp* is tellingly named "Nick Belane," obviously echoing "Mickey Spillane." Of course, Bukowski's gift for dialogue, monosyllabic Anglo-Saxon vocabulary, and skeletal, pared-down prose derives from Hemingway, supplemented with elements he often said he found lacking in Hemingway: humor, as well as liberal doses of slang, swearing, scatology, and obscenity. The title "The Bell Tolls for No One" is an obvious reference to Hemingway's novel *For Whom the Bell Tolls*, while in another story a pornographer husband and his wife carry on a humorous dialogue about Hemingway.

Bukowski often returned nostalgically to the legendary outlaws of the 1930s, and in the poem "the lady in red" recalled: "the best time of all / was when John Dillinger escaped from jail, and one of the / saddest times of all was when the Lady in Red fingered him and / he was gunned down coming out of that movie. / Pretty Boy Floyd, Baby Face Nelson, Machine Gun Kelly, Ma / Barker, Alvin Karpis, we loved them all."[7] For Bukowski, as for a writer in every way his opposite, William S. Burroughs (one of whose favorite books was Jack Black's 1926 autobiography chronicling his adventures in the underworld, *You Can't Win*), the American power structure was criminal at its very core and found its mirror image in the violent figures who struggled against it.[8] Cain, Spillane, Dashiell Hammett, and Raymond Chandler depicted a hard, amoral universe that shows no mercy and provided Bukowski a tradition within which to dramatize his mythicized autobiography. His 1947 meeting with Jane Cooney Baker at the Glenwood Bar on Alvarado Street becomes a tale endlessly told and retold, shaped and refined. In a 1967 story for *Open City* he declares that Jane "had delicious legs and a tight little gash and a face of powdered pain. And she knew me. She taught me more than the philosophy books of the ages"—casting Jane in the *film noir* role of *femme fatale*. And the violence of this broken world is continual. Wallace Fowlie once wrote about Henry Miller: "I believe the quality which first attracted me in Mr. Miller's writings was his violence. Not the violence of the things said, but the violence of the way in which they were said. The violence of feeling has become in his work the violence of style which has welded together all of his disparate passions and dispersed experiences into the one experience of language."[9] Similarly, Bukowski evolved his own original finely modulated "language" to portray a modern world in which the redemptive power of love was under continual threat.

"Nothing is true, everything is permitted" was a phrase of Hassan-i Sabbah (ca. 1050 CE–1124 CE), the Ismaili founder of the *Hashshashin*, repeated like a mantra by William Burroughs. In *The Brothers Karamazov*, Dostoevsky proclaims: "If God does not exist, then everything is permitted," and Karamazov is cited in "A Dirty Trick on God." Another Bukowski favorite, Friedrich Nietzsche, declared in *The Genealogy of Morals*:

> When the Christian crusaders in the Orient encountered the invincible order of the Assassins, that order of free spirits par excellence, whose lowest ranks followed a rule of obedience the like of which no order of monks ever attained, they obtained in some way or other a hint concerning that symbol and watchword reserved for the highest ranks alone as their secretum; "Nothing is true, everything is permitted." Very well, that was freedom of spirit; in that way the faith in truth itself was abrogated. Has any European, any Christian free spirit ever strayed into this proposition and into its labyrinthine consequences? Has any of them ever known the Minotaur of this cave from experience?—I doubt it.[10]

"The labyrinthine consequences" of such a philosophy become the subject matter of Bukowski's repeated portrayals of his characters' encounters with the Minotaur of the cave of unrelenting chaos. Crime becomes a metaphor for an unjust universe in which reward and punishment often seem unrelated to virtue: The unyielding, brutal, and powerful "Break In" contains an explicit speech on the unfairness of society, and in Bukowski the narrator often observes the occurrences helplessly, without commentary. He is at once quasi-participant and observer.

Yet these stories also demonstrate Bukowski's wide range; he can be witty, casual, intimate, and ingratiating, and he tries his hand at a variety of genres: science fiction, a send-up of Westerns, stories of jockeys and football players. While he is devoted to chronicling the *Sturm und Drang* of his private, emotional life, the political and social upheavals of the mid to late sixties are frequently portrayed, as in "Save the World," which depicts his relationship with his partner Frances Smith. Although he pokes fun at Frances's devotion to liberal causes, Bukowski had met—and liked—Dorothy Healey, giving her inscribed copies of *Cold Dogs in the Courtyard* and *Crucifix in a Deathhand*. He wrote Will Inman, editor of *Kauri*: "Dorothy Healey, spokeswoman for the Communist Party, came to visit me. I was honored. I have no politics, but I was, nevertheless, honored."[11] One tale imagines an apocalyptic 1968 presidential victory of George Wallace and his vice-presidential choice, the Air Force general Curtis Le May; others make incisive comments on the return of American POWs following the end of the Vietnam War and allude to Bukowski's own questioning by the F.B.I. during the period he was under investigation for his supposedly incendiary writings for the underground press.

The political ferment of the period—from approximately 1967 to 1973—corresponds exactly with one of Bukowski's most brilliant and prolific phases. One might argue that the eruption of Dionysian sexual energy was directly related to the anti-war stance of the time: Make love not war. The gradual loosening of censorship restrictions allowed writers and artists new freedom for self-expression. Centered in San Francisco's Haight-Ashbury district, the "comix underground" had taken off with the appearance of the famous *Zap #1* in 1968.[12] Bukowski himself continued to draw and paint prolifically and would ultimately get to know personally or have professional association with the three major figures of underground comics: Robert Crumb, Spain Rodriguez, and S. Clay Wilson.[13] An admirer of Bukowski's writing, Robert Crumb demonstrated his genius at capturing its German Expressionist tragicomic essence in his illustrations for *Bring Me Your Love, There's No Business*, and *The Captain is Out to Lunch and the Sailors Have Taken Over the Ship*.[14] Bukowski himself now began to draw cartoons for his stories in *Open City* and the *Los Angeles Free Press*. He also created several stand-alone comic strips such as "Dear Mr. Bukowski"—a hilarious account of a more-than-usually crazy day in his life—which appeared in the

June 27, 1975, issue of the *Free Press* and was then printed as a silkscreen set of fifty signed copies in 1979, as well as a series titled "The Adventures of Clarence Hiram Sweetmeat," which appeared in the October 24, 1974, and September 19, 1975, issues. The installment that appeared in the October 3, 1975, *Free Press* was published in 1986 in book form as *The Day It Snowed in L.A.*

Just as Burnett had in the forties, John Martin—who had begun publishing broadsides of Bukowski's poetry in 1966—urged Bukowski to write a novel. He worked on a manuscript titled *The Way the Dead Love* that was never completed, but several chapters were published in magazines.[15] One chapter, which appeared in *Congress* (1967), vividly described some sexual hijinks involving "Hank" (Bukowski), "Lou," and a young lady in a cellar, and demonstrates Bukowski's newfound, jaunty, erotic style. In the early 1970s, it now seemed natural for him to begin writing for the men's magazines in order to supplement his income. Four stories in this volume—"The Looney Ward," "Dancing Nina," "No Quickies, Remember," and "A Piece of Cheese"—were submitted to *Fling*, published by Arv Miller in Chicago. Bukowski created the title "Hairy Fist Tales" as the rubric for the series, and the phrase likely derived from a poem he had published in the *Grande Ronde Review* 6 in 1966, "the hairy, hairy fist, and love will die," a fierce and frightening description of total spiritual defeat: "your soul / filled with / mud and bats and curses, and the hammers will / go in / there will be hairy / hairy / fists and / love will / die."[16] These tales, however, are lighthearted and rambunctious. Bukowski had read Boccaccio, and the *fabliau* technique of folk-story telling familiar from Chaucer can be seen as well in "No Quickies, Remember" in which, as in a joke, the same story is repeated several times, leading to a surprise ending.

Bukowski began writing a series of stories about the women he met during the period 1970–1976 which would ultimately take shape as the novel *Women*, and the *Los Angeles Free Press* began serializing them in the February 13–19, 1976, issue with an editor's note calling the sequence a "novel-in-progress" under the title *Love Tale of a Hyena.* (The title was kept for the German edition of the novel: *Das Liebesleben der Hyaene.*)[17] His relationship with Linda King is portrayed. Liza Williams appears in several; at one of her parties, Bukowski describes meeting Robert Crumb (but declines the invitation to meet the editor of *The Realist*, Paul Krassner). Writing and women form a constant counterpoint in his stories. He plunges into the cauldron of love, passion, sex, attempting to heal the wounds of his past, attempting to find in romantic love a salve for the demons that try him. Yet he can only momentarily find such redemption, and returns to his self, and gains distance from his solitude by crafting the experiences into narrative. His life exists mainly to be transcribed and transformed into words. He goes to Arizona, describing himself writing, and immediately refers to Gertrude Stein and Hemingway, weaving in his encounters with women and children and the life immediately taking place around him at the moment. Sex is a matter of occasional ecstasy and frequent laughter; love is a matter of life and death: He gives us both, in alternation. The stories also exemplify the gender wars of the period, during which women's liberation had begun. Bukowski typically reverses the situation to show how the "politically correct" stance can be easily turned on its head. He also, however, satirizes men, and shows the absurdity of the whole romantic love complex. Pathos, farce, tragedy: Often, humor saves the situation. He is able to defuse the pain by poking gentle fun at the entire absurdity of love relationships. Massage parlors, a pornographer engaging in late-night discussions with his wife, adult bookshops, older women picking up younger men: The entire panoply of the fading sexual revolution is held up to satire and ridicule.

Bukowski's shift to becoming a "professional writer" in 1970 in some ways altered his method of composition. He had always reshaped the same material into poem and story, but now he was devoting his time to writing novels as well as submitting to the adult magazines. Several of the stories included in this volume demonstrate how he worked and reworked this material. He creates the same narrative anew; he doesn't copy, but starts over. He is always telling his autobiography but selecting different details, reinventing instead of rewriting. For example, "An Affair of Very Little Importance" about Mercedes exists in another version in *Women*, but the narrative and emphasis are different. And the story "I Just Write Poetry So I Can Go to Bed with Girls," for example, also exists as the "Dirty Old Man" installment included here: It keeps some of the plot, but takes a completely different approach to the meeting with Gregory Corso.[18] It is typical of Bukowski's method of selecting episodes from his life and reworking them, adding specific details and usually elaborating on reality by adding invented plot elements. He is constantly engaged in telling and retelling his life, giving it the structure of myth so that the two become inseparable. The basic structure of his life is mythic, a variation on the hero's journey, the genius as hero: his abandoned childhood, primal wounding by his father, and his skin disfiguration, his wanderings in the wilderness, his near-death by alcoholism in 1954, and his resurrection.[19]

These stories from 1948–1985 demonstrate Bukowski's growth as a writer of short fiction. He gradually hones his craft and learns how to combine the tragic and comic modes effortlessly. In his late phase, Bukowski had mastered his style to the point of making the laconic, finely modulated prose we see in "The Bell Tolls for No One." The mood is swiftly established, and not a word is wasted. His goal in his fiction was to entertain, yet he was driven to explore the dark places, the Nietzschean cave with the monstrous Minotaur. As he once said: "I can't name it. It's just there. The thing is there. I have to go see it. The monster, the god, the rat, the snail. Whatever's out there I have to go see it and look at it and endure it and maybe not endure it but it's needed. That's all. I really can't explain it."[20] The unspeakable, monstrous, inscrutably violent and tender mystery at the heart of existence will not leave him in peace.

INTRODUCTION NOTES

1. "The Reason Behind Reason," *Matrix*, vol. 9, no. 2, Summer 1946 in *Absence of the Hero*, ed. David Stephen Calonne (San Francisco: City Lights, 2010).
2. Charles Bukowski letter to Whit Burnett, Box 19, Folder 13; Princeton University Library.
3. François Rabelais, *Gargantua and Pantagruel*, p. 677; "Ultimate Religion," in *The Essential Santayana*, ed. Martin A. Coleman (Bloomington: University of Indiana Press, 2009), p. 344.
4. *Absence of the Hero*, pp. 255–270.
5. See David Stephen Calonne, *Charles Bukowski* (London: Reaktion Books, 2012), pp. 31–32; also see footnote 8, p. 185).
6. See Erin A. Smith, "Pulp Sensations" in David Glover and Scott McCracken, *The Cambridge Companion to Popular Fiction* (Cambridge University Press, 2012); on Bukowski and *Pulp*, see Calonne, *Charles Bukowski*, pp. 171–173; Paula Rabinowitz, *American Pulp: How Paperbacks Brought Modernism to Main Street* (Princeton University Press, 2014), pp. 296–297.
7. Charles Bukowski, "the lady in red," in *Dangling in the Tournefortia* (Santa Barbara, CA: Black Sparrow Press, 1981), p. 13.
8. Jack Black, *You Can't Win*, Introduction by William S. Burroughs (Edinburgh: AK Press/Nabat, 2000).
9. Wallace Fowlie, "Shadow of Doom," in *The Happy Rock: A Book About Henry Miller* (Berkeley, CA: Bern Porter, 1945), p. 102.
10. Friedrich Nietzsche, *On the Genealogy of Morals; Ecce Homo*, trans. Walter Kaufmann (New York: Vintage Books, 1967), p. 150.
11. *Kauri* 15, July-August 1966, p. 4; on Healey, also see "Eyes Like the Sky" in Bukowski, *Tales of Ordinary Madness* (San Francisco: City Lights, 1983), pp. 175–180.
12. Hillary Chute, "Graphic Narrative," in Joe Bray, Alison Gibbons, and Brian McHale, eds., *The Routledge Companion to Experimental Literature* (London and New York: Routledge, 2012), p. 410. Also see Patrick Rosenkranz, *Rebel Visions: The Underground Comix Revolution, 1963–1975* (Seattle: Fantagraphic Books, 2002).
13. For reproductions of Wilson's illustrations of Bukowski stories, see Patrick Rosenkranz, *Demons and Angels: The Mythology of S. Clay Wilson, Volume 2* (Seattle: Fantagraphic Books, 2015).
14. Crumb remarked about Bukowski: "I like his ironic humor and his alienated attitude about the world in general. He expresses that in very succinct and eloquent terms." See D.K. Holm, ed., *R.*

Crumb, Conversations (Jackson: University of Mississippi Press, 2004), p. 208.

15. On *The Way the Dead Love*, see Abel Debritto, *Charles Bukowski, King of the Underground: From Obscurity to Literary Icon* (New York: Palgrave MacMillan, 2013), pp. 127, 135–6.

16. The poem may be found in *Pacific Northwestern Spiritual Poetry*, ed. Charles Potts (Walla Walla: Tsunami Inc., 1998), pp. 48–51.

17. *Los Angeles Free Press*, Feb 13–19, 1976, p. 20.

18. See *Absence of the Hero*, pp. 99–111.

19. David Stephen Calonne, "Bukowski and the Romantic Conception of Genius," *Jahrbuch der Charles-Bukowski-Gesellschaft 2011/12/13*, pp. 217–218.

20. *The Charles Bukowski Tapes*, DVD, directed by Barbet Schroeder (Detroit, MI: Barrel Entertainment, 2006).

The
BELL TOLLS
for NO ONE

A Kind, Understanding Face

The parents died younger than it is usual to die, the father first, the mother soon afterward. He didn't attend the father's funeral but he was at the last one. Some of the neighbors remembered him as a boy and had thought him a "nice child." Others only remembered him grown, on sporadic one or two week stays at the house. He was always in some far off city, Miami, New York, Atlanta, and the mother said he was a journalist and when the war came without his becoming a soldier, she explained a heart condition. The mother died in 1947 and he, Ralph, entered the house and became a part of the neighborhood.

He became the victim of scrutiny, for the neighborhood was decently average, home-owned, home-lived rather than rented so that one was more aware of the permanence of things. Ralph seemed older than he should have been, so quite worn. At times, though, in favorable shades of light he was almost beautiful, and the left lower eyelid would sometimes twitch behind an almost gaudily lit eye. He spoke little and when he did he seemed to be joking, and then he would walk off, either too fast briskly, or he would slouch-swagger off, hands in pockets and flat-footed. Mrs. Meers said he had a "kind, understanding face." Others thought he sneered.

The house had been well cared for—the shrubbery, the lawns and the interior. The car disappeared, and soon in the backyard were three kittens and two puppies. Mrs. Meers, who lived next door, noticed that Ralph spent much time in the garage breaking the spider webs with a broom. Once she saw him give a crippled spider to the ants and watch them cut it to pieces alive. This, beyond one incident, gave vent to the most early conversations. The other: coming down the hill he had met Mrs. Langley and had said, "Until people learn to excrete and copulate in public they will be neither decently savage nor comfortably modern." Ralph had been intoxicated and it was understood that he was grieving. Also, he seemed to give more time to the kittens than the puppies, almost teasingly so, and this, of course, was strange.

He continued to grieve. The lawns and shrubs began to yellow. He had visitors, they kept late hours and were sometimes seen in the mornings. There were women, stout, heavy-laughing women; women too thin, shabby women, old women, women with English accents, women whose every other word referred to the bathroom or the bed. Soon there were people day and night. Sometimes Ralph was not to be seen for days. Somebody put a duck in the backyard. Mrs. Meers took to feeding the pets and one evening Mr. Meers, in an anger, attached his hose to Ralph's faucets and gave the place a good soaking down. He wasn't stopped, wasn't even noticed, except by "a thin, terrible-looking man" who came out of the screen door with a cigar in his mouth, walked past Mr. Meers, opened the incinerator, looked into it, closed it, walked past Mr. Meers and back into the house.

Sometimes at night the men fought in the backyard and once Mrs. Roberts (on the other side) called the police, but by the time they arrived everybody was in the house again. The police went into the house and remained some time. When they made their exit they were alone.

It began to be almost too much when suddenly the neighbors noticed that the people were gone. The duck was gone too. It began to be quiet nights. In the days there was only one woman, thin-faced, with an English accent and rather snobbish, though cleanly dressed and younger than the others had been. Ralph was seen coming home with library books and then leaving every morning at 7:15 A.M. in overalls. He began to look better, though Mrs. Meers smelled whiskey on the woman the few times she spoke to her. Ralph began to water and trim the yard. The left lower eyelid was improved. He spoke more. "People are good. Everybody's good. I hope we can be good friends," he spoke to Mrs. Roberts. "I guess I've been a kid most of my life. I guess I'm just growing up. And don't mind Lila. She's . . . she's really . . . " He didn't finish. He just smiled and waved a hand and turned the hose onto a bush.

Sometimes on weekends they saw him intoxicated, and her, of course; but he always made work and was very kind, really a good-natured person. "If she could only be like Ralph. Oh, I know he takes a drink! But he's a brilliant boy—and that job, you know! He is so nice. But I guess he needs her."

"Once she saw him give a crippled spider to the ants and watch them cut it to pieces alive."

He must have needed them too. They started coming back, first a few, and then the rest. The woman, Lila, seemed to dislike it most. She was in a fury but Ralph just laughed. Then the duck came. When the duck came Lila went into silence. The kittens and puppies were almost full-grown and the poor duck, once master, had its troubles. The "thin, terrible-looking man who went to the incinerator" was seen building a pen and thereafter the penned duck was understood by the neighbors to belong to the "thin, terrible-looking man who went to the incinerator."

One of the dogs died. They bought a piano and played it almost continually, day and night, for a week then left it alone. They buried the dog behind the garage, setting up a cross in the neck of a whiskey bottle half sunken in the soil. But they had buried the hound shallow and it set up an odor. One night a husky woman invaded the grave and burned the remains in the incinerator, cussing loudly and violently, laughing and then vomiting and crying. "It's not death that aches us, it's the getting older, older . . . wrinkled hands, wrinkled face . . . Christ, even my keester's wrinkled! Christ, Christ, old age: I hate it, hate it!"

They evidently sold the refrigerator. Everybody tried to help the moving van men get it into the truck. There was much laughing. The piano went too. It was understood that Lila had tried a suicide and failed. For several days she was very drunk, dressed in an extremely short skirt and four inch spiked heels. She spoke to everybody, even the neighbors.

Some of the crowd thinned out. It was understood that Ralph was charging rent. He was getting thinner and quieter. He bought some seed and planted a lawn, fencing off the new soil with stakes and string. He was seen leaving early every morning in his suit, and several weeks later he was leaving at 7:15 A.M. in his overalls. The crowd remained, though, but weren't quite as noisy. In a fashion, the neighborhood had accepted the house. The lawn came up fine, and it wasn't unusual to see Ralph, in the evenings, speaking to Mr. Meers as they worked about the yards. The other inhabitants seemed to have a certain disdain and central fancy in mind, but Ralph was nice, even on the weekends when he did take a drink. He was just too easy-going putting up with those people; and you could see, he did care much for Lila.

The piano came back. The refrigerator came back. Lila began to wash Ralph's clothing, though Mrs. Meers still smelled whiskey when she spoke to her. Lila had something though. She was really an upper class girl meant for Ralph. She wasn't, in spite of it all, as Mrs. Roberts said, quite like those others. They both had education and good upbringing. You could see that. Ralph had been a journalist . . .

So Ralph's suicide was a real surprise. Of course, they all are, though they say it's old stuff, nothing new. The note seemed written in a moment of agonized frenzy. And on the back of the note were some disconnected notations taken from his readings, as strange as everything else had been:

I saw some manticores, a most strange sort of creatures, which have the body of a lion, red hair, a face and ears like a man's, three rows of teeth which close together, as if you joined your hands with your fingers between each other: they have a sting in their tails like a scorpion's and a very melodious voice.—Rabelais.

The absolute love of anything involved the love of universal good; and the love of universal good involves the love of every creature.—Santayana.

Warcollier established himself before World War I through an invention for the manufacture of artificial jewelry from the scales of a fish. Factories were opened in France and the United States . . .

The lawn went to pot.

Save the World

She came in and I noticed that she was banging into the walls and her eyes didn't seem to focus. It was the day after her writer's workshop, and she always seemed that way as if she had been taking dope. Maybe she was. She hit the kid for spilling her coffee and then got on the telephone and had one of her everlasting "intelligent" conversations with somebody. I played with the little girl who was my daughter. She hung up. "Are you all right today?" I asked.

"What do you mean?"

"I mean, you act kind of . . . distracted."

Her eyes looked like the eyes of people in movies who played at being insane.

"*I'm* all right. Are *you* all right?"

"Never. I'm always confused."

"Have you eaten today?"

"No. Mind throwing some potatoes in the pot to boil? The pot's in the sink, soaking."

I had just come out of the hospital and was still weak.

She walked into the kitchen, then stopped and looked at the pot. She propped, stiff, swaying in the doorway as if the pot were an apparition. It couldn't have been the kitchen that scared her because she had been the worst housekeeper of all my ex-wives.

"What's the matter?" I asked.

She didn't answer.

"The pot's all right. It just has soapwater in it. Just scrub it out a bit and dump it."

She finally came out, walked around a bit, bumped into a chair, then handed me a couple of magazines: PROGRAM OF THE COMMUNIST PARTY U.S.A. and AMERICAN DIALOGUE. DIALOGUE had a cover of a baby asleep in a hammock made out of a couple of gun belts with bullets protruding. The cover also indicated the contents: THE MORALITY OF OUR TIMES. ON THE SUPERIORITY OF THE NEGRO.

"Look, kid," I said, "I'm not much on politics of any kind. I'm not much good that way, you know. But I'll try to read this stuff."

I sat there and went through it, a bit of it, while she put some meat on in the kitchen. She called me in and the kid and I went in. We sat down to it.

"I read about the superiority of the Negro," I said. "You know, I am an expert on the Negro. Down at work most of them are Negroes . . . "

"Well, why don't you just be an expert on Whites?"

"I am. The article spoke of the 'fine, tough muscular system. The beautiful, rich color, the full broad features, and the gracefully frizzled hair of the Negro' and that when Nature got to the white man she was pretty well exhausted, but she pinched up his features and did what she could."

"I knew a little colored boy once. He had the softest, shortest hair, his hair was beautiful, beautiful."

"I'll try to read the Communist Party Program tonight," I told her.

"Have you registered to vote?" she asked.

"I never have."

"You can register at your nearest school on the 29th. Dorothy Healey is running for County Tax Assessor."

"Marina is getting more beautiful every day." I spoke of my daughter.

"Yes, she is. Listen, we've got to go. She goes to sleep at 7. And there's something I must hear on KPFK. They read one of my letters over the air the other night."

KPFK was an FM radio station.

"All right," I said.

I watched them leave. She pushed the kid across the street in the stroller. She had the same old wooden stride, nothing fluid at all. I watched them go. A better world. Jesus. Everybody has a different way, everybody has a different idea, and they are all so *sure*. She's sure too, that wooden woman with the insane eyes and grey hair, that woman running into her walls, crazy with life and fear, and she would never quite believe it that I didn't hate her and all her friends who gathered 2 or 3 times a week and praised each other's poetry and were lonely and who made each other, and carried signs and were very enthusiastic and sure, they would never believe that the solitude, the privacy I asked for, was only to save myself so I might guess who *they* were and who the enemy was supposed to be.

Still it was nice to be alone.

I walked in and slowly began washing the dishes.

The Way the Dead Love

My head hurt for a week and a half. I had some beautiful hangovers that way. Lou would get on the wine and apologize until I felt like vomiting. I even worked a couple of days uploading boxcars. Lou found a wallet in the crapper of a bar with $35 in it. So we went on. A while. But I felt like I owed Lou something. I think I got it one night. Lou was talking about his girlfriend.

"What a body! What breasts! And she's *young*, Hank, *young!*"

"Yeah?"

"Only she can't stop drinking. She's drunk all the time. She can't pay her rent. She's down in the cellar."

"Down in the cellar?"

"Yeah, that's where they put 'em when they can't pay their rent."

"Is she down there now?"

"Yeah."

We drank a while. Then I said, "Lou, I gotta call it off early tonight. I've got something to take care of."

"Sure, kid."

He left and I went out and got a fifth of whiskey. I went down to the cellar. There was only one door down there. I knocked. The door opened and here stood this young piece in panties and bra, in high heels, with just this thin negligee on. I pushed my way in. She screamed:

"Get out of here! You get out of here!"

I took the fifth out of the bag and held it before her eyes.

"Get out," she said in a lower voice.

"You've got a nice place here. Where are your glasses?"

She pointed. I went over and got 2 waterglasses, filled them half up and we sat on the edge of the bed.

"Drink up. I live upstairs."

I worked her breasts loose. They were fine. I kissed her on the throat and mouth. I was in form. We had another drink, then I worked her pants off and put it in. It was still good. I stayed all night, we went another round, and then once again before I left in the morning. She seemed to like me. And she was a very good piece.

I was sitting up in Lou's place one night and I asked him, "You seen your girlfriend lately?"

"No, no, I meant to tell you. They threw her out. They threw her out of the cellar. I can't find her anywhere. I've looked everywhere. God, I'm sick. What a piece she was! You don't have any idea how I feel!"

"Yes, I do, Lou."

We both drank one to her in silence.

have met enough writers, artists, editors, professors, painters, none of them were truly natural men, interesting individuals. They looked better on paper or in paint, and while you can't deny this has importance, it is still very uncomfortable to sit across from these same creatures and listen to them talk or look upon their faces. The life-seed, if there is any, is lost in their work. For my amusement and fill and grace and look-upwardness I have had to seek elsewhere. And in the manswarm, stamped so alike, there is still always the individual madman or saint to be found. I have found many but will tell you about a few.

There was this hotel at Beverly and Vermont . We were on the wine, my ladyfriend and I. Jane was a natural, and she had delicious legs and a tight little gash and a face of powdered pain. And she knew me. She taught me more than the philosophy books of the ages. We'd see some man or woman walking down the hall and they would reek of the death and the plague and the vomit of sell-out, and I'd feel it but stand silent in some morning hangover shade, rather cleaved in half again about how low the human being could descend without effort. And I'd be thinking this thing and then I'd hear her voice: "That son of a bitch! I can't STAND him! He makes me sick!" Then she'd laugh and she always made up some nickname for the creature—like Greenjaws or Anteyes or Deadears.

But to get on with it, one time we were sitting around our room drinking our port wine and she said, "Ya know, I think you'd like to meet the F.B.I." She worked as a maid in the place and knew the roomers.

"Forget it, sweetie," I told her, "I've already met the F.B.I."

"Well, o.k."

We gathered the half empty wine bottle and the two or three full ones and I followed her down the hall. It was the darkest hall of hell, dozens of people leaning up against the wallpaper, all behind in the rent, drinking wine, rolling cigarettes, living on boiled potatoes, rice, beans, cabbage, hogshead soup. We walked a little way down and then Jane knocked, the insistent little knock that said: this is not trouble.

"It's Jane. It's Jane."

The door opened and here stood a fat little bitch, rather ugly, a bit dangerous, demented, but still all right.

"Come in, Jane."

"This is Hank," she introduced me.

"Hello," I said.

I came in and sat down in a straightback chair and one of the ladies went around filling the large waterglasses full of deathstink wine.

Meanwhile, in the bed, unintroduced, sat, no *sprawled*, was this male creature ten years later than I.

"What goes, shithead?" I asked him.

He didn't answer. He just looked at me. When you get a man who doesn't care to rejoinder in common conversation, you've got a wild one, you've got a natural. I knew that I was in deep. He just SPRAWLED there under that dirty bedsheet, wineglass in hand, and worse, he looked quite handsome. That is, if you think the vulture is handsome and I think that he is. It is. He had the beak and eyes of living and he lifted that glass and ran the wine down his throat, one run down, all that deathstink wine, without a blink, since I was the heaviest drinker born in the last two centuries there was nothing for me to do but throw that filthy poison into my stomach, hold mentally to the sides of the chair and keep the straight pokerface.

A refill. He did it again. I did it again. The two ladies just sat and watched. Filthy wine into filthy sadness. We went around a couple more. Then he started to babble. The sentences were energetic but muddled in content. Still, they made me feel better. And all the time, this big bright electric light overhead and these two drunken madwomen talking about something. Something.

Then it happened—the sprawl was over. He pushed upward in the bed. The beautiful vulture eyes and the big electric light was upon us. He said it very quietly and with easy authority.

"I am the F.B.I. You are under arrest."

And he would arrest us all, his woman, mine, me, and that was all. We would submit, then, the rest of the night would go on. I don't know how many times in the next year that he put me under arrest, but it was always the magic moment of each evening. I never saw him get out of bed. When he crapped or urinated or ate or drank water or shaved, I had no idea. Finally, I decided that he just didn't do these things—they happened in another way, like sleep or atomic warfare or snow melting. He realized that the bed is man's greatest invention—most of us are born there, sleep there, fuck there, die there. Why get out? I tried to make his woman one night but she said that he would kill me if he ever found out. That would have been one way to get him out from under the sheets. Killed by an F.B.I. agent in dirty underwear. I let her go; she didn't look that good.

Then there was another night when Jane set me up for another. We were drinking. The same cheap stuff, of course. I had gone to bed once or twice with her and there wasn't much else to do when she said: "Howja like to meet a killer?"

"Wouldn't mind," I said, "wouldn't mind a-tall."

"Less go."

She explained the whole thing to me on the way. Who he'd killed and why. He was now out on parole. The parole officer was a good guy, kept getting him these dishwasher jobs, but he kept getting drunk and losing them.

Jane knocked and we went on in. Like I never saw the F.B.I. agent out of bed, I never saw the killer's girlfriend get out of bed. She had this *totally* black hair on her head and this whitewhitewhitewhite skim milk terribly white SKIN. She was dying. Medical science be damned: all that was keeping her alive was port wine.

I was introduced to the killer:

"Ronnie, Hank. Hank, Ronnie."

He sat there in a dirty undershirt. And he didn't have a face. Just runs of skin. Veins. Little fart eyes. We shook hands and started in on the wine. I don't know how long we drank. One hour or 2, but he seemed to get angrier and angrier, which is rather commonplace with commonplace drinkers, especially on the wine. Yet we kept talking, talking, I don't know about what.

Then, suddenly, he reached over and grabbed his black and white wife and picked her out of bed and began using her like a willow rod. He just kept banging her head against the headboard:

                                                                     bang bang

      bang bang bang
             bang bang bang bang

bang

Then I said, "HOLD IT!"

He looked over at me. "Wuzzat?"

"You hit her head one more time on the headboard and I am going to kill you."

She was whiter than ever. He placed her back in bed, straightened the strands of her hair. She seemed almost happy. We all began drinking again. We drank until the crazy traffic began running up and down the streets far below. Then the sun was really up. Bright, and I got up and shook his hand. I said, "I have to go; I hate to go; you are a good kid; I gotta go anyhow."

Then there was Mick. The place was on Mariposa Ave. Mick didn't work. His wife worked. Mick and I drank a lot together. I gave him 5 dollars once to wax my car. I didn't have a bad car at the time, but Mick never waxed it. I'd find him sitting on the steps. "It looks like rain. No use waxing if it looks like rain. I'm gonna do a good job. Don't want it spoiled." He'd be sitting on those steps drunk. "O.K., Mick." Next time he'd be sitting there drunk and see me. "I'm just sittin' here lookin', deciding what I'm gonna do. You see, you got those scratches on there. First thing I'm gonna do, I'm gonna paint in those scratches. I'm gonna get me some paint . . ."

"Jesus Christ, Mick. Forget it!"

He did, but a fine fellow he was. One night he insisted that I was drunk although he was the one who was drunk. And he insisted that he help me up the 3 flights of stairs. Actually, I helped him up. But it was a lumbersome, cumbersome journey and I think we awakened everybody in the apartment building with our cussing and falling against walls and doors and stair-rails. Anyhow, I got the door opened, and then I tripped over one of his big feet. Down I went, straight and flat upon a coffeetable with a one-quarter-inch glass covering. The whole table smashed straight to the floor—I weigh around 218—and all 4 legs crushed under, the top of the table cracked in 4 places, but the slab of glass itself remained perfect, unmarred. I got up. "Thanks, old buddy," I told him. "Nothin' to it," he said. And then I sat there and listened to him crashing into doorways and falling down the steps. It was like the whole building was under bombardment. He made it on down, gravity was on his side.

He had a good wife. I remember one time they cleaned up my face with cotton and some kind of sterilizer when it was all smashed-in from a bad night out. They seemed very tender and concerned and serious about my smashed-in face, and it was a very odd feeling to me, that care.

Anyhow, the drinking got to Mick, and it gets to each of us differently. With him, the body swelled up, doubled, tripled in size in various places. He couldn't zip his pants and had to cut slits in the pant legs. His story was that they didn't have a bed for him in the vet's hospital. My feeling was that he didn't want to go there. Anyhow, one day he made a foolish move and tried the General Hospital.

After a couple of days he phoned me. "Jesus Christ, they're killing me! I've never seen a place like this. No doctors anywhere and nurses don't give a damn and just these fruit orderlies running around like snobs and happy that everybody's sick and dying. What the fuck is this place? They're carrying the dead out by the dozens! They mix up the food trays! They won't let you sleep! They keep you awake all night fucking around with nothing and then when the sun comes up, they wake you up again. They throw you a wet rag and tell you to get ready for breakfast and then breakfast, if you want to call it that, arrives around noontime. I never knew that people could be so cruel to the sick and dying! Get me outa here, Hank! I beg you, pal,

I beg you, let me out of this pit of hell! Let me die in my apartment, let me die with a chance!"

"Whatcha want me to do?"

"Well, I asked to get out and they won't give me my release. They've got my clothes. So you just come on down here with your car. You come up to my bed and we'll bust out!"

"Don't you think we better ask Mona?"

"Mona don't know shit. Since I can't fuck her anymore she don't care. Everything about me swelled up but my dick."

"Mother nature is sometimes cruel."

"Yeah, yeah. Now listen, you comin' on down?"

"See you in about 25 minutes."

"O.K.," he said.

I knew the place, having been there 2 or 3 times myself. I found a parking spot near the entrance building and walked on in. I had the ward number. It was the stink of hell all over again. I had the strange feeling that I would die in that building some day. Maybe not. I hoped not.

I found Mick. The oppressive helplessness hung over everything.

"Mick?"

"Help me up," he said.

I got him to his feet. He looked about the same.

"Let's go."

We went padding down the hall. He had on one of those chickenshit gowns, untied in back because the nurses wouldn't tie them for you, because the nurses didn't care about anything except catching themselves some fat young subnormal doctor. And although the patients seldom saw the doctors, the nurses did—in the elevators, pinchy pinchy! oh hee hee hee!—with the smell of death everywhere.

The elevator door pulled open. There sat a fat young boy with pimples sucking at a popsicle. He looked at Mick in his gown.

"Do you have a release, sir? You have to have a release to get out of here. My instructions are . . . "

"I'm on my own release, punk! Now you move this

thing down to the street floor before I jam that popsicle up your ass!"

"You heard the man, son," I told him.

We moved on down, smartly, and straight through the exit building where nobody said a word. I helped him into the car. In 30 minutes he was back at his place.

"Oh fuck!" said Mona. "What have you done, Hank?"

"He wanted it. I believe a man should have his own wishes as much as possible."

"But there isn't any help for him here either."

I went out, bought him a quart of beer and left them in there together to fight it out.

A couple of days later he made the vet's hospital. Then he was back. Then he was at the hospital. Then he was back. I'd see him sitting on the steps.

"Jesus, I could sure use a beer!"

"How about it, Mona?"

"All right, goddamn it, but he shouldn't!"

I'd go get him a quart and he'd light up all over. We'd go inside and he'd show me photos taken when he'd first met Mona in France. He was in his uniform. He'd met her on a train. Something about a train. He'd gotten her a seat on the train when the brass had wanted to kick her off. Something like that. The photos were of 2 young and beautiful people. I could not believe that they were the same people. My guts hurt like murder. They gave me some kummel they said Mick couldn't have. I made fast work of the kummel. "You were a very handsome man, Mick." There he sat, puffed out of belief, all chance gone. "And Mona. What a babe! I still love you!" I said. Mick really liked that. He wanted me to know that he'd caught a good one. I think it was about a week later I saw Mona outside the apartment house.

"Mick died last night," she said.

I just kept looking at her. "Shit, I don't know what to say. Even all puffed up like that I didn't think he would die."

"I know," she said. "And we both liked you very much."

I couldn't handle it. I turned around and walked into the apartment house entrance, right past apt. #1 where we had had so many good nights. He wasn't in there anymore. He was gone like last year's Christmas or an old pair of shoes. What shit. I made my way up the stairs and started in. The Coward. I drank, I drank, I drank, I drank. Escapism. Drunkards are escapists, they say, unable to face reality.

Later, I heard, she went to Denver to live with a sister.

And the writers keep writing and the artists keep painting but it doesn't mean too much.

was always rather indifferent to politics, but before the election, I couldn't help but see some of the fools while turning toward the race results. Horserace results, I mean. They all said Nixon was in. Which I felt was a little worse than Humphrey, but when Wallace won by a landslide I was as stupefied as the next. And when he was sworn into office, things began to happen. Le May stated that unless the war were won within a month or the enemy surrendered he might have to H-bomb N. Vietnam, maybe China. Maybe Russia. "A man's got to be a MAN!" he stated. "He's got to show his guts! Old Teddy Roosevelt knew how to handle bums!" Wallace simply grinned. He grinned simply. "Atta boy, baby!" he said. "Wow!"

They set up machine guns in the black districts and rapidly began solving the housing problem. "I'm not a racist," said Wallace, "but I figure if a man is poor or black, it's his own fault."

Le May grinned, "Yeh."

Layoffs began everywhere. One man had to do the work of two at half the wages of one man. The relief rolls were closed down, old age pensions terminated. The police force was tripled, new concentration camps and jails were built. At any hour of the day or night you could hear machinegun fire. Blacks were only allowed on the streets between sunup and sundown, and they were restricted to designated areas. An underground product hit the market: WHITEWASH, a white coloring to cover black. A white man's wig and a bit of WHITEWASH and you had a bit of a better chance. But most Negroes refused to use it. The Mexican and Indian population received similar treatment, though not as harsh.

There were 30 million unemployed and aged wandering the streets. When a man or woman or child fell dead of starvation or were murdered by the police or troops, they had what were called "A" cars—"A" for assholes who didn't know HOW to survive, baby. The "A" cars patrolled the streets constantly, working something on the order of street sweeper machines. Only instead of sucking up leaves and paper, various trash, the "A" cars sucked up the newly dead bodies of women, children, the aged, and various unfortunate men. "We must keep our cities sanitary," President Wallace stated. The bodies were burned just like the books in the library. Not all the books in the library were burned, but a good 85 percent. A good 95 percent of paintings and statuary were destroyed as being "decadent to a good American Society." All editors of left-wing newspapers were tortured before hundreds of thousands of spectators in the baseball and football stadiums of America. And as the editors screamed in their agony, being cut and torn slowly to bits, a record was played over the loudspeakers: GOD BLESS AMERICA! While the torturers said to their victims as they worked: "Remember Hungary! Remember Prague!" And evangelical Baptist ministers stood behind the victims' heads, dangling huge silver crucifixes before their eyes. No admission was charged, whether the man to be tortured was black or white.

Of course, I had lost my job and was sitting on my last month's rent. The end was working toward me. They had just finished the demolition of the L.A. County General Hospital so I had no place to go. I had lost 48 pounds, was starving, but still, in a cowardly way, I thought, well, at least almost ALL of my writing has been non-political. I will be allowed to die of starvation instead of being murdered, but like George said, it was my own fault: I just couldn't play a good game of chess. God protects those who protect themselves. All that shit.

So I was somewhat surprised when the 3 men arrived and showed me their badges. They seated themselves about me.

"Well, Slim, we gotta ask ya some questions."

"Shoot!" I said.

One of the motherfuckers drew out a gun and leveled it at me, clicking off the safety latch.

"WAIT, MAN! THAT'S JUST AN EXPRESSION!"

"Oh?" he said and put the gun back.

"You're Charles Bukowski?" the big one asked.

"Yeh."

"You used to work for that son of a bitch Bryan?"

"Yeh."

"We've gone over your stuff. Mostly sex shit. I kinda liked it. Especially where you stuck your dick up your buddy's ass because you were drunk and you thought you were in bed with your girl. Did that really happen?"

"Yeh."

"So we checked out the 192 articles you wrote in 192 weeks and only ONE of them wuz about POLITICS . . ."

"The one on the merits and demerits of Revolution. Yes, I remember it."

"But we don't quite understand it. What did it mean?"

"It meant that unless your soul and hand were straight, Revolution was useless—it only meant substituting one kind of Economic Slavery for another. It meant, if you were going to kill somebody make sure you had something at least 5 times as good to replace it with."

All three of them sat back writing in little notebooks.

"Is Hitler really alive in Argentina?" I asked.

"Uhh, huh," the big one said. "He's coming up next month to vacation in Vegas. He keeps asking for postcards of those chorus girls. You know, the last thing to die on an old German is his dick."

"Yeh?"

"Hey."

They all put their pencils down and looked at me. They didn't say anything for 5 minutes. Part of some kind of training they were put through. Finally the big one said, "Mr. Bukowski?"

"Yeh?"

"Would you allow your daughter to marry a nigger?"

"Yeh."

"WHAT?"

They all leaned a bit forward.

"Oh," I said, "I mean, it's all up to *her*. I mean, the kid's only four. I don't think she wants to marry anybody yet."

They stared at me a long time again.

"Did you like the hippies?" (The hippies had long ago been exterminated.)

"Not really. But they never hurt me or bothered me. What more can you ask?"

"Are you for the war in Vietnam?"

"I've never been for any war. I wasn't even for the war against Hitler."

"Atta boy!" said the middle-sized one, putting his gun back.

Again they sat for a long time, just looking at me.

"Well, I'm afraid we gotta take you in, Bukowski," the big guy said.

"All right, at least I'll get some food in jail."

They all laughed at that.

"No, the new jail system is juz jail them. Don't feed them. Saves a hellulota money for the state."

"God bless the State," I said, "and while He's at it He might as well bless the *Saturday Evening Post*."

"Oh no," said the big one. "The *Saturday Evening Post* has been burned."

"Why?" I asked.

"Too left-wing," said the fat boy.

"Jesus Christ," I said, "let's get out of here and get it done with."

"Before we get you down there and work you over," said the fat boy, "I just want to let you have one bit of mental unhappiness."

"Shoot!" I said. "No, I mean, tell me about it."

They put the bracelets on me. And walked me toward the door. The middle-sized one farted. A sign of happiness.

"Since you are being taken out of circulation, I am free to tell you this."

He looked at his watch. "We have been careful not to have any leaks, so I can tell you this. A shit like you deserves unhappiness."

"All right. Let me have it."

We walked toward the door. Fat boy looked at his watch.

"In exactly 2 hours and 16 minutes Vice President Le-

May will push the button that will set a fusillade of H-bombs upon N. Vietnam, China, Russia and other selected spots. What do you think of that?"

"I think it is a tactical mistake," I said.

Fat boy reached to open the door. As he opened it, a sheet of red and grey and green and purple spread everywhere. There was lightning. And lily slivers. There were teaspoons and half-dogs, ladies stockings, torn cunt, history books, rugs, belts, turtles, teacups, marmalade and spiders flying through the air. I looked around and Fatso was gone and middle-size was gone and the little little shit was gone and the bracelets were broken on my wrists and I was standing in a bathtub and I looked down and I had one ball, a piece of cock, and there were eyes rolling along the ground like ants. Green, brown, blue, yellow, even albino eyes. Fuck. I got out of the tub. Found half a chair. Sat down. I watched my whole left arm shrivel up at once like a piece of burning cellophane.

How you gonna keep 'em down on the farm? Everything gone: Picasso, Shakespeare, Plato, Dante, Rodin, Mozart . . . Jackie Gleason. All the lovely girls. Even the pigs eating any kind of swill, so godly. Even the cops in their tight black pants. Even the cops that I had felt so sorry for, trapped in their nastiness. Life had been good, horrible but good and a few heroes had kept us going. Perhaps wrongly chosen heroes, but what the fuck. The polls had been wrong again—the old Harry Truman shit—Wallace had *won*, sitting in his mountain top hideaway. Spitting out redneck teeth of hatred—2 hours and 16 minutes too late!

Hiroshima was re-named America.

I was in the *King's Crow Bar* and this guy sitting next to me asked, "You got any place to stay tonight?"

And I said, "Hell, no, I don't have any place to stay."

"O.K., come with me. My name's Teddy Ralstead."

So I went with him. That first night I sat in their front room while Teddy and his wife wrestled on the floor. Her dress kept slipping up around her ass and she smiled at me and pulled it down. They wrestled and wrestled and I drank beer.

Teddy's wife's name was Helen. And Teddy wasn't always around. Helen acted like I had known her for years instead of one night.

"You've never tried to fuck me, have you, Bukowski?"

"Teddy's my friend, Helen."

"Shit! This is your friend too," she said pulling her dress up. She didn't have any panties on.

"Where's Teddy?" I asked.

"Don't worry about Teddy. He wants you to have me."

"How do you know?"

"He told me."

We walked into the bedroom. There was Teddy sitting on a chair, smoking a cigarette. Helen pulled her dress off and climbed onto the bed.

"Go ahead," said Teddy, "do it."

"But Teddy, it's your wife."

"I *know* it's my wife."

"I mean, look Teddy—"

"I'll give you ten bucks to do it," he said. "Is it a deal, Bukowski?"

"Ten bucks?"

"That's right."

I took off my clothes and got on.

"Give her a long ride," said Teddy. "No quickies."

"I'll try, but she's got me going."

"Just think of a stack of horseshit," said Teddy.

"Yeah, think of a stack of horseshit," said his wife.

"How tall?" I asked.

"Real tall. *Wide.* Covered with flies," said Teddy.

"*Thousands* of flies," said Helen, "all eating shit."

"Flies are sure strange," I said.

"Your ass looks funny," Teddy said to me.

"Yours does too," I said.

"How does *my* ass look?" asked Helen.

"Please," I said, "I don't wanna think about your ass or I'm not gonna last."

"Try singing the National Anthem," said Helen.

"*Oh, say can you see? By the stars early light? Oh—*"

"What's the matter?" she asked.

"I don't know the words."

"Say anything that comes to your mind then," said Helen.

"I'm coming," I said.

"*What?*" she asked.

"I said, 'I'm *coming!*'"

"Oh, my gawd!" she said.

We clutched and kissed, moaning. I climbed off. I wiped off on the sheet and Teddy handed me a ten.

"Next time," he said, "try to last longer or it's only five bucks."

"O.K.," I said.

"Oh, Teddy!" said Helen from the bed.

"What, dear?"

"I *love* you . . . "

The second night was a bit different. Teddy and his wife had wrestled on the floor. Then Teddy had disappeared. I was drinking beer and watching television. Helen snapped off the TV and stood in front of it.

"Hey—that was a good program, Helen. Why'd you turn it off?"

"You're not much of a man, are you?"

"What do you mean?"

"Did you like that fried chicken tonight?"

"Sure."

"Do you like my legs, my hips, my breasts?"

"Sure, sure."

"Do you like the color of my hair? Do you like the way I walk? Do you like my dress?"

"Sure, sure, sure."

"You're not much of a man, are you?"

"I don't understand."

"Beat me!"

"*Beat* you? What for?"

"Don't you understand? *Beat* me! Use your belt! Use your hand! Make me cry! Make me *scream!*"

"Look—"

"*Rape me! Hurt me!*"

"Look, Mrs. Ralstead . . . "

"Oh, for Christ's sake, get going!"

I took off my belt and slapped her across the thigh.

"*Harder*, you fool!"

"Mrs. Ralstead . . . "

"Be a beast!"

I slammed her across the ass with the buckle. She screamed.

"MORE! MORE!"

I laid the belt to her. All up and down her legs. Then I slapped her and knocked her down, picked her up by the hair.

"Rip my dress!" she said. "Rip my dress to shreds!"

"But Mrs. Ralstead—I *like* your dress."

"Oh, you fool—*rip* my dress!"

I ripped it straight down the front. Then I kept ripping until she didn't have anything on.

"What do I do now?"

"*Hit* me! *Rape* me!"

I hit her again, picked her up and carried her into the bedroom. Teddy was sitting there smoking a cigarette. Helen was sobbing, crying.

"Beautiful!" said Teddy. "*Beautiful!*"

"You beast!" Helen screamed at me.

"Get her!" said Teddy. "Slam it to her!"

I leaped onto his wife and inserted my penis.

"Make it last," said Teddy, "no quickies."

"But she's got me hot," I shouted.

"Just think about eating shit," said Teddy.

"Eating shit?"

"Yes," said Helen, "with the flies still on it."

"The flies would fly away if I got the shit close to my mouth," I said.

"Not *these* flies," said Helen. "These flies are different. You swallow them with the shit."

"O.K.," I said.

"No quickies," said Teddy.

"Little boy blue," I said, "come blow your horn, the cow's in the meadow, the sheep's in the corn . . ."

"You haven't learned the National Anthem yet?" asked Teddy.

"No."

"You're not a very good American, are you Bukowski?"

"I guess I'm not."

"I've never failed to vote," said Teddy. "This is a great country."

"Little Jack Horner," I said, "sat in a corner, eating a pumpkin pie . . ."

"And along came a spider and sat down beside her," said Helen.

"Wait a minute," said Teddy, "is *that* the way it goes?"

"I don't know," I said. "Mary had a little lamb and its fleece was white as snow and everywhere that Mary went—I'm coming!"

"What—?" asked Helen.

"I'm coming!"

"Oh, my gawd!" she said.

We clutched and kissed, moaning. I climbed off. I wiped off on the sheet and Teddy handed me a ten.

"Next time," he said, "try to last a little longer or it's only one buck."

"O.K., Teddy," I said.

"Oh, Teddy!" said Helen from the bed.

"What, dear?"

"I love *both* of you . . ."

The third night we were all sitting watching TV. I got up and walked behind Helen. I grabbed her by the hair and pulled her backwards out of her chair. I fell on her and began kissing her legs. Then I heard Teddy get up and he pulled me off of his wife.

"What's wrong?" I asked. "What's wrong, Teddy?"

"Shut up!" he told me.

He picked Helen up by the hair, then slapped her and knocked her down.

"You whore!" he screamed. "You dirty rotten whore! You filthy whore! You've betrayed me with this man! I've seen it with my own eyes!"

He picked her up, ripped her dress, slapped her. Then he took off his belt and worked her over good.

"Betraying bitch! You rotten bitch! You're a disgrace to all womanhood!" He took a moment to look at me: "And *you*, you bastard, you better get out while you can!"

"But Teddy . . . "

"I'm warning you, Bukowski."

He picked Helen up and carried her into the bedroom. I got my coat and walked out, walked down to the *King's Crow Bar* and sat down and had a beer. That Teddy. What the hell kind of friend he turned out to be.

D riving in to Los Alamitos racetrack one night I passed this small farm and saw this large creature standing in the moonlight. There was something very odd about this creature, it drew me to it. It seemed a magnet, a signal. I mean, I braked my car and got out and walked toward the creature. I always got off the freeway early and drove past these little farms. It gave my mind time to relax, getting off the freeway like that and driving down a side road to the track took the pressure off of my mind and made a better gambler out of me. I didn't say a winning one, I said a better one. I really didn't have time to stop. I was already late for the first race, but there I was walking toward this fenced-in enclosure.

I walked up to the fence and there it was—a huge hog. I'm not much of a farm hand but I felt that this must simply be the largest hog alive, but that wasn't the thing. There was something *in* that hog, something that forced me to stop my car. I stood at the fence looking at it. There was the head, and well, I'll call it a *face* because that's exactly what was on the front of the head. This face. Never had I seen a face such as that. I am not sure what had called me to it. People often joke about my ugliness saying I am the ugliest old man they have ever seen. I am rather proud of this. My ugliness was hard-worked for; I was not born that way. I knew it meant a passing through of areas.

I forgot about the races, about everything but that hog's face. When one ugly admires another there is a transgression of sorts, a touching and exchange of souls, if you will. He, this hog, had the ugliest face I had seen in a lifetime of living. He was covered with warts and wrinkles and hairs, these long single hairs that cropped out obscenely and twisted—every place a hair shouldn't be. I thought of Blake's tiger. Blake had wondered how God had created such a thing, and now here was Bukowski's hog and I wondered what had made *that*, and how and why. The deep ugliness reoccurred everywhere—it was wondrous. The eyes

were small and mean and stupid, what eyes, as if all the
evil and crassness that existed everywhere was registered
there. And the mouth, the snout was horrible—gross, demented, slobbering, it was a stinking asshole of a snout and
mouth. And the flesh of the face was actually decaying,
rotting, falling off in pieces. The overall total of that face
and body was beyond what could seem to register upon
my brain.

My next thought came quickly—it's human, it's a human being. It came upon me so strongly that I accepted it.
The hog had been standing ten or twelve feet off and then
it began moving toward me. I couldn't move although I felt
some terror at its approach. Here it came toward me in the
moonlight. It walked up to the fence and raised its head
toward me. It was very close. Its eyes looked into my eyes
and we stood there that way for some time, I believe, looking into each other. That hog recognized something in me.
And I looked into those mean and stupid eyes. It was as if I
were being given the secret of the world, and the secret was
obvious and real and horrible enough.

It's human, the thought came again, it's a human being.

Suddenly it was too much, I had to break off; I turned
and walked away. I got into my car and drove toward the
racetrack. The hog rode in my brain, in my memory.

At the track I began to look at the faces. I saw a part of
this face that fit the hog's face and I saw a part of that face
that fit the hog's face, and here was another part, and here
was another. Then I went to the men's room and saw my
face in the mirror. I am not one to linger before mirrors too
long. I went out to bet.

That hog's face was the sum total of that crowd, somehow. Of crowds everywhere. That hog had added it up
and it stood there. It stood there behind that fence on the
little farm two or three miles away. It was a night when I
didn't remember too much about the horses. After the races
I didn't have any desire to see the hog again. I took another
road up . . .

A few nights later I explained to a friend of mine about
the hog, about what I had seen and felt, mainly that the hog

was a human caught in that body. My friend was an intellectual, well read.

"Hogs is hogs, Bukowski, that's all there is to it!"

"But John, if you had seen that hog's face you would have known."

"Hogs is hogs, that's all."

I couldn't explain it to him, nor could he convince me that "hogs is hogs." Certainly not this hog . . .

I remember the first night I had worked in a slaughterhouse. They would kill the steer in another room and it would come to us skinned and gutted through this space in the wall, headless, hanging by the rear legs raw red, and we had to take the steer upon our shoulder and hang him up in the waiting trucks, this time by the gristle up near his shoulder. It was heavy work and the steer kept coming, a maze of steer, on and on. As the hours went on and I became more and more fatigued, the whole mass of oncoming freshly-murdered steer and working men became a bit mixed in my mind; sweat ran into my eyes and my vision became foggy. I was so tired I felt drunk. I laughed at the smallest things. My feet hurt, my back, everything. I was pushed into an area of fatigue beyond belief and I felt as if I were losing my identity. I no longer remembered where I lived or why, or what I was doing or why. The animals and the men mixed, and then I had the thought, why don't they murder me? Why don't they murder me and hang me in a truck? Why was I different from a steer? How could they *tell?* This thought was very strong because I could no longer tell the animals from the men except that the animals, I remembered, had been hanging by their legs.

As I left that night I felt that it would be my last night there and it was. So they never got to hang me in their bloody trucks . . . . no Bukowski steak for you, my dear. Steers is steers, of course, but some weeks later going into meat markets I couldn't help but think that I was looking at murdered human flesh, transformed . . .

And it's absurd, of course, but there are places, restaurants, and markets that have signs on the doors: NO ANIMALS ALLOWED. These signs are usually on a tin plate with white background and the letters are in red. NO ANIMALS ALLOWED. The sign is usually up near where the hand pushes the door open. When I see that sign there is always a small pause. I hesitate. Then I push on in. Nobody says anything. They go about their business.

One time, just to test the reactions of others, I stood outside a supermarket door with one of those red signs upon it. I watched the people. They simply walked in without hesitation or delay. It must be wonderful to have a mass mind— somebody tells you that you are a human being and you believe it. Somebody tells you that a dog is a dog and you go out and buy a dog's license and some dog food. Everything is so neatly pocketed. There is no room for overlap or admixture . . . NO ANIMALS ALLOWED IN OUR ZOO . . .

I suppose that most people have seen these cooked pigs in restaurant windows, eyes gouged out, snout facing the window with an apple in the mouth and slices of pineapple spread along the back. I was in New York City once, starving and miserable, walking along the sidewalk when I came upon a restaurant window with one of those pigs as the frontispiece. I stopped. Where the eyes had been dug out two long holes went into the skull. The holes had this burnt out appearance and gave off the flavor of something betrayed and mutilated beyond common sensibility. As hungry as I was I couldn't imagine sticking a fork into the side of that thing and slicing off a hunk of meat. It sat on a silver plate, obedient and sending off rays of horror. The New Yorkers hurried on or sat inside eating and wiping their mouths. My alliance with the human race became less and less. They never considered anything; they simply accepted. What a crowd they were—without honor, sensibility, and whatever feeling they had was only limited to self. That pig—to simply display that atrocity as something valuable to them—that was the key to their going-on, that was the door that opened and showed what they were. I said goodbye to my pig and walked through the crowd . . .

Last week a young woman came to see me from Costa Mesa. She said she was a reader of my books. She was a handsome girl, about 21, and since I was a writer always in search of material, I let her in. She sat in a chair across the room looking at me, not speaking. The silence lasted some minutes. "Beer?" I asked.

"Sure," she said.

"Then you can speak."

"Uh huh."

"I'm going to Mexico to study creative writing. I'm taking a six week course," she added.

"The best way to study creative writing is to live."

"I think a course helps."

"No, it hinders. It tightens. Too much bad praise and bad criticism. Too much admixture of similar personalities. It's destructive. Even if you want to meet a man, that's the worst place to meet a man."

She didn't answer.

We drank some more beer and I talked. Then the beer was gone.

"I like bars," she said, "let's go to a bar."

We walked on down the street and went in. I ordered two scotch and waters. When she went to the restroom the bartender came back on down.

"God o mighty, Bukowski," he said, "you've got another one. They're all young. How do you do it?"

"It's all platonic, Harry. Plus a matter of research."

"Balls," said Harry and walked off. Harry was a crude guy.

She came back and we had another after that one. She still didn't talk. What the hell's she want? I thought.

"Why did you come to see me?" I asked.

"You'll see . . ."

"O.K., babe."

Scotch and waters in a bar add up a bill fast. I suggested we get a 5th and go back to my place.

"All right," she said . . .

I filled her glass with half scotch and half water. Likewise, my own. I talked about this and that, being a bit embarrassed by her continual silence. She drank right along with me. Then, after the 3d or 4th drink she began to change. Her face changed. Her face began to take on a strange shape. The eyes became smaller and different, the nose seemed to become sharper, the lips seemed to show teeth. I am serious about this.

"I want to tell you something," she said.

"Go ahead," I said.

"I'll get right to it," she said. "I am a rat in the body of a woman. The rats have sent me to you."

"I see," I said.

"Rats, you see, are more intelligent than people. We have been waiting for centuries to take over the world. We're getting ready now. Do you understand this?"

"Wait," I said. I went out and poured two more drinks.

"Tell me more," I said.

"It's simple," she said, "the rats have sent me to you to help us take over the world. We want your help."

"I'm honored," I said. "I haven't been too fond of people for some time."

"You'll help us then?"

"Well, I'm not too fond of rats either."

"Well, all right," she said, "you have to choose a side. Which side do you want? The rats are going to win. If you're wise, you'll side with us."

"Let me think it over."

"All right," she said, "I'll write you from Mexico."

She stood up.

"You going now?"

"Yes," she said, "my mission is completed."

"O.k.," I said. I walked her to the door, in fact, I walked her to her mother's new Cadillac, a white Cadillac, and she got in and drove off.

Now I'm waiting for the letter. I'm not quite sure what my answer will be. Those rats are getting there—drinking scotch, driving white Cadillacs and taking creative writing courses in Mexico. I suppose the final war will be between the rats and the cockroaches. I suppose they have an edge on the human race; I doubt they concentrate on killing each other . . .

Yesterday my girlfriend brought over her dog and came to see me. I live in a front court and there are a great many cats who belong to people in the other courts. One cat came and stood on my porch. The dog barked up a great racket, I couldn't quiet him. The guy from next door who owned the cat came over to get him.

"What kind of dog is that?" he asked. The guy was drunk.

"He's just a mutt, a low-life mutt."

"Let him out. My cat can handle him."

"Maybe. Maybe not. It's not my dog."

"Whose dog is it?"

"It belongs to a friend."

"Let him out."

"No," I said, "I like animals."

"They've got a lot more sense than people," he said.

"You're goddamned right," I said.

And that's not a very profound way to end this but I figure it's good enough. Hang in, observe, and I'll probably send you instructions for the future.

The Looney Ward

When the student nurses came in, some of the fellows masturbated under their gowns, although one or two of them simply took their things out and did it in the open.

The student nurses wore these very short uniforms and you could see through them. So you could hardly blame the fellows. It was an interesting place, this hospital. Then the doctor would come in. His name was Dr. McLain, a very fine fellow. He'd walk around, look at us and say, *"Yes, 140 cc's for this one, and, ah, give this one . . . ah, 100 cc's of . . . "* And then he'd look at me and snap his fingers, *"Ha, ha! Drugs! Drugs! Let's have a big party! Where's the big party, Bukowski?"* he'd ask.

I was in . . . well, they'd caught me with an overdose and I was trying to stay in a while because I'd passed a few bad checks and was waiting for the heat to die down.

"The big party's right under my balls, doctor. I can hear it down there!"

"Under your balls, hey, my man?"

"Yes, directly under. I can even hear it down there."

It usually went on and on like that.

In the evening they'd bring us our juice. We always made a big thing about the juice.

"I think they're coming with the juice," somebody would say.

"Yes, the man is coming with the juice!"

Then I'd leap out of bed. "Who's got the juice?" I'd ask.

"The juice! The juice! We've got the juice!" Anderson would shout.

I'd spin on Anderson. "What'd you say? Did you say *you* had the juice?"

"What?"

I'd point to Anderson. "Look, fellows, here's the man with the juice! He said *he* had the juice! Give us our juice, man!"

"What juice?"

"I heard you say you had the juice! What'd you do with our juice?"

"Yes, give us our juice!"

"Give us our juice!"

"Hey, man, give us our juice!"

Anderson would back off.

"I don't have the juice!"

I would follow him. "Listen, I heard you say you had the juice! I distinctly heard you say you had the juice! What did you do with our juice, man? Give us our juice!"

"Yeah, yeah! Give us our juice!"

Then Anderson would scream at me, "God damn you, Bukowski—I don't have the juice!"

Then I'd turn to the fellows: "Look, men, now he's lying! He claims he doesn't *have* the juice!"

"Stop that lying!"

"Give us our juice!"

Anderson and I went through that every night. As I say, it was a very pleasant place.

One day I found a broken hoe in the yard. The hoe itself was all right but somebody had broken the handle almost all the way down. I brought the hoe back into the ward and hid it under my bed. I also found a trash can where they used to throw the empty medicine bottles. I'd keep dipping in there and hiding the stuff under my gown and carrying it back to my cabinet. I hid it all in my cabinet. They were careless. Some of those bottles were 1/5 full. You could still get some good highs off them.

Then they found the hoe under my bed. I was called in Dr. McLain's office.

"Sit down, Bukowski."

He pulled out the hoe and sat it on the desk. I looked at the hoe.

"What were you doing with this under your bed?" he asked.

"It's mine," I said. "I found it out in the yard."

"What were you going to do with this hoe?"

"Nothing."

"Why did you bring it from the yard?"

"I found it there. I put it under my bed."

"You know we can't let you have things like that, Bukowski."

"It's just a hoe."

"We *realize* that it is a hoe."

"What do you want with it, doctor?"

"I don't want it."

"Then give it back. It's *mine*. I found it in the yard."

"You *can't* have it. Come with me."

The doctor had a male nurse with him. They walked up to my bed. The male nurse opened the doors of my bedstand.

"Well, look at this!" said the doctor. "Bukowski's got a regular pharmacy here! Do you have a prescription for this stuff, Bukowski?"

"No, but I'm saving it. It's mine. I *found* it."

"Dump it out, Mickey," the doctor said.

The male nurse pulled up a trash can and threw it all in there.

I was denied my juice for the next three nights. Sometimes they were quite unfair, I thought.

It wasn't very hard to get out. I just climbed a wall and dropped to the other side. I was barefooted and in my gown. I walked down to the bus stop, waited, and when the bus stopped I got on. The driver said, "Where's your money?"

"I don't have any," I answered.

"He's a looney," somebody said.

The bus was moving. "*Who's* a looney?" I asked. "Who said I was a looney?"

Nobody answered.

"They took my juice because of a hoe. I'm not staying there."

I walked down and sat next to a woman.

"Let's make it, baby!" I said.

She turned away. I reached out and pulled her breast. She screamed.

"Hey, look, fellow!"

"Somebody call me?"

"I did."

I looked around. It was a big guy.

"You leave that woman alone," he told me.

I got up and hit him in the mouth. When he rolled from his seat I kicked his head two or three times, and although I didn't have shoes on, I never cut my toenails.

"Oh, God oh Mighty, help, help!" he screamed.

I pulled the bus cord. When the bus stopped, I got out the back door. I walked into a drugstore. I picked up a pack of smokes from the counter, found some matches and lit a cigarette.

There was a little girl in there, about seven, with her mother. "Look at that funny man!" the girl said to her mother.

"Leave the man alone, Daphine."

"I'm God," I told the little girl.

"Mommy! That man says he's God! Is he God, Mommy?"

"I don't think so," said Mama.

I walked up to the little girl, lifted her dress and pinched her behind. The little girl screamed. Mama screamed. I walked out of the drugstore. It was a hot day in early September. The little girl had had on nice blue panties. I looked down upon my body and grinned as the sky fell down. I had a whole day before I decided to go back or not.

Dancing Nina

Nina was what you might call a flirt, a vamp. Her hair was long, her eyes strange and cruel, but she knew how to kiss and dance. And when she kissed and danced, she had a way of offering herself to every man that few women had. That made up for a lot of deficiencies and Nina had a hell of a lot of deficiencies.

But Nina was what she was.

She was a tease. She'd almost rather tease than do the actual thing. What Nina lacked was the ability to choose— she simply couldn't tell a good man from a bad one. The American female, in general, has this same frailty. Nina simply had an overdose.

I met her through a circumstance in Los Angeles that I will not bore you with.

She was hot and she was laughter and she made good love on the bed. Neither of us wanted marriage (she was married before) and I thought, at first, I have finally met my miracle woman.

I noticed her absentness of mind, her repeating of phrases, her telling the same stories again and again. Most of her speech and ideas were borrowed, heard from other minds. But she had this certain invisible *flair* which I didn't recognize then as the ability to tease.

I thought she simply loved *me*.

But at the first party I took her to, I looked up and thought, great god, what have I got hold of here? She didn't simply dance, she actually copulated in front of everybody. It was her right, of course, to copulate in front of everybody. Of course, she didn't copulate, it only appeared that she did.

Nina was the hit of the party. Nina was the hit of *all* the parties.

She was the Eternal Whore come to tease the Genes. We had arguments over her dancing because I still loved part of her.

"I'm too smart for them," she said. "When the party's

over and I've turned the male on, I'll slip out the back door and vanish."

"But that's a lie, you see. You offer yourself to men and then you run away. That's a lie. You're trying to get even with something."

"Listen," she said, "you've got this fuck-chain on your leg. I don't. I float *free*. When I'm dancing, I don't even think of you. I think of the music and I think of *his* dancing, whoever I'm dancing with. I float free—I am a great white bird in the sky."

"O.K., fine."

"You've said before that when I dance, I betray you. How can I betray you?"

"You know how," I replied. "Dancing can be more sexual than copulation. There's more movement and people watching. There are the eyes, the getting closer and closer. I know *you*, bitch. You're no great white bird—you're the Whore of the Centuries . . . "

"You're a son of a bitch, Charlie. You just don't understand."

I don't know why I hung on.

Maybe I just wanted to hear a story, maybe I just wanted to write a story. I suppose the tragedy of her dancing was that she thought she was a great dancer. I had seen great dancing—things that people practiced months, years, lifetimes to bring out.

Nina just brought sex right on out, she did that well, but it was hardly great dancing.

I once saw a white woman in a Turkish café one night. It was one of those places where you ate downstairs, then went upstairs to drink. The dark girls were doing their natural quiet movements alone, and then the American woman, a nicely-shaped blonde got up and did her thing. She did it well but it was ugly because it was so obvious. They asked the woman and her escort to leave and the white American woman screamed obscenities at us—all the way down the stairway. What she never realized was the difference between art and artlessness. Then I turned my eyes upon the dancing dark girls who flowed like rivers of real-ness to the sea . . .

Besides the parties, I got other bits of information from Nina, mostly upon the love bed, before or after. One might call them confessions or perhaps, in her case, exhilarations.

"Yeah. Well, there was this clothing store. I went in to get my husband something. There was this guy there. He was very sarcastic to me. Oh, I always go for these sarcastic guys . . ."

She looked at me but I avoided her cruel eyes.

"He took me behind a curtain and kissed me. There was a little room in the back. He walked behind me and had his cock out and there were some guys there and everybody laughed. I came back later and I told him, 'You're just a queer, aren't you? You're just a queer!'"

"Was he?" I asked.

"I think so."

"O.K. . . ."

"You know," she continued, "I didn't cheat on my husband much. Just maybe once or twice. This one guy, well, I told my husband I had taken his cock out and kissed it but I hadn't screwed him though." More stories: she'd placed an ad in an underground newspaper and gotten 50 answers. One guy left his phone number so Nina called him. She met the young, thin guy in a coffee shop. Then he asked her to drive him down to the park because he'd left his car at the park. "I drove him down," Nina told me, "but I should have known better. He got me real hot, he knew he had me hot, and he had this huge curving cock like a scythe. I never saw anything so big. But he wouldn't tell me his name. I didn't want to get pregnant so I said no. He got angry and said, 'I'd rather screw a guy—at least they don't bother me with all this shit!'"

"And you let him go?"

"Yes, and you should have *seen* it—Huge, curving, like a scythe!"

I don't know. There were many battles and many turn-ings between us. I made a living as a writer which meant I didn't have much money but much time. Time to think—

time to love. I suppose that I was in love with Nina. Even though I was 20 years older than her.

One weekend I drove her all the way to Arizona where she put on a special three-hour dance show in a ranch-house with a homosexual. She wore a pair of red pajamas with strands that flopped open to show her belly and bellybutton.

I drank most of the night in the game room, looking at dead and mounted animals, feeling quite a knowledgeable relationship with them.

Finally, I walked into the poolroom of the ranch-house where they were dancing. I lifted the homosexual high over my head, but decided not to crack his skull on the ceiling. I set him down and then gave my own drunken version of the Dance—the Great White Bird Flying.

When I finished, the fag walked up and said, "Pardon me."

I gave way and he danced with Nina and nobody seemed to object, not even I . . .

Time and things went on, they do, you know.

I gave a few poetry readings, got some minor royalties from a novel. Then I was up in Utah with Nina waiting for the big Fourth of July dance.

"That's the only time when things happen up here," she told me.

So we made the little town big-time dance, and Nina met her big, dumb cowboy. Or maybe he wasn't big and dumb.

I watched him a bit and I thought, hell, he'd even make a writer if something got up and really sliced his soul, showed him where it was at. But nothing had bothered him too much, and so, let's say he had soul of a sort and Nina knew it. She kept looking back at me as she kept offering it to him in the Dance. And I thought—here I am, a stranger in a shit town. I just wish I could get out and leave the Nina's and their people and themselves to each other, but Nina kept slicing in closer and closer and offering herself.

And that was it for me, because if she wanted him, she

could have him. That was my way of thinking: the two that wanted each other should have each other.

But she had to keep bringing him back to me after each dance. "Charlie," she said, "this is Marty. Doesn't Marty dance nice?"

"I don't know much about dancing. I guess he does."

"I want you two guys to be friends," she said.

Then the floor squared off and they danced together, everybody clapping and laughing and joyous. I smoked a cigarette and talked to some big-titted lady about taxes. Then I looked up and Nina and Marty were kissing while they were dancing.

I was hurt but I knew Nina. I shouldn't have been hurt. As they danced they kept on kissing. Everybody applauded. I applauded too. "More, more!" I demanded.

They danced again and again.

The townspeople became more exhilarated. I simply lost hope, came down to reality, and became terribly bored. Bored, that's the only state I can name it. There is something about the beat of dance music. It can only hold me so long then I feel as if I have been flattened with hard and meaningless hammers.

Nina and I had been living in a tent at the edge of town. I was sitting alone against a tree one evening outside the tent when she came running down the road, "Charlie, Charlie, I don't *want* Marty, I want *you*! Please *believe* me, goddamn you!"

Her car was parked along the downward road and evidently Marty was chasing her in the moonlight. The big, dumb cowboy was on a horse. He caught up with her in the path and lassoed her and she screamed in front of me in the dirt. He pulled her blue jeans and panties off and put it in. Her legs raised into the pitch black sky.

I couldn't watch anymore so I walked down the pathway to the main road.

I had a good five-mile walk to the nearest bus station in town.

I felt good.

I knew that they were finished by then and that I was free. I thought of Shostakovich's Fifth Symphony. And as I walked along, I knew that for the first time in years, my heart was free.

The gravel that crunched under my feet provided the best dance of all. Better than all the kissing and dancing that Nina could offer me.

"You ain't a real cowboy until you got some steer dung on your boots." . . .

Pall Mall McEvers—July 29, 1941

Phoenix, Jan. 13th, 1972

Well, being a writer means doing many things so that the writing is not too lousily aligned from one base, and one doesn't always choose the obvious—like Paris or San Francisco or a COSMEP meeting—so here I am typing standing up, à la Hemingway, only on an over-turned table spool somewhere in an Arizona desert, a yellow monoplane with propeller going overhead—Africa and the lions far away—the lessons of Gertie Stein ingested and ignored—I have just stopped a dogfight between a small mongrel dog and a German police dog—and that takes some minor guts—and the mongrel lays on the cable spool below my feet—grateful and dusty and chewed—and I left the cigarettes elsewhere—I stand under a limp and weeping tree in Paradise Valley and smell the horseshit and remember my beaten court in Hollywood, drinking beer and wine with 9th rate writers and after extracting what small juices they have, throwing them physically out the door.

Now a little girl walks up and she says, "Bukowski, what are you doing, you dummy?"

Now I am called in for a sandwich in the place to my right. Literature can wait. There are 5 women in there. They are all writing novels. Well, what can you do with 5 women?

The sandwiches are good and the conversation begins:

"Well, I worked for this lawyer once and he had this guru on his desk and I got hot and took it into the woman's john, and the head was just right, the whole thing was shaped just right, it was pretty good. When I finished I put the thing back on the lawyer's desk. It took the paint right off the thing when I did it and the lawyer came back and noticed it and said, 'What the hell happened to my guru?'

and I said, 'What's the matter? Is something wrong with it?'
Then he phoned up the company he got the thing from and
complained because the paint had come off after he'd only
had the thing a week . . . "

The girls laughed, "Oh hahaha ha, oh, hahaha!" I
smiled.

"I read in *The Sensuous Woman*," said another of the
novelists, "that a woman can climax 64 times in a row, so I
tried it . . . "

"How'd you make out?" I asked.

"I made it 13 times . . . "

"All these horny guys walking around," I said, "you
ought to be ashamed."

Here I am, I thought, sitting with these women, sleeping with the most beautiful one of them, and where are the
men? Branding cattle, punching timeclocks, selling insurance . . . How can I bitch about my lot as a starving writer?
I'll find a way . . . Tomorrow I'll go to *Turf Paradise* and see
if the gods are kind. Surely I can outbet these cowboys and
the old folks who come out here to die? Then there's the
poem. Patchen died Saturday night of a heart attack and
John Berryman jumped off a bridge into the Mississippi Friday and they haven't found his body yet. Things are looking better. These young guys write like Oscar Wilde with
a social consciousness. There's room at the top and nothing at the bottom. I can see myself walking through TIMES
SQUARE and all the young girls saying, "Look there goes
Charles Bukowski!" Isn't that the meaning of living immor-
tality? Besides free drinks?

I finish my sandwich, let the beautiful one know that
I still love her, soul and her body, then walk back into the
desert to my overturned wooden reel, and I sit here typing
now. I *stand* here typing now, looking at horses and cows,
and over to my left are mountains shaped differently than
those tiresome mountains north of L.A., and I'll be back
to L.A., it's the only place for the literary hustler: at least
I hustle best there, it's my Paris, and unless they run me
out like Villon I have to die there. My landlady drinks beer

from the quart bottle and forces them upon me and takes ten bucks off the rent (a month) because I take out the tenants' garbage cans and bring them back in. That's more advantageous than a *Great Writer's Course*.

I got worried about the girls, though, they dance sexy with the cowboys at the local tavern and make big cow eyes at them; sun-tanned raw dudes who ain't even read Swinburne yet . . . Nothing to do but drink beer, act stoical, indifferent, human, and literary.

The little girl comes back:

"Hi, Bukowski, dummy! Without no shirt on, without no shoes on, without no pants on, without no panties on, bare-naked typing outside . . . ."

She's 3 years old and drives a toy tractor by, stops, looks back again:

"Hi, Bukowski, dummy! No pants on, no panties on, bare-naked typing in the sun . . . No hair on, bare-butt typing, drowning in the water . . . "

No hair on? The female, of course, is the eternal problem as long as that thing stands up. And living 50 years doesn't bring a man any closer to solutions. Love still arrives 2 or 3 times in a lifetime for most of us, and the rest is sex and companionship, and it's all problems and pain and glory . . .

And here *she* comes across the dust, 31 years' worth, cowboy boots, long red brown hair, dark brown eyes, tight blue pants, turtleneck sweater; she's smiling . . .

"Whatcha doin', man?"

"Writing . . . "

We embrace and kiss; her body folds into mine and those brown eyes reflect birds and rivers and sun; they are hot bacon, they are chili and beans, they are nights past and nights future, they are enough, they are more than enough . . . Where she learned to kiss I'll never know. As we part, something stands out in front of me.

"We'll go to the track tomorrow," she says.

"Sure," I say, "and how about *this* thing?"

I look down.

"Don't worry. We'll take care of it," she says.

We walk about and lock again over by the rabbit pen. Appropriate.

"You're the horniest old man I ever met . . . "

I send her away soon so I can finish this column. I watch the movement of her ass as she walks across the desert toward the house. She bends over to pet a dog. Freud, this is what the wars are all about, you had some truth going there, even though it was slightly hyped . . .

I stop another dog fight. This time 2 young girls walk through with a larger dog. The German police dog attacks. It is a good fight. I leap in with a stick, grab the large dog by the collar.

"Thanks," says one of the girls.

She reminds me of one I knew, married wrong, who used to beat on my door for consolation . . .

Charles Bukowski—his writing style . . .

Well, he designed it by drinking beer from quart bottles, rolling *Prince Albert* in *Zig Zag* and interfering in dog fights . . .

Now I see that I have fallen into one of my bad habits: I have written this in both the present and past tense. Instead of correcting it I will throw it at the editors to test their liberality . . . Now two kids come home from school and the boy throws me a ball. I've got all my sharp and catch it, wing it back with a deft and nonchalant accuracy . . . Ernie would have been proud. Now, I'd like to tell you something about Phoenix whorehouses . . . but that's going to take a bit of research. A blind writer told me yesterday that it's the 3rd largest dope center in the U.S. The blind writer also told me that he thought those (writers) who had lasted through the ages were badly chosen. I've had that thought for some time. Such boring fellows.

Now if you think I've always stood out in the desert standing up by an overturned reel, mixing my tenses and clowning, you're wrong, babies. I've starved in tiny rat-filled, roachfilled rooms without enough money for stamps.

I used to lay down drunk in alleys waiting for trucks to run me over . . . Here are those two kids standing here . . .

"We've come to bug you, man!"

"Yeah? I say.

"Do you like 7-UP?"

"Hell no. I like hard liquor."

Now the young girl is climbing up on my precious reel, bugging me. But since the brought me some 7-UP I will tolerate their indecencies. Now the young boy gets up on my precious reel and dances. Now here comes two more kids. One gets up on the table.

"What's your name?" I ask.

"Genie," he says.

"You guys do something exciting so I can write about it. Then GET THE HELL OUT OF HERE!"

They don't do anything but bug, bug, bug . . . How would Ernie handle this? Who owns all these? There they go . . .

There's hardly enough sex to this column . . . I thought if I stayed in the desert I would get me some solitude. This is worse than Hollywood with all those drunks getting me out of bed at 11 a.m. to hear the sounds of their diminishing souls. I can't recommend outdoor writing. At least the birds haven't shit on me. One of those desert kids suggested that I wrote my next on horseback. Well, I tried Phoenix and Phoenix tried me. The sun's going down now and my legs are immensely disgusted. I suppose it's too obvious: Writing on an overturned reel in this place. I probably brought some Hollywood with me. If the races aren't any better than this writing, then I'm a sure loser tomorrow. Meanwhile, it's pack this machine back and sit down and listen to the ladies tell about screwing broom handles, cucumbers and the like . . . which reminds me of the guy who told me he stuck his into a vacuum cleaner . . . quack, quack, quack. I hear ducks. I whirl with this machine and stride toward that houseful of dirty female novelists . . .

awakened in a strange bedroom in a strange bed with a strange woman in a strange town. I was up against her back and my penis was inserted into her cunt dog-fashion. It was hot in there and my penis was hard. I moved it a little and she moaned. She appeared to be asleep. Her hair was long and dark, quite long; in fact, a portion of it lay across my mouth—I brushed it away to breathe better, then stroked again. I felt hungover. I dropped out and rolled on my back and tried to reconstruct.

I had flown into town a few days earlier and had given a poetry reading . . . . when? . . . the night before. It was a hot town. Kandel had read there 2 weeks earlier. And just before that the National Guard had managed to bayonet a few folk on campus. I liked an action town. My reading had gone all right. I had opened a pint and gone on through it. The regents and the English dept. had backed down at the last moment and I had to go on backed by student funds.

After the reading there had been a party. Vodka, beer, wine, scotch, gin, whiskey. We sat on the rug and drank and talked. There had been one next to me . . . . long black hair, one tooth missing in the front when she smiled. That missing tooth had endeared me. That was it, and there I was.

I got up to get a drink of water. Nice place. Large. I saw two babies crawling in a crib. No, it was one baby. One was in the crib, crawling. The other was outside walking around naked. A clock said 9:45 a.m. Well, it didn't *say* 9: 45 a.m. I went into the kitchen and sterilized a bottle and warmed some milk. I gave the baby the bottle and he went right at it. I gave the walking kid an apple. I couldn't find any seltzer. There were 2 beers left in the refrigerator. I drank another glass of water and opened the beer. Nice kitchen. Nice young girl. Missing tooth. Nice missing tooth.

I finished the one beer, opened the other, cracked 2 eggs, put on chili powder and salt, and ate. Then I walked into the other room and this kid said, "I can see your Peter." And I told him, "I can see your Peter too." Over on the mantle I saw a letter, opened, addressed to a Mrs. Nancy Ferguson. I walked back into the bedroom, placed myself down behind her again.

"Nancy?"

"Yes, Hank?"

"I gave the kid a bottle, the other one an apple."

"Thanks."

"Your husband?"

My penis got hard again. I inserted it into her butt.

"We're . . . . ouch!—go easy there! . . . we're separated."

"Did you like my reading?"

"Oooh, goddamn it! Easy there! Yes, the reading was great. I liked it better than Corso's reading."

"Corso? You've heard him? How about Kandel?"

"I missed the Kandel . . . ."

"I met Corso the other night," I said.

"Ah, you've met him?—Please! It doesn't feel bad, but go easy . . . . What was Corso like?"

"Fine, he was fine. I'd heard he was very mouthy, but really he wasn't. Really gentle and entertaining . . . ."

"Listen, don't rip me up!"

"He wore this white outfit with little rivulets and strings hanging off of it. He wore beads, an amulet . . . ."

"That's good, that's good . . . ."

"What's good?"

"You're going good, or maybe I'm getting used to it."

"Oh yeah?"

"OW! Not that!"

"Corso read the cards. He said I was POWER!"

"Oh, I believe it!"

"Corso asked me why I didn't wear any beads or rings. . . ."

"What did you tell him?"

"I . . . ."

"Listen, take it OUT, you're KILLING ME!"

I pulled it out. She turned around. I was right. It was the one with the missing tooth. She looked down at me.

"Do you mind if I kiss it?" she asked.

"Not really," I said.

"They say I'm the greatest poet since Rimbaud," I said.

"Go ahead," I said, "go ahead."

"I gave the one kid a bottle," I said, "I gave the other one an apple."

"You've got a nice place here," I said.

"Go ahead," I said. "Don't worry about it."

"Oh Jesus!" I said.

"Uh uh uh uh uh, oh uh oh uh," I said.

She went to the bathroom. When she got back she climbed into bed and looked at me.

"I've bought all your books, I've read all your books."

"Greatest since Rimbaud," I said.

"How come they call you 'Hank'?"

"Charles is really my middle name."

"Do you like to give poetry readings?"

"Yes, when they end like this one."

I got up and began to dress.

"Will you write me?" she asked.

"Nancy, please write your address on this piece of paper."

I handed her paper and pen. Twenty minutes later I was taking a taxi back to the place of my host. He wanted to know where I'd been. I told him, other side of town. The next day I took the plane back to L.A. I remembered the lady with fondness for several days, then I forgot about her. I'm not using her real name in this story but she was then just separated from an underground poet of some reputation. Well, the way I remembered her again was this. I'd had some poems accepted by this mag up near Frisco and the editor liked to write these long letters. Well, in this letter the editor said he was up drinking with this underground poet the night before and the poet made them all laugh by telling them how he screwed this certain lady in the ass in a Portland hotel room, and this lady was one of the powers in The National Foundation of the Arts outfit, the one that awarded grants. Well, I answered the letter, since K. likes to laugh so much, you tell him that I met his wife one night after reading at the University of . . . . I didn't hear from the editor again or the underground poet, and I didn't write the lady and I never met Corso again, and if anybody sees

Corso you tell him that I don't like to wear rings just because I don't like to wear rings, and that's sufficient enough
and that's also the end of this story.

S he drove him down Sunset and they had breakfast in the afternoon at a place with a Japanese waiter with long hair. There were long hairs and Hollywood types all about. Vicki ordered. Vicki was buying. Vicki suggested the waffles and eggs, plus. He said, "All right, I'll take the sausage, and it feels good to be a gigolo." She suggested a drink—something new to him—champagne and orange juice. Hank said that would be all right.

"Is it over?" she asked.

"Yes."

"What are you going to do?"

"Continue. And eat waffles with nice ladies. And talk."

"What are you going to do about me?" she asked.

"I'm not going to try to force myself on you," he said.

"There's no way you can."

The drinks arrived.

"Did you love her?"

"Shit, yes. My second love. I've been in love twice in 50 years. That's not bad, is it?"

"All you need to beat it," Vicki said, "is time, time and doing your work and meeting other people."

"That's what I'm doing. How're you doing?"

"Two marriages. Ten years and four years. Other men, plenty of other men, but not for too long."

"Nothing seems to last," said Hank.

"Have you ever known of a happy marriage?"

"No, and no happy shackjobs or relationships either."

"What goes wrong?"

"Well, I'd say, presuming that everything else is fairly in order, that somehow the chemical admixture always seems improper."

They finished their drinks. Breakfast had arrived.

"Tell me about the admixture."

"It's always the same. There is one person who cares very much and one person who doesn't seem to care, or who only half-cares. The one who doesn't care too much is

79

in control. The relationship ends when the one who doesn't care gets tired of the game."

"Which ends have you been on, Hank?"

"Both ends. This last time, I cared."

"The waffles are good, aren't they?"

"Damned good."

They ate quietly, then had another drink. Vicki picked up the tab. Nine dollars. Jesus. He walked back and left a tip. They walked to the car.

"You're going to stop drinking, aren't you?"

"Sure. First stages of the split, you know. Self-pity."

"Listen, ever since I've known you, you've been in some kind of turmoil, sitting with a drink in your hand."

"You don't know me."

"I know you. I used to come visit you. Don't you remember?"

"I think I do."

Vicki backed the car out. "Why do all the young girls take the old men? Why don't they leave me some of the old men?"

"They just did. Last Friday afternoon."

She turned down Sunset. "Well, where do you want to go?"

"Ta ta . . . you know I'm in agony. What's appropriate?"

"How's your sense of humor?"

"They say it's all right."

"What do *you* say?"

"I say it's all right."

Vicki drove along. Hank sat in the sunshine thinking, well, I'm out of it now. If I'm intelligent at all I'll stay out of the woman game. But it's difficult. I had four years of perfect solitude and strength, and then one knocked on the door . . .

Vicki turned into a driveway and they were in The Hollywood Cemetery. She followed the circling drive, then she parked and they got out.

They began to walk. There wasn't anybody else about. They had the whole cemetery to themselves on a Sunday.

"Look, this is it . . . "

They walked about, looking at the stones.

"Look," she said, "Tyrone Power is a *bench*. Let's sit on Tyrone Power!"

They went and sat on Tyrone Power. He was a bench and he was made of cement. They sat on him.

"Oh," said Vicki, "I just *loved* Tyrone Power and now he's made himself into a bench and he allows me to sit on him. I think that's nice!"

They sat on Tyrone Power a while and then got up and walked about. And there was Griffith, one of the beginners, he had this huge spike snarling into the sky.

There were many separate tombs above the ground, like little cement houses with locked steel front doors. Hank walked up and tried his keys on one of the doors. No good. You couldn't visit them.

They walked some more. Then they saw the tomb of Douglas Fairbanks. Douglas Fairbanks was really laid out. "Goodnight, Sweet Prince . . . " They all got overdosed on Goodnight Sweet Prince.

His tomb was above the ground and Douglas had his own private lake, quite a large one. They walked up the steps to the tomb and then went around behind it and sat on a bench there.

"Look," she said, "the ants are getting into Douglas."

It was true. There was a little hole in the tomb and the ants were going in there.

"We should fuck back here," said Vicki. "Don't you think it would be nice to fuck back here?"

"I'm afraid I couldn't get it up back here."

Hank reached out and kissed her. It was a long slow kiss among the dead . . .

"Let's go see the Sheikh," she said, "let's go see the fag."

"All right."

"What was his name?"

"Rudolph Valentino."

They walked into the large building and began looking for Rudolph.

"The newspapers used to make a lot of it. People used to come on his death anniversary. Along with a lady in black. Now they don't come anymore. People die. But love dies faster."

"Well, we're going to see him."

It took some searching. Rudolph had had an economy layout, it seemed. He was down near the bottom and near the corner and in between and below all those other bodies. His vases had something standing in them, something very stale.

They turned to walk out. A young girl in an orange sweater, purple slacks and smiling, was walking with a very fragile white-haired old lady.

"We're looking for the Sheikh," said the young girl laughing.

"He's down there," pointed Hank, "down there in that dark corner."

They walked over and looked.

"Oh my god," said the old woman, "look at all these empty vaults. I'm too close to these empty vaults!"

"Oh, Mary, you've got a long way to go yet!"

"No, I haven't. No, I haven't!"

"Mary . . . "

"Let's get out of here!"

They hurried past Vicki and Hank.

"Peter Lorre is just around the corner," said the young girl to Hank as they went past.

"Thanks."

They walked around and looked at Peter. He looked just like the rest of them. They moved on. They walked about casually. It was pleasant. All clean and secure and dull. No pain.

Vicki wanted to steal a glass vase but she wanted a hand-cut glass vase. Hank talked her out of it. "They may search us. With a face like mine . . . "

"You've got a beautiful face. I've always admired you. You're one of the few real men I've known . . . ."

"Thanks, but leave the vase."

"Tell me I'm pretty."

"You're pretty, and I like very much being with you."

They kissed in the tombs. Then they walked toward the

entrance. Three men were up front. They were locking the door.

"Oh," said Vicki.

They ran. "Hey! Hey!" yelled Hank, "wait a minute!"

The door was locked. They beat on the door. The men turned. One came forward and put a key in, opened the door.

"It's closing time," he said.

"O.K. thanks . . . "

The keepers walked off and Vicki and Hank walked down toward the car. They got in and Hank bummed a cigarette.

"Of course," he said, "it's no good now, but think if we had been locked in there? Wouldn't it have been wonderful?"

"Well, you can think of it that way. I figure we got all the benefits . . . We didn't get locked in but we *almost* did."

"Maybe you're right."

They were on the street again. "Look, Vicki, let's stop off at my place . . . "

"Why? You want to see if she left a note? You want to see if she might phone?"

"That's over, I tell you. It's history, deader than a Douglas Fairbanks tomb. I just want to leave a note for Marty. Marty said he was coming by tonight. I don't want to hang him up. I just want to leave a note on the door."

"You've still got her on your mind."

"I just don't want to hang up Marty. Now don't spoil a good afternoon."

"It has been a good afternoon, hasn't it?"

"Yes."

They got to the place. Hank had the front court.

"Just drive up on the lawn."

Vicki parked it and they went on in.

"God," she said, "this place is filthy! Got a broom?"

"Trauma," he said, "forget it. Sit down."

He gave Vicki three or four books and she sat there. He let the water run in the tub. He heard her laughing. Well, they were pretty fair books. He had written them.

He got into the tub. *The Wormwood Review No. 44* was on the edge of the tub. He began to read the first page:

From a Letter by Henry Green to G.W.—dated June 9, 1954 in W.R. Archives:

A man falls in love because there is something wrong with him. It is not so much a matter of his health as it is of his mental climate: as, in winter, one longs for the spring . . .

It went on, and ended:

It is the horror we feel of ourselves, that is of being alone with ourselves, which draws us to love, but this love should happen only once, and never be repeated. If we have, as we should, learnt our lesson, which is that we are, all and each of us, always and finally alone.

Hank got out and toweled. Vicki was still laughing. "Your writing's so raw. You're too goddamned much."

"Thanks, kid . . . "

He walked into the bedroom and got into some fresh clothes. He got the shoes on and then checked the place out. He decided to see if the back screen door was locked. He stepped into the back porch. There was something in the way. A batch of tin and on top of it a bottle of pills and under the bottle of pills a note scrawled on the back of an old envelope:

Hank—
I'm leaving this cooler
For the fifteen collars
I owe you—
The pills for your tired
Blood
The panties to smell
While you masturbate—

                              Carol

Hank hooked the back door, threw the latch on the porch door and walked out front.

"Let's go."

"Where?"

"Your place would be nice."

"Sure, but don't you want to wait for a phone call?"

"There won't be a phone call."

"Why not?"

"I told you: one loves, the other decides."

"Don't be so dramatic."

They got into the car and drove off. She turned down Normandie.

"Wait," said Hank, "I've got a pair of panties in my pocket. I wonder if they'd fit you?"

"Don't get vicious with me," she said.

"I'm not getting vicious."

"I know you're not."

"Look, we're not even shacked and we're having our first argument," Hank said.

"Look," she said, "it's a beautiful evening."

"Yes."

She took Franklin to Bronson, then up north on Bronson.

"And look—there's a Backyard Sale! Let's go to the Backyard Sale. You buy me something and I'll buy you something," Vicki said.

They got out and walked up the drive. There was a hippy-looking guy and a young girl sitting way up the drive. As they passed a row of shrubs he took the panties out of his pocket and threw them into the brush. They hooked on a lower branch. They were yellow and they swung slightly in the breeze.

He took her hand. She looked handsome, like a woman who knew things, or a woman who wanted to. He supposed he'd find out.

Joe went in to take a shower and when he came out naked there was another guy on the bed and the guy had his clothes on and he was kissing with Julie. The guy looked at Joe and then kept on kissing. Julie had gotten dressed and so there they were both dressed and kissing while Joe stood there watching.

The guy's cock was hard and Julie reached for it, grabbed it. Then she pulled the zipper back and got it out and began tonguing it. Joe's cock began to get hard. Then Julie had the guy's penis in her mouth, working on it. The guy just groaned and stretched out there. The sunlight from the window glanced off and on of Julie's head as it bobbed. Joe began masturbating. He stood right over them and began to masturbate. Then the guy came and Julie got it and then Joe pulled her head off of his tool and worked his penis into her mouth and then he came and Julie got that too.

Julie went to the bathroom. When she came out the guy was zipped and sitting in a chair smoking a cigarette. Joe was dressed except for getting his shoes on.

Julie said, "Joe, this is Artie. Artie, this is Joe."

They shook hands.

"It finally rained the other day," said Joe. "It was good to get that rain. First in about a year."

"Yeah," said Artie, "we needed that rain."

"I'm hungry," said Julie, "let's go get something to eat."

Joe got his shoes on and they walked outside. They turned south and then right and they were on the boardwalk. There was a young black guy walking toward them. Julie drifted out as if she didn't see him and she walked into him.

Julie said, "I'm sorry, I didn't see you."

"That's all right." said the black guy.

Julie put her face real close to his. As close as she could get without touching. Her body was the same way.

"I should watch where I'm walking," she laughed. She stood there and stared deeply into the black guy's face.

Neither of them said anything. They just stood there like that.

When Julie walked back over to Artie and Joe, the black guy followed. The black guy said his name was Lawrence. They turned into *The Happy Hunting Ground* and sat at a table. Joe ordered draft beers from the waitress. Julie was to Joe's left. She leaned forward and whispered into his ear, "Listen, Joe, I love you. I really *do* love you. But you've got to give me room, lots and lots of *room*."

"Sure," said Joe.

They got the beers and made small talk. Then Julie stood up and said, "I'm going to liberate this bar!" She walked over to the jukebox and put in some money. Then as she walked away she grabbed a guy who had just come out of the crapper. "Will you dance with me, mister?"

They danced.

Julie was great. She danced like she was fucking the guy right on the floor. Only it was better than fucking because she could get in more movements. All the men watched. Julie's ass mashed and turned. She gave the feeling that she was out of control. Julie could really dance. Meanwhile she put her eyes on the guy with the most inviting look one could imagine. When the dance ended the guy came over and sat at their table. His name was William.

"I wish I could really dance the way I wanted to," said Julie.

"How's that?" asked Lawrence.

"I mean, I really dance WILD! I mean, I just wouldn't dare dance the way I actually feel! Sometimes I feel like I'm going to fly! Oh, I feel so WILD! If I could only let it go!"

"You're doing fine," said Artie.

Julie got up to dance with Lawrence. It did seem wilder than the preceding. At the end of the dance Julie and Lawrence whirled into the men's room and locked the door. While they were in there Artie ordered three rounds of beers.

"You've got quite a girlfriend there, Joe," said Artie.

"A real sexpot," said Joe, "and she loves me. She just came off a ten-year marriage. The woman's lib gave her the strength to break it. She's a liberated woman. Intelligent. She's got a lot of soul."

"And how," said William.

After a while Julie and Lawrence came out of the men's room. They sat down at the table.

"Lawrence *sculpts*," said Julie, "isn't it wonderful?"

"You any good?" Joe asked Lawrence.

"Pretty good."

"How about the money?"

"Well, I haven't made any money yet but it will be along."

Then Julie danced with the bartender. Near the end of the dance she got in real close and rubbed her box against him. When they broke the bartender had a hard on. He got around the bar and gave himself a double whiskey with water.

"Where I come from in the country," said Julie, "dancing is just natural. The trouble with some city men is that they think dancing is dirty. Out in the country dancing is just natural. Why, we have this big 4th of July dance every year and it's just more *fun!* One old guy actually leaps around like some kind of frog."

"Dancing's all right," said Joe. "I got nothing against dancing."

"Me neither," said Lawrence.

"It's just that," said Julie, "some men just can't dance good so they get jealous when I dance."

"Sure," said Joe, "that's it."

Then Julie went over to another table and asked a blonde kid to dance with her. They had been eyeballing each other. Julie began to dance and she really turned it on for him. Every man in the place had a hard on. The cat walked by and even the cat had a hard on. Julie was liberating the bar.

"I could dance for hours," said Julie afterwards. "I could dance night and day. I just love to dance."

Nobody said anything. Joe bought another round of beers.

"We came here to eat but to hell with it," he said.

"You're not getting nasty, are you Joe?"

"What do you mean?"

"I mean you don't mind me dancing with all these men?"

"No, it's all right."

"I mean, if you don't like the way I act maybe I can find a man who *does* like the way I act."

"I'm sure you can."

"Now what do you mean by that?"

"Oh, shit . . . "

"Now what's the matter? Why are you swearing?"

"Oh, Christ . . . "

"Look, Joe, you're just *jealous*. I never met a more *jealous* man! You think I can't *feel* your jealousy?"

"I don't know what you can feel."

"Listen, Joe, there's something *wrong* with you. You oughta go see a shrink and get yourself untangled. This is the modern age. You act like some guy out of 1900. Look around and see what's happening. This is the modern age . . . "

"Shit . . . "

"See? See? If you don't want me, Joe, maybe I can find . . . "

Joe got out of his chair and walked toward the door. Then he was outside on the boardwalk. He walked down to the grocery store and got a pint of scotch and a six-pack. Then he went to his place, peeled the bottle, and opened a beer. He'd make the track tomorrow and the fights Thursday. He had to get out of it. Maybe he was 1900. Maybe there was a reason to be 1900.

The phone rang. It was Julie. "Listen, Joe, if you ever get over your stupid jealousy, let me know. There might be a chance for us then. But right now there's no way."

Joe didn't answer. She hung up. Then he went to the refrigerator and made a salami and cheese sandwich. He ate it with a beer. Then he had a shot. Then he stretched out on his bed and looked at the little cracks in the ceiling. The cracks made designs. He discovered an elephant, a horse and a bear. And they were all dancing.

Pete Fox is a gem. My friends wondered why I can laugh at, with, and during Pete Fox. Pete is 1930. Pete is 1940. Pete is a fat Bogart. Pete is early Edward G. Robinson. Pete is James Cagney. Pete is dull as warm piss and funnier and more tragic. Pete is myself when I am drunk, very drunk. Pete is all the worst parts of me put out where I can see them.

Pete usually arrives around midnight with something to drink. He places himself on my couch almost flat, just the head looking up at me.

"Where's Linda?"

She's gone. This is Liza."

"Oh, Liza. *Liza!* Oh . . . "

He looks at me. "Hank, you don't mind if I try to make it with Liza? I couldn't make it with Linda. I tried to make it with Linda. Do you mind if I try to make it with Liza?"

"Pete, no man ever owns any woman, nor does any woman ever own any man."

"But Linda was so *pretty* . . . What happened between you and Linda? . . . *Geeez!*"

I take a drink and don't answer.

He looks at Liza from flat on his back. "Linda . . . I mean, *Liza*, hahaha . . . do you mind if I try to make it with you?"

"Yes, I mind *very* much. I don't want you."

"Ah, hell, you don't have to be *that* way! I'm just trying to be friends! Don't get mad!"

He straightens up from the couch, pours himself another wine.

"This is good shit, ain't it, Hank?"

"It's o.k."

"It must be. You're stayin' right up there with me. That's what I like about you . . . I can drink with you and *talk* to you. I can't talk with most people. Hey, you know what happened when I left your place last time?"

"No."

"I got rolled."

"Rolled?"

"Yeah. I went up around Cahuenga Blvd., they call it Siff Gulch. Anyway, I'm drunk, you know, and I'm walking down the sidewalk and here comes this young girl, she looks pretty good, you know, and she puts it to me, ten bucks, she says. So I say o.k. Well, we get in my car and I give her the ten and she starts going down on me. She's pretty good, you know."

He looks at me and I nod. Of course, we are both guys who get so much of it that we can tell the pretty good from the other. So I nod.

"Well, she's working away, you know. She's taking a lot of time, doing it right. Suddenly she pulls away. 'What the hell's wrong with you?' I ask. 'I don't want to do it!' she says. 'What ya want to do?' I say, 'leave me with a *rock?* You can't leave me with a *rock!* I'll beat the shit out of you!' 'I don't care,' she says, 'I won't do it!'

'All right, baby,' I say, 'just give me my ten back then!' She gives me back the ten and I let her go. Man, she hasn't been gone five minutes . . . I look for my roll, I always take it out of my wallet, you know. I had it all rolled up with rubber bands. You know, she found it? And everything was in there, my i.d., driver's license, and the money. She found that."

"A real pro," I say.

"I've been rolled dozens of times," says Pete.

"Me too, Pete."

We drink our wines and wait for something. Then Pete looks at Liza.

"Linda . . . I mean, Liza, hahaha . . . Boy, Hank can really pick 'em, one after another . . . You know, I knew Frances too. Well, she had a little grey in her hair, and now she's got those snaggles straightened out in her teeth, she looks pretty good . . . "

He pours another wine. "What I'm really saying is that I could *go* you, baby!"

Liza and Pete are both sitting on the couch. Pete stretches out sideways, put his head near Liza's leg, looks up . . . "Baby . . . "

I start laughing and Liza gets angry. "You big hunk of shit," she says to Pete, "move off!" Pete sits up. "Listen, I was here when Hank smashed all of Linda's teeth out. She was a bloody mess! You shoulda seen her. I ain't never hit a woman. I'm a real MAN!"

We don't see him any more for two or three nights, then around midnight he shows. He is in bermudas and t-shirt and has a bottle of wine and a woman and a little girl with him.

"Hi!" he says.

I let him in. There are introductions. The lady is Tina. A very severe face. She has been hurt by a dozen men. Now she goes to the Unitarian church and is filled with causes, and she finally knows the kind of man she wants but it's too late because the body is gone and the charm and the originality are gone. Her hair is white. She'd make a fine nun. Her daughter exuberates. Her daughter hasn't met any men yet. Her daughter is 7. Liza tells the daughter that there are some toys in the corner. The daughter's name is Nana.

I open Pete's bottle and began pouring drinks into the glasses. Pete has already been drinking.

"You know, Hank," he says, "I heard you out the window last time I left. I heard you say to Liza, 'Liza, the gods have sent this man to me! I am so fortunate!' You did say that, didn't you?"

"I did."

"You know that Nana knows Marina, don't you?"

(Marina is my 7-year-old daughter.)

"No, I didn't know that."

"Well, they know each other."

"That's fine."

Then he looks at the severe Tina sitting very upright upon the couch, clutching her wine glass in her crucified hand. Then he looks back at Liza and myself.

"You know, I been trying to make Tina for a long time!"

Pete drinks some wine, looking down into his glass, then looks up.

"Yeah, ha, ha, ha, I been trying to make Tina for a long time . . . but I can't seem to make it . . . can I, Tina?"

He looks at her. Tina doesn't answer.

"Of course, I can't get it *up*, anyhow. I can't get the damned thing up! So even *if* I made her . . . ? . . . ?"

Pete drinks again at the wine. "This is good shit, ain't it?"

"Sure, Pete."

"I notice you're stayin' right with me. It has to be good stuff. I like to talk with you Hank. Even though you did smash all of Linda's teeth out . . . " He looks at Liza. "I told you he smashed all of Linda's teeth out, didn't I?"

"You told me," said Liza.

"Yeah, I been trying to make this woman . . . " he looks at Tina ". . . for a long time. But, hell, I can't get it up. I doubt that I can get the damned thing up . . . "

"Listen," says Tina, "I've got to go. I've got to get Nana to bed!"

"Oh, what the hell, baby!" says Pete.

"No, we've got to go."

Nana and Tina leave. I pour some more drinks.

"You're a tough guy, Hank. But I'm a tough guy too. Did I ever tell you how I got these cauliflower ears?"

"Yeah, Pete."

"Well, you heard some of the stories but you haven't heard all of them. How come, Hank, you ain't got no cauliflower ears?"

"I'd rather give than receive."

"Linda, I mean Liza, have you ever seen my cauliflower ears?"

"Yes."

"But you ain't looked at them real close, have you?"

Pete gets down on his hands and knees and starts crawling along the rug. Liza is sitting in a chair by the fireplace. He crawls toward her.

"I got these cauliflower ears, Lisa."

Pete crawls toward her. He is a very heavy man, close to 250 pounds, all beerfat and whiskeyfat and the easy life of some money. The rug hurts his hardshell knees and his butt is rammed upward quite awkwardly. His face is eaten by flat afternoons and greasy foods. He has never considered suicide or that life might be meaningless. He likes football, bad poetry, Iceberg Slim, and more than enough to drink. He crawls forward.

I know what is going to happen. It is the unfolding of a slow movie that one can't stop. It is preciously great. I can't stop it. I don't want to stop it. It's Cary Grant. Dimple in chin, forever. It's all the sad and wonderful and horrible things. It's everything, lousy things that I have done without feeling and all the lousy things that I will do in the future without feeling, and all the lousy things that will be done, thusly, to you and to me and to all. Pete crawls toward her, the snail in the china closet, the holy grail filled with $1.69 of cheap wine . . .

"See, I got these cauliflower ears Liza? Now see this one?"

He turns his head sideways. He is a child of a mountain of a man. He is infinite and distant, yet like a horseshoe or a turnip.

"That's the one. Now look at this other one."

Liza sits there looking at the other one. And then the thing that we all know is going to happen, happens. He straightens his head, opens his eyes wide, then pokes his head forward between Liza's knees. It is entirely too much: it is too wonderful and horrible and beautiful and foolish to believe. I begin laughing. I can't stop. Pete holds his pose. Liza leaps up.

"You son of a bitch! I don't have to take that!"

"But Liza . . . "

"I warned you from last time . . . "

"What the hell's the matter, Liza, honey?"

Pete turns and looks at me over his back, over his ass crouched in bermudas.

"Now what the hell's the matter with her?" he asks me.

He leaves soon after that. But I'm sure he'll be back. Our wonderful Cagney. Our Alan Ladd. Our 1937 hero. I hereby light altars to him. Let it be known. Somebody must be sacrificed. Do you remember the tiny grains of sand in the old-fashioned hourglass? Out of one globe and into another, dripping. And when one globe was empty, an hour was gone or 12 hours or 24 hours or however they were constructed? But I always cheated. I kept turning the globes back and forth, frustrating the machinery . . . Pete Fox is something like that. I use him. I am sorry if I have used him and I realize that it isn't quite right, but I like to laugh whenever possible, and Pete will never know and if he did finally find out, he'd only be proud.

Precious holy things finally lack accurate glory.

'd had a breakup with Jane and she was the first woman I had ever loved and my guts were hanging out by a string, and I started drinking, but it was the same, it was worse, drinking only shot the pain upwards, but I was angry too because she'd slept with another man, and a real idiot sort too, as if to punish me, and it killed some of the love but not all of it, and to make sure I wouldn't find her in one of the bars in town and start the agony all over again, I took a bus (I'd had my driver's license revoked for drunk driving) to Inglewood that afternoon and started drinking in a bar full of rednecks, a bar decked out to look like Hawaii, and since Hawaii seemed the falsest place in the world to me I walked into the bar and started drinking, hoping for a good fight with some redneck, hoping for a good fight with anybody, but they didn't bother me and Jane kept lighting up in front of me, scenes of her walking across the floor or putting on her stockings or laughing, and I drank faster, played songs and conversed wildly with people, completely out of reason, but they laughed and the more they laughed the worse I felt.

Finally, late that night, I was 86'd and I walked along the sidewalk wondering how in the hell you could get a woman out of your blood and your gut, and I found another bar and drank quietly until closing time; it was Saturday night, well, it was Sunday morning and I walked along outside not quite knowing where I was going.

Then I saw this large mortuary, one of those colonial structures with long rows of steps very well lit by all these lights and I walked up to the next to the top step, stretched out and went to sleep.

I awakened to what seemed a traffic jam on the street below. Cars were honking, people were screaming and laughing, and as I sat up to look at them I heard laughter and catcalls and saw two cops rushing up the steps toward me . . .

When I awakened I had forgotten what had happened.

The walls were hung with tapestries. It was a very fine place. Perhaps somebody had, at last, found out what a good person I was and I was getting my reward. A class place.

Then I looked at the door. Bars. The window. Bars. I was in jail. I walked to the window and there was the ocean.

I later found out I was in Malibu. It reminded me somewhat of the time I had awakened to piped-in music and there was a long row of guys standing in the sand all handcuffed to this chain of handcuffs. There was a loose set hanging at the end. I walked up to the loose set and held out my hands. The cop looked at me and laughed. "Not you, buddy, you're just a drunk. Here, you get your own special pair." He snapped them on. As usual—too damned tight.

Two cops came and got me. They pushed me into a squad car and drove me to the Culver City courthouse. When I got out of the car one of the cops took the cuffs off and walked into the courthouse with me and sat next to me. I was third or fourth.

"You are charged," said your honor, after informing me of my rights, "with intoxication and blocking traffic. What do you plead?"

"Your honor?"

"Yes?"

"The intoxication was deliberate. Blocking traffic was not."

"Do you realize that those people thought you were a corpse stretched out on that mortuary step?"

"I suppose so."

"Do you realize that you caused the worst traffic jam in the history of the city of Inglewood?"

"No, your honor."

"What do you plead?"

"Guilty, your honor."

"32 dollars or ten days."

I'll pay the fine, your honor."

"Please see the bailiff . . . "

I got off the bus at Alvarado across from the park and

walked into the first bar I saw and there was Jane sitting down at the end of the bar. She was sitting between two guys and she had this long silken hanky or scarf flopped over her purse and she was either drinking a vodka or a gin and smoking a cigarette and not talking, and when she saw me her eyes got very wide and I walked toward her slowly. Then I stood near her. "Listen," I said, "I tried to make a woman out of you but you'll never be anything but a goddamned whore."

"If I wanna . . ." she started to say. I knew what she was going to say. My hand went out. I couldn't hold it back. The left hand, open palm. She landed on the floor, screamed. One of the guys helped her up. It was very quiet in that bar. I walked to the entrance. Then I turned and faced them. There were twelve or thirteen guys in there.

"Now, listen," I said, "if there's anybody in here who didn't *like* what I just did, JUST SAY SO!"

I waited. It was a most quiet quiet. I turned and walked out the door. The moment I got to the street I could hear the sound in there, they were all talking.

She's right, I thought, if she wants to be a whore that's her business. I had no right to hit her. I fell in love with a whore. She didn't ask me to.

I walked into the next bar and there sat Judy Edwards. Judy would do anything for five dollars. Judy would do anything for a drink. I bought her a scotch and told her I was going to buy a fifth and go up to my place. She said, "What about Jane?" "We're split," I said.

"For good?"

"For good."

We got on up to my place and Judy sat in a chair, crossing her legs and twisting her ankles. She was ready. "Are you sure it's over?"

"Yeah, baby," I said, "yeah, baby, I wouldn't lie to you."

I pulled her up from the chair and then I gave her a long slow kiss, watching myself do it in the full-length mirror. Judy pushed me off.

"You sure she's gone?"

"Yeah. I just knocked her on her ass down at *Shelby's*."

Judy walked over and opened the closet door. "Her clothes are still here. She'll kill me if she finds me here."

"She doesn't own me."

"Are you sure?"

"Sure I'm sure."

"How long you been with her?"

"Five years."

"She owns you."

I grabbed her again. She seemed to be fighting me. We fell backwards over the bed. I fell on top of her. "I blocked traffic in Inglewood, was jailed in Malibu, and tried in Culver City. No wonder our taxes are so high."

"Your eyes are open," she said. "You have the most beautiful eyes. I've never seen when you open them. Why don't you open your eyes more often?"

"I don't know."

I spread her lips open with mine and then locked my mouth against hers. Her tongue came out and then the door opened. It was Jane. Judy leaped up. They started screaming at each other. Their voices became more and more pitched, yet they seemed to hear each other and answer back and forth.

I walked over and poured a tall straight one, drank it down, poured another one and sat in a chair and listened and watched. They got closer and closer.

Suddenly one reached out, I don't know which, and then they were upon each other, scratching and biting, pulling hair, kicking, screaming. They fell to the floor and rolled over and over. They both knew how to dress—long spiked heels, garter belts, all that feminine wondrous stuff—ankle bracelets, earrings, the works.

At last I've really done something, I thought. I caused the worst traffic jam in the history of the city of Inglewood.

Their long lovely legs kicked through the air, a lamp leaped from the table and broke. Then I drank half my drink and reached over and turned on the music station. I was in luck. Shostakovich. I hadn't heard Shostakovich in a long long time.

A Piece of Cheese

Rena was hot, that's all. She had a ground floor apartment in the middle of a row of apartments. They were all one story high with beamed ceilings, fireplaces, beds and pillows all about—at least there were beds and pillows all about in Rena's place.

The place was just steeped in sex, even a red telephone, red gown, red pillows, well, and there was Rena and although she wasn't red, she was hot, that's all.

I am oversexed myself. There is definitely something wrong with me, but the best thing for an oversexed man is an oversexed woman. I didn't say a nymph. A nymph can kill a man. Rena was just *hot*, that's all.

It was summertime so I went over to Rena's at night.

Those daytime workouts just got too sweaty. It was just one round of sex after another but it was far from work, it was almost humorous. It was like being in a trance only it was a very good trance.

We'd decide to wash off after resting up from a good one and we'd get in the shower and begin soaping up and rubbing each other's parts, laughing, the water first too cold, then too hot, then me hogging the spray. And the next thing you knew, I had it in again, back or front, anywhere. And it's more difficult standing up, but it can be done.

We did it everywhere. In the large park behind the brush, in the car, in the kitchen, in the front room, in the bedroom, wherever it struck us

This one night I came over a bit drunk and I sat in the front room drinking from a good bottle of French wine I had brought along. Rena and I began kissing, and Rena could KISS. She did things to me with her lips and tongue that no other woman ever did.

Rena had verve and imagination. My imagination isn't bad either. Soon we were both naked and I was tonguing her all about and vice versa.

Pretty soon I got hungry and Rena brought me a cheese sandwich. She stood on the coffee table. Rena liked to stand

101

on coffee tables, naked. It brought her thing right about to my face when I stood up. I looked at her there. Then I took the piece of cheese, rolled it up and stuck it in there. Then I stood up and slowly began to nibble at the cheese.

This had quite an effect on Rena.

She liked new things. She boiled and cursed, she got so hot she got mad, her lips flecked out and she flushed in the face and along the neck, cursing, her body trembling.

When I got to the end of the cheese I just kept on eating. She erupted like a damn volcano, then pushed me backwards upon the couch and threw herself upon me.

It was like being raped. I didn't mind. We had nothing left after that one.

I dressed and went home and read one of those many books on the life of Ernest Hemingway, and I thought, I wonder if Ernie did all the things with women that I did? If he did, he must have stopped doing it or he wouldn't have gone the shotgun way. Such things were too good to leave voluntarily.

The phone rang. It was Rena.

"Bukowski, I'm scared."

"What's the matter?"

"I think there's a man at my window. A peeping Tom. I see his head in the window now. I'm in the bedroom. I'm scared. He can come right in here."

"I'll be right over!" I hung up.

I got in my car and ran two red lights and ignored the stop signs. As I parked, sure enough—here was some guy in a white t-shirt standing behind this bush by Rena's window with his head sticking in there. I leaped out of the car.

"Hey, you son of a bitch!"

It was a young kid, about 19, blonde, goodlooking. He looked scared though, plenty. And as I ran toward him, he broke from behind the bush and started running down the street. I raced after him but his fear and his youth were too much for me, and I was soon winded.

About the only exercise I got was hitting the typewriter, plus the sex workouts with Rena.

He was soon around the corner and gone.

I walked back.

It was senseless for a kid like that having to peep. It was just that women were unavailable to some, hard to get. It really wasn't fair.

I had decided long ago never to go through all that, but I had simply been lucky all my life. Women tend to like men who tend to disregard them. I was psychologically lucky.

I rang the bell.

"Who is it?"

"Bukowski, Rena."

She let me in. "Is he gone?"

"Yeah—I ran his ass off. But I couldn't catch him."

"Come on outside a minute," she said. "I want to show you something."

She had a heavy robe on over her pajamas. I stepped outside with her.

"Look," she said.

Rena pointed to the curtains that covered the front room windows. From inside, the curtains had a heavy look as if they concealed everything. The lights were on inside. But you could see right through the curtains. The front room, the coffee table, the couch. It was like a stage.

"My god!" I said.

"He could see everything we've done in there and we've done about everything."

I looked at the tall apartment that stood facing her front room windows. It seemed as if all the shades were pulled almost down to the bottom with just a small portion to look out of. People could have invited their friends if they wanted to.

"We've given half the neighborhood rocks," I said, "and we've created a peeping Tom. Our souls ought to rot in hell."

"Tomorrow," Rena said, "I'm going to the store and buy some more material and sew it onto the curtains."

"O.K., either do that or we begin charging admission," I laughed.

"Please, Bukowski, I want you to stay with me tonight. I'm afraid."

"Sure," I said, "let's take a shower together before we hit the sack."

"Alright," she said, and we walked in. Whoever invented the shower was one horny guy . . .

The next night, with the additions to the curtain, I tried the cheese bit again. Only this time, I stuck in two slices.

I was just at the bottom of the last slice when I heard a brushing sound outside and then somebody running. I got dressed as quickly as possible and went outside. One of the kids from the apartment down the way was standing out there. He was about 12.

"Hey, mister," he yelled, "I came outside when I heard the ice cream truck and I saw this man looking in your window. When he saw me, he ran away."

"Was it a young, blonde guy in a white t-shirt?"

"Yeah, that's who it was."

I looked at the curtains that Rena had repaired. You could *still* see in there. I walked back in.

"We've got to stay out of this front room, Rena, or we've got to work in the dark or something."

"Can you work the cheese bit in the dark?" she asked.

"I suppose so."

"But I like it better when I can watch you," she said.

"All right, we'll get a flashlight or something."

"O.K.," she agreed.

I had to leave town for a week and I called on Rena one night without phoning. She let me in. A young guy was sitting on the couch. He looked about 19, blonde, almost handsome.

"This is my friend, Arnold," said Rena.

"Hello, Arnold, how's it going?"

"Oh, real good," he said. "Everything's fine, just fine."

"Listen, Rena," I whispered, "this guy is the peeping Tom."

"Who, Arnold?"

"Yes, Arnold."

"Bukowski, you're just a jealous man. I won't have you saying such things about Arnold."

"How'd you meet him?" I shot back.

"Arnold's a bag boy at the local market. He's a nice boy. He was a straight-A student in high school. I won't have you talking bad about him."

"Damn it—this is the guy I chased down the street that night."

"You son of a bitch, I won't have you talking that way. Please leave."

Rena was really mad. I walked to the door, opened it, closed it, and I was gone. I got in my car and was half-way home on the freeway when I realized I had left my top coat back in her apartment.

I pulled off the freeway, got it going the other way, and drove back. I parked and got out.

I walked up to the apartment and was about to ring when I saw something through the curtain. Arnold and Rena were kissing, a long hard kiss. He had her down upon the sofa, her dress up around her hips, one of her breasts out, and she was grasping his penis in her hand.

It looked exciting. I watched.

She began to rub his joint. He lifted his head, sucked at her breast, then leaped back from the breast to the mouth, one of hands going down and pulling at her panties. Then I heard somebody coming down the walk and I pulled away from the curtain quickly and walked toward my car. A little drop of sweat rolled down my neck.

I started the car and drove off. Hell—I could get the coat in the morning or they could keep it. As I drove off, though, I had the feeling that I would have liked to have watched the rest of that scene. It had to be good.

That kid Arnold had a lot of technique. He should have—after watching me all those nights with Rena.

"All these guys," he said, "walking around the room with just their shorts on, not naked but with their shorts on, some with hard-ons, some with half hard-ons, soft soft, walking around the room, saying, 'I'm tough. I hate those goddamn fags. I'll beat the shit out of a fag!' They had a shit-thing going," he said, "everybody liked to shit. Another thing they liked to do was run across the street naked from one house to another. One time a guy was running across the street naked with half a hard-on and hollering and there was this guy sitting in his car and the guy jumped up on the hood and shit on the windshield. The other guy didn't know what to do."

"Well," I said, "I guess he could have turned on his windshield wipers."

"Another time this guy was an All-American tackle and he was fucking this girl with this shade open and about twenty-five or thirty guys were watching. Suddenly he stopped, got up on her and shit on her."

"Well," I said, "it's sexual, I guess. Then there are some guys who pay women to shit and piss on them. Then there are some guys who like to be shit and pissed-upon, spiritually. Not me. I've had enough. I ask kindness out of a woman but most American women can't give it, not under the age of forty. For that matter, neither can men. But women are colder than men because it's much easier for them to get picked up, fucked, possibly loved. I guess a lot of men go fag simply out of disgust."

"The whorehouse," he said, "has been a great saver of man's spirit."

"Amen," I said, "but where can a woman go? Even though it's easier for them, it's not always easier. There ought to be whorehouses for women too. Clit-licking guys with giant cocks and muscular bodies. But I suppose it's all a matter of supply and demand. If women needed whorehouses badly enough they'd arrive."

"It's like you say, it's too easy for them. A woman can

walk into a bar and there will be twelve guys sitting there, ready to go, ready to fight over her. Where's a bar a guy can walk into and have twelve women sitting there ready to fuck him, fight almost to the death for him?"

"Nowhere in America," I said. "Nowhere in this land and in this time."

"What's a man to do?" he asked.

"Nothing. Most men settle for 2nd or 3rd or 4th best simply because they are lonely, simply because they are afraid, simply because they lack the guts to live alone. They accept all the flaws in another person simply to have them around."

"What do you mean by 'flaws'?"

"I mean what people do to you because they simply don't care enough. 98 percent of the people in America live together but don't love each other. It's a compromise and a lie."

"Yeah," he said, "and then the games begin. The flirt-ings, the cheatings, the fucks on the side, meanwhile each one claiming innocence and love."

"Yeah, they sure use the word LOVE easily. 'Oh, I love you, o my god I love you!' They usually say it after you send your cock home after a good warm-up. But they don't mean it."

"And we're chauv pigs, you know, our ideas on women are all wrong."

"Of course," I said.

We sat silent, drinking our beers. Then he said, "Yeah, those guys at S.C. were just too much, especially the ones from the higher-income families. They had a thing they learned from the boys at Yale, it was called 'Drifting Dili-gently.' Nobody ever saw them study. They studied in the early morning hours, like from 3 a.m. to 7 a.m. Nobody ever saw them study. They were always lolling around the ten-nis courts or bullshitting on the lawn. It always confused the other guys."

"Life is good for some," I said, "but you know, the pressure must get off a man's back in one way or the other before he can really become clever. It's hard to be clever standing in a line outside the Union Rescue Mission waiting for some watery beans."

"I wonder what these guys do for women?"

"They forget them. At least they're at peace in that area."

"You've heard the old joke about the screw in the bellybutton, how it falls out and your cock and asshole drop off?"

"No, I haven't heard it," I said. "Tell it to me."

"Oh no, I don't want to tell it."

"Oh, go on."

"No, no, no."

"This screw drops out," I said, "and the asshole and cock drop off. That's good, How about the balls?"

"The balls too."

"Then what happens?"

"Forget it," he said. "You know when we were kids it was hard to get fucked. Now everybody fucks. Even the dolts and morons get it. But when we were kids it was something else. Remember the old Stink-Finger?"

"Yeah, I remember it."

"Yeah," he said, "these guys used to come around and hold their finger under your nose and say, 'Smell that, baby, you know where it's been?'"

"The old Stink-Finger."

"You could get it," he said, "by rubbing your finger against mutton. Guys used to go around rubbing their fingers against mutton. That's what it smells like: mutton."

"It sure does," I said. "And remember the old Dry-Fuck?"

"Memories," he said. "Stop it, you're going to make me cry."

"The Dry-Fuck," I said. "The girls didn't want to give it up. The word got out too fast and that killed marriage prospects. Girls used to want to get married."

"Stop it," he said, "you're going to make me cry."

"Grass used to be called Tea, and if you had some Tea the girls sometimes gave way because they claimed they were under the influence and it didn't really count. You couldn't get them to drink though, and most of us couldn't get any Tea."

"Yeah, mostly the musicians had it."

"So you'd go to work on a girl in the back seat. Hot kisses. We'd kiss 5 or 6 hours. You'd get one hot enough you'd finally get that finger up under those tight panties and get it in there. Or you'd dry-fuck. Once in a while you'd climax. But mostly you'd bluff it. 'Oh, my GOD, I'm coming!' And the girl would laugh, she'd like that. And you'd get out behind the car and pretend to wipe off with a hanky. Then you'd get back in. Sometimes you'd do that 2 or 3 times and the girls really liked it, they'd thought they'd brought you on."

"How about the old rumble seat and the banjo?" he asked.

"I don't go back to Jack Oakie, the raccoon coat and the college banner. I'm old but not that old."

"Yeah. Now everybody fucks," he said. "It's just like breathing."

"Better," I said, "no smog."

"You mean smog can't get into that thing?"

"I guess it can. Everything else does."

"You're talking about my mother. That's sacred."

"Sure," I said, "but to go on when you got a real wild one you'd get the hand-job. You'd pull the thing out and she'd sit there whacking you off. That was pretty exciting when you came, that semen spurting out and her watching."

"Still, I'm glad we have modern times," he said.

"Yes," I said, "we've fucked so much we don't even need it anymore. We shit on windshields."

"The delicate perversions," he said, "leather and leather and leather—thongs, dildoes, automatic pussies, beatings, cagings, murder . . . "

"It's a much better life," I said.

"Socially acceptable," he said.

"Socially acceptable," I said.

"Freedom," he said.

"Freedom," I said, "we're liberated."

Then we sat silent, drinking our beer.

"We have all of us been scoundrels in our time"
—Sir Lord Henry Hawkins

Karen and I fought continually; it was a misunderstanding of wills and ways, mostly my will and her way. Anyhow, it had been something over a wrong number, a telephone call by a stranger that I felt had been exceeded in length and intimacy on Karen's part, especially after we had just finished making love, oral, regular, and otherwise. Trivialities can sometimes be more destructive than tragedies. Anyhow, I decided to get out for a while and Karen told me, "If you go to the goddamned racetrack now I won't be here when you get back."

I got in my car and drove to the racetrack. It was a fairly good card and I managed to make $28. When I came back Karen was gone—clothes, possessions and all. I took a bath, changed into clean clothes and drove down to the liquor store for a fifth of whiskey and a couple of six packs. I got back in, turned on the radio and proceeded to get drunk. I drank for a week: days and nights, noons and evenings ran together. One morning the phone rang:

"Bukowski?"

"Yeh?"

It was Karen.

"How you doing?"

"Just fine."

"I'm in Wyoming," she said, "will you please forward my mail? I'd do the same for you."

She gave me the address and I hung up. For the first time in a week I walked out on the back porch. There was an air cooler sitting there with a note on it and a bottle of pills. I read the note:

"Here's your air cooler and some pills for your tired blood. I took your watch to pay for all my tears. Here's to one very important wrong number. And here's a pair of panties to masturbate in."

Karen had lived in a court three doors down, although I had slept there every night. We had been together a year and a half. Which just about fit my theory: about all you can expect out of any run is two years. I took the pills, the vitamin E's and the panties, a yellow pair. I threw the panties in a drawer and opened a beer.

I got out Lila Wiggins' phone number. I had met her years back—though not intimately—while I was working for *Open City*. And I had met her again recently, by accident, and had gotten her phone number. She had gone up from being a sophisticated hippie. She was now president of a record company. Her secretary put me through. I told her that I was loose and disoriented. Lila said she was working late that night but to come by any time.

I arrived at the record company that night, drunk. Quite. Lila Wiggins was in the back with a fairly famous female vocalist. They were running off a tape. There were two male instrumental accompanists. Lila sang backup. She did it well. I sat there with my pint and smoked and listened. They kept going over the same song trying to get it right. It became monotonous. When they began again I joined in. It made everybody very unhappy. I stopped and listened while Lila and the female vocalist berated me. Then I read them both off good and walked toward the door. Lila followed me to the door. We kissed in the doorway.

"Some other time," she said . . .

The next night it was at her house, in her bedroom, her "Arabian tent bedroom" as she called it. A large rug hung down over the ceiling. There were braids and trinkets everywhere. There were pills, dope, good wine, and champagne. And a huge colored television set.

"Pain, pain, pain," I said, "that bitch killed me by running off. You have no *idea* of the pain. It's immense, immense, like a buffalo charging through my guts! Lila, save me, save me, you'll never regret it!"

She just looked at me.

"And I'm a great lover, I'm the world's greatest lover, you'll see!"

Lila waited. She waited four days and four nights.

"Listen," she said, "you told me you were the world's greatest lover and you haven't even done anything. How long do I have to wait?"

I mounted her and gave her a standard old-fashioned screw, rolled off.

"Was that it?" she asked.

"No, that was hardly it," I said, "you'll just have to wait."

She waited another couple of nights and then I did it. Lila screamed and talked and moaned all the way through it. "YES!YES!YES! Oh, my god! My god!"

I had worked all the tricks and movements on her that Karen had taught me and I had added some of my own.

"You *are* the best," she said, "you are the best of all the men I've had . . . really . . . "

"I'll bet you tell that to all the boys."

"No, I mean it."

"Listen, do you have any more of those green pills and those yellow pills and some of that champagne?"

"Of course, my darling . . . "

After that when I awakened each morning there would be a love note waiting for me. Some bothered me more than they flattered me, like: "This is what it all means, all the days and all the years have come down to this, this is what it means, my love . . . "

I'd read the notes, make the bed, put the heart-shaped pillow up against the headboard. Then I'd look at television for a while, get into my car, drive to my place, check the mail, change my clothes and drive to the racetrack, lose out there. Lila asked me, "Do you have the rent money?"

"Sure," I said, "it's all right. I have it."

I knew I was getting in deep so I told her one morning, "You know, this isn't love. I'm still in love with Karen but that's all over. I want you to know where it is."

"It's all right, I understand."

Lila took me to dinners and rock concerts, long week-end drives up and down the coasts and into the mountains. She wanted to keep me away from telephone calls to Karen in Wyoming. I was bored with rides and I was bored with her rock and roll stars, publicists, agents, writers, artists. She knew everybody. "I'm going to have dinner with Paul Krassner," she said, "do you want to meet Paul Krassner?" "No," I said. Robert Crumb came by one night followed through the door by 17 admirers. Crumb was all right but the whole rock music world gang was inept, facile, and sycophantic. They made subtle little jokes and dropped names and dropped names and dropped names all night long. And none of them had the guts to get drunk. I cursed and railed against them and retreated to the Arabian tent with my bottle and watched the large colored tv while they giggled and gossiped and gagged on their lives in the other room. The tv was almost as bad but not quite. And when my friends came over with their crude and straightforward longshoremen acts, Lila then retreated to the Arabian. So, as far as that went we were even. I managed to get to my place and phone Karen several times but she was still cool. She had her sisters there to guide her against the beast that was Bukowski. I supposed that she was getting some good advice . . . .

A photographer friend of Lila's came over and took about 50 photos of Lila and myself about the house. The situation was getting nervous. Next I knew Lila was on vacation and she had me on an island looking out of a second floor window at the ocean and the bathers and the boats and the tourists while I crouched over her electric typewriter. I couldn't write. I laid around and drank beer and watched the small black and white tv. I watched the doctor programs and the cowboy movies. Lila ran about the shops, talked to people, rode boats, took photos. "This is it," she said, "I could live here forever." There wasn't a racetrack within 50 miles. We ate at every café, nightclub, and restaurant on that island. And the man at the liquor store got to know me very well. After two weeks of dismal drudgery and damnation we made it back.

We stopped at my place to check the mail. There was quite a bit of it. Lila lay on the bed while I read it. The phone rang. I went out to answer it. Lila usually took the phone off the hook when we weren't there, afraid that Karen would call. I had told her never to do it again. I walked toward the phone. Lila began to moan. It made me angry. I answered the phone. It was Karen.

"Yes," I answered her, "sure I'll come up."

Lila's moans got louder.

"Yes, I still love you, of course, I love you. It never stopped."

Lila moaned louder and louder. I covered the mouthpiece when I could; I was afraid Karen would hear. Lila's dramatics pissed me. Karen and I talked quite awhile. When I hung up, I went to the refrigerator for a beer and sat in a chair and looked out the window. Lila was quiet. I finished the beer and walked into the bedroom. Lila appeared to be asleep. She had a very strange look about her. I lifted one of her arms and it fell back like something almost not attached to her. I lifted the other arm, I moved her body, her head. She had a strange and limp heaviness. "Lila! Lila! What the hell have you done?" I finally awakened her. "Listen, have you taken any sleeping pills?" "I swallowed the bottle," she said. Her voice was heavy, dark, garbled. "You're trying to scare me. You're playacting." "No," she said.

I stuck my hand in her mouth to induce vomiting. She vomited, then stopped and I stuck my hand down her throat again and again. She kept vomiting. "More, more," I said, "keep it up!" I stuck my hand in her mouth again and an upper plate leaped out, it leaped through the air like a frog and landed on the sheets. "My teeth, oh, my teeth . . . I didn't want you to know . . . o, my god . . . my teeth . . . I didn't want you to know about my teeth . . . o . . . "

"Fuck it! I don't care about your teeth! Keep vomiting!"

Lila reached for her teeth and tried to put them in. She was too out of it. I took the teeth and put them in an ashtray out of reach. I put my hand down her throat again. "All right, I'm not going to Wyoming! I'll phone Karen in the morning and tell her I can't make it!"

"My teeth, o, my teeth . . . I didn't want you to know!"

I was thinking of taking Lila to a hospital for a stomach pump but as she kept vomiting I noticed that her body was losing the heavy and disattached feel. I finally gave off and drove her over to her place, back to the Arabian tent. I washed her face and neck and hands and we sat there and drank a little wine and smoked some pot.

"If you ever write that scene about my attempted suicide and my teeth I am going to kill you," she said.

"Listen, Lila," I said, "I may be a son of a bitch but I'm not that much of a son of a bitch."

Some days later it was my birthday and my car had a flat. I put the spare on and we drove down to Mark C. Bloome's in Hollywood and Lila got me two tires and two shock absorbers for my birthday. The bill was over $70 . . .

In September Karen had to come back to Los Angeles and put her boy in school. Also, her ex-husband lived in North Hollywood and wanted to see the boy each weekend. I found out where she was living and went over. At first she wouldn't let me in. I pushed in and began talking. I turned on all the charm and reason and dialogue. I have never known I had had all that. But it took that, and some more. That, in itself, is almost a separate story. Story? Anyhow, in three or four days we were together again and in a week we were living together again. Karen confessed to an affair of her own in Wyoming. I didn't like *that* but it did tend to equalize things and made a truce and new beginning more possible . . . Meanwhile, there was Lila Wiggins, record company executive. I told Karen that I must go to see her and explain why everything was as it was . . .

I phoned and her friend Judy was staying with her. Judy said Lila was in and I said to keep her there. I'd be right over. It wasn't a long drive and I parked in the same old place and got out, walked through the garden and up to the sliding glass doors at the side of the house and tapped. I had phoned Lila several days back that I was with Karen again and that it was over between us. Judy let me in and pointed toward the Arabian tent. "She's back there."

I walked on back. Lila was on her stomach on the bed. All she had on were a pair of blue panties. An empty pint of whiskey was on the floor and there was a dishpan on the floor filled with vomit. A very sour smell was in the air. I sat down on the edge of the bed. "Lila . . . ."

She turned her head. "You . . . "

"I just wanted to explain . . . "

"You rotten lousy bastard . . . "

"Lila, listen . . . "

"You rotten foul stinking . . . "

"Listen, Lila, I've been left, too. I've been left *cold* a few times by myself by the female . . . no note, no sound, no word . . . I'd like to be as human as possible about it . . . "

Lila got up on her knees. She moved across the bed toward me. "Human? Human? You stink all the way to hell and back!"

She doubled her fists and started winging at me. I sat there. Some of the punches hit me on the chest, some missed, others got me about the face. She kept swinging and swinging. My nose bled and some of it dripped on my shirt. Finally I grabbed her hands.

"Lila, I told you it wasn't love. I told you I loved Karen . . . "

She put her head over the edge of the bed and vomited into the dishpan. Then she stretched out on the bed.

"Just hold me. Hold me a little . . . "

I held her. "Kiss me . . . "

I kissed her. Her mouth tasted stale, sour.

"Don't go back . . . Don't go back to her. Stay with me. The world's so horrible out there. You're crazed, you're so crazed . . . but you're a great writer . . . I want to protect you from that world."

"A great writer? That's got nothing to do with anything."

"I've always loved you, from the first time I saw you years ago. You were down at *Open City* drunk and laughing and cursing . . . "

"I don't remember that . . . "

"I remember that . . . "

I held her and didn't say anything. Suddenly she sat up again. "You rotten bastard, o, you rotten rotten bastard!"

She began swinging again. She got me some good ones.

"Listen, Lila, all you do is kick the shit out of me . . . "

"You have it coming! Hold still so I can give you some more."

I held still as her fists punched against my face. Then she stopped. "You're going back to her, really?"

"Really. Listen, Lila, you won't try to do anything."

"What for? For you? You're not worth it!"

"You're right. Well, listen, I'll be going now."

"You won't forget me, you'll see, you'll never forget me."

"Of course I won't."

I got up and turned away from the bed, began to walk away. The empty pint whiskey bottle flew after me over my right shoulder. I knew then why you had to leave them cold instead of humanly: it was kinder.

I slid the glass doors back and walked through the garden. Her two cats were out there. They knew me. They rubbed against my legs and followed me as I walked away.

The POW propaganda plant is still grinding against all sensibilities. We lost the war, got our asses kicked out by starving men and women half our size. We couldn't bomb, con, or beg them into submission so we got out and while getting out, somebody had to come up with a smokescreen to make the populace forget we got our asses kicked. Let's build the POW angle, they said, and so it began. Bob Hope became concerned about the POWs; his wartime Santa Claus kick had rather petered out in the last two trips. The word was out and the act was in. The arrival of the first POWs was put on tv. Here came the plane in. And we waited and waited and the plane taxied and taxied. You never saw a plane taxi that much in any airport at any time in the world. The cameras waited and they bled it to death. Then out came the first grand POW and patriotism was back.

Here were men who had flown in bombers and dropped thousands of tons of explosives upon cities and people. Here were killers being honored as heroes. The sympathy pangs, of course, were for these poor fellows whose aircraft had happened to get hit, forcing them to bail out, become captured and imprisoned where they were forced to eat meals not chosen from a menu. We here in America have imprisoned men for much less, fed them badly, and they were hardly heroes when they came out.

George Wallace got himself trapped. The man who once vowed to maintain segregation forever in Alabama was photographed shaking hands with Sgt. Thomas W. Davis, former POW, who returned to his hometown in Eufaula, Alabama. Sgt. Davis is black.

A POW is a man who went to war knowingly, knowing he might kill or be killed, capture or be captured, maim or be maimed. There is no special quality of heroism in this. There are few real patriots anymore, there have been too many useless wars and they have come too fast.

Most American men of war age merely took a gamble;

119

they figured by going that the odds against them actually getting killed were high. By going and returning, whether they believed in the war or not, they would still retain their decent citizen status and be able to return to their women and their jobs and their homes and their baseball games, their new cars. By refusing to go they faced imprisonment and / or hiding.

Most weighed it all and considered that going to war was the easier way, especially those with college educations and ROTC training who were able to fly above the muck and blood, only pushing buttons. That some of them became POWs was just tough shit of the spinning of the wheel and they know it better than anybody. And if they are given a free fuck now or a free automobile or applause or a good job, they're going to take that, too.

The other night at the Olympic Auditorium boxing matches, a former POW was introduced and he got up into the ring and was given a standing ovation. I once had an almost-admiration for boxing fans. I now see them in a different magenta lavender brownsmear hue . . .

A friend came over the other night with some stories about the Arctic. They had been up there filming the life of a drunk, he said, who looked just like me. Anyhow, this drunk took an airplane up there and used it regular, helping people out, flying supplies, rescuing, stunting and making money. One of the tricks of this drunk was to stand on his head and drink a tumbler of scotch.

Anyway, for the average civilized man not at all used to the space and silence and the six month's night and the six month's day, it's crack-up territory. There's a term for it which I have forgotten. Anyhow, it gets to many men.

There was a cook up there and the cook kept frying eggs for the men. And you know how it is with eggs. Some want them straight up, some want them scrambled, some want them boiled (soft, hard, medium-hard, medium-soft), some want them over easy, some want them over medium. Everybody seems to want his eggs in a different way and that way must be just so. If it isn't just *so*, they become terribly annoyed. Ask your waitress or cook at your local café. They have suffered enormous swarms of annoyed egg-eaters.

I was sitting in this place one time when a guy in a baseball cap and a black sweater with holes in the sleeves walked in and said, "Baste two." I asked the waitress, "Now what does he mean, 'baste two'?" "God," she said, "I don't know what he means. I'll just let the cook worry about it."

Well, this cook in the Arctic also had space, time, silence, eggs, snow . . . he went on and on doing different eggs for different men, all of them without women, making money and waiting . . . all day or all night. Finally, one day (or one night?) the cook took all the eggs in camp, every last egg and hard-fried them all. He let them dry out a bit and then took them all to his room and nailed them to his walls. When it came time for breakfast they couldn't find the cook so they went to his room and there he sat in a chair. He said, "There's your eggs. Just cut down what you want."

The new cook was a boy from Boston who kept talking about John Dillinger and Baby Face Nelson and Fats Domino every time he got drunk . . .

They tell me that there are Eskimos and Indians up there, the Indians a little further south and that the Eskimos don't like the Indians and the E's favorite thing is to watch cowboy movies and get their sperm with each Indian killed.

I suppose that the extreme north is the last west in the world, or as my buddy John Thomas might infer, the Last Frontier. Jack London got some gravy out of it. Old London was the Hemingway of the frozen nothingness, wolves instead of lions, the bible of Joe Conrad in his pocket. All I know about is Wile Post, A. Earhart, and Will Rogers being lost forever in the whiteness, and also a millionaire ex-wife who couldn't stand me who married a Japanese fisherman with very nice manners in upper Alaska.

There's room for artistry and the word up there and I might suggest that some of you people who sit on those benches by the parking lot at the end of Rose Avenue in Venice and hit me for 20 cents everytime I go into that Jewish market for a corned beef sandwich, I might suggest that you go up there and give it a run.

Then there's another one. They have these guys in out-stations, usually in twos. So it happened, you know. There's nothing to do but do your job and drink. Sometimes your job is to intercept coded messages from the Russians and Chinese, sometimes your job is hardly a job at all but somebody is paying you and there aren't any women and there's nothing to do but drink. And as any wise man knows, sometimes even where there are women, the best thing to do is to drink.

There were these two guys in the out-station. They did their job but there was nothing. Waiting and drinking. One of the finest things about drinking up there is you can get very drunk, extremely drunk, and all you have to do is to step outside the door into all that clear cold pure whiteness of oxygen and just breathe it in and you sober up and can get drunk all over again. It's the same with a hangover, you just walk outside, breathe, and the hangover is gobbled up by the whiteness.

So, once upon a time, one night, one of these two guys walks outside and breathes in the whiteness. It felt good out there. He just stayed out there a while. His buddy just kept drinking and listening to old Eartha Kitt records. Then he missed something. He went outside to look for it. His buddy was frozen. There was nothing to do but leave him out there. It would be four months before human contact would bring them back to civilization. Open another bottle, set the machine, get the coded message that the Red Chinese bastards are meaning to H-bomb every thrift shop in the city of Pasadena.

Time went on and there really isn't any time up there. It sits still. It doesn't move. You may urinate and defecate, but there isn't any such thing as time, not in that white silence frozen. There isn't anything at all if nothing is there. You need to be reminded that something is there. He needed to be reminded that something was there. And he got a little lonely. So he went out and got his buddy and leaned him up against a chair. He opened the window so his buddy would stay solidified and he kept his buddy by the window. And he began drinking and talking to him.

Things seemed better. He drank and talked to his buddy. He made it better by having his buddy answer him. He'd say something and his buddy would answer him. It was like old times.

But one night (day?) it got bad. It got to be over Clare. He had always felt that his buddy had crossed him with Clare the time he had gone to Sears to get the new muffler, although both of them (Clare and his buddy) had always denied it. The argument mounted; denial followed accusation, accusation followed denial and the drinks flowed. The anger and the lie became too much and after a triple jolt of hundred proof he got a gun and shot his buddy. Then he slept.

The months did go. When they arrived they found him and a dead man who had been shot. He was accused of murder. Luckily the autopsy proved that his buddy had been dead long before he had been shot.

I liked the one about the cook better.

This Sunday, April 15, 1973, was the first Sunday of horse racing in the State of California. It was a crowd just a bit different from a Saturday crowd, although some of the Saturday crowd was back; at least those with anything left from the paycheck. The crowd was 40,954 and for some it was the first day at the track.

Tables were set up and booklets handed out free, explaining the delicacies of the game. There were more babies in strollers than I had ever seen before. And you could tell that much of the crowd was new; they stood ganged-up and squeezed together at the finish line. Where these people once hid on Saturdays is your guess. But something had to be done to jive up the attendance so the track asked to trade their Tuesday for a Sunday. I believe the track was given three Sundays to work with as a beginning. After that, it was to pass through Sacramento.

The churches and other Sunday business groups are fighting hard against Sunday racing. But I would surmise that nothing will hold it back now, even God Himself. The track and the state roughly divide the take on each betting dollar, which is about 15 percent. The extra tax revenue from Sunday racing will be almost impossible to reject.

Hollywood Park states that over two million dollars a day is wagered at the track. This doesn't mean that 40,000 people come to the track with two million dollars. It means that the same people bet the same money back into the mutual machines for nine races (those who stay) and that the state and the track take their bite over and over again from the same dollar.

For instance, it's possible to go to the race with two dollars, and with a win here and there, it's possible to bet that same two dollars back again and again for nine races. You may even lose it at the end, but meanwhile that mutual machine out there that flashes the numbers has automatically extracted 15 percent of $18 (nine times two). It's magic, isn't it? You might say that if you bet two dollars nine times with a 15 percent take, that you are bucking a take of nine times 15 percent, which on that theory is bucking a 135 percent take, which might explain why most people leave all they brought with them at the track.

Other math boys say, no, it's not so, the take remains at 15 percent. I don't know. I only know that only one person out of 20 leaves the track a winner. In all decency those places should be closed, but the tax dollar just won't allow it. It's just like rebuilding Vietnam, there's just too much money made by blowing it to hell and gone in a shit wind. That's magic too: profit in destroying and profit in rebuilding. But both are done under the guise of morality and righteousness.

Of course, somebody suffers someplace in between. The racetrack is a war, too. Get yourself a camera and get those faces leaving after the ninth race. Tricked again. The workings of a democracy. The tortured submit to the torture, volunteer for it.

Sunday racing is with us to stay. The war is everywhere and the little man will never be let go of. He will be squeezed and taxed and tricked and percentage-wised out of a chance. And he'll scream and drink green beer, he'll lose everything, and on the way out he'll say, "Well, hell, I lost but I had a good time." What he means is that he didn't have the imagination to know what to do with his time or his money so he moved it over to somebody else who solved that problem. What he means by a good time is that he didn't have to be inventive and he just slid down the slide. And Monday morning the timeclock will be there and somebody else will arrange things for him to do.

You see why I go to the racetrack? I learn all these things about humanity.

Anyway, Sunday racing is *in* just like the massage parlors. I'll see you out there this Easter Sunday. I am a solid California citizen. I am paving the roads and building the schools and paying the cops and trying to keep some of the insane asylums open. And if you approach me quietly and with any manner of grace I might suggest the winner of the up-coming race. If you think I'm just a guy who goes around writing dirty stories, *you're* crazy. Although next week I should be back with one. This straight writing lacks the divinity and the flame. How can those other guys keep on doing it? I don't even know how to end one of these things. I guess like this: END.

I t was in Washington, D.C., a private party but well-attended, a little over 200, and Danny James (it was rumored that he had given $50,000 to the administration for the last election) and his girlfriend were standing about, drinks in hand. Danny James, former entertainer, now retired. Not entirely retired for it was rumored that he had blown a Master of Ceremonies role to Bob Hope—losing his temper when the Secret Service refused to allow one of his Las Vegas buddies to perform without security clearance. Among other rumors was one that James often entertained the Vice President at his home.

While Danny and his girlfriend were standing there with drinks in hand, Danny was approached by a woman columnist who asked a question. James answered, "Who the hell do you think you are? If you want to see me, write me a letter."

The woman columnist vanished to be replaced by another. Danny said: "Get away from me, you scum. Go home and take a bath. I don't want to talk to you. I'm getting out of here to get away from the stench of you." He turned to his girlfriend: "That stench you smell is from her."

Then Danny James turned back to the woman columnist: "You're nothing but a $2.00 cunt. C-U-N-T, you know what that means, don't you? You've been laying down for $2.00 all your life!"

Mrs. Blanche Delmore, the female columnist, laughed at first. Then she moved off and began to cry. Danny James had stuffed $2.00 into her cocktail glass, along with the remark, "Here's $2.00, baby, that's what you're used to."

Her husband, Henry Delmore, found a paper towel and Mrs. Delmore cried into it. Everybody at the party had heard the remarks. Her husband consoled her a bit more, then took her home. Henry poured two drinks when they arrived at home and they talked about it as they undressed.

"Oh, Henry, it's awful, awful, awful! I think I'm going to die!" She threw herself face-down on the bed.

"You'll feel better in the morning, dear." Henry drank his drink, then drank Blanche's. He turned off the light and they slept . . . .

After Henry left for work that morning, Blanche sat up in bed with her pink telephone. First she dialed the office: "Briget? Oh, Briget, I just *can't* come to work this morning . . . . I . . . .oh, it's in the papers? *All* of them? Oh, Lord, no!" She hung up quickly, then sat over the pink telephone, thinking. She got up, went to the bathroom and urinated. She was back at the bed, sitting by the pink telephone when her mother entered.

"My god, Blanche, you look AWFUL! What happened?"

"It was the party. Danny James insulted me! It was just terribly awful! I've never had such a gross, unjust thing happen to me in my whole life!"

"What did he say?"

"Oh, mother, *please*!"

"Blanche, I want to *know*!"

"Mother, *please*!"

"Blanche, I *am* your mother!"

"He called me a $2.00 cunt."

"What's a 'cunt,' Blanche?"

"What?"

"I said, 'What's a cunt?'"

"Oh, mother, you must be joking. I don't *feel* like joking. Not at all. Hardly."

"I want to know what a 'cunt' is, Blanche."

"Mother, *please* leave me alone! Please, please, *please*!"

Blanche's mother left the room and she lifted the pink telephone, dialed it.

"Hello, Annie. Is Wayne Brimson in? What? He died last night? In an elevator? Oh, my god, what's happening? What's happening?"

Blanche hung up. Wayne Brimson had been her attorney.

The door opened and Blanche's mother appeared.

"Mother, will you leave me the hell alone? Will you, before I go crazy?"

The door closed.

I've got to get another lawyer, she thought. But Wayne and I were such good friends, and he was reasonable.

The phone rang. She picked it up. It was a man's voice, deep, low, slow and full.

"Your $2.00 cunt stinks like a monkey's hemorrhoid asshole."

He hung up.

Then she remembered John Manley. He was a fairly decent attorney and his reputation was good. She dialed. John answered.

"Listen, John . . . . Oh, you've heard? It was terrible, John, and all true . . . . What? No, no, that's all right. All I want is an apology. That's all, just an apology. That isn't asking too much, is it, John? Yes, Henry's doing just fine. Of course, he's as upset about this thing as I am. All right, you'll go to work on it? Just an apology, that's all I ask."

She hung up, walked around the room, looked out the window, then sat down at the dresser and began combing her hair. The phone rang. She walked over and picked it up.

It was a man's voice again, but this time higher-pitched and much more juvenile.

"Listen, baby, you may have a $2.00 cunt, but I don't mind. I'll stick my cock right into that $2.00 cunt and I'll jam it home, 12 inches, I'll come, I'll squirt this white juice right into that $2.00 cunt. Doesn't that make you hot, thinking about it? It makes me hot. I'll squirt right into—"

Blanche hung up. She walked into the bathroom and let the water run into the tub. She took a slow, hot bath, took a sleeping pill, toweled herself, brushed her teeth, got back into her nightgown and went back to bed. After an hour of waiting, she slept.

She had no idea how long she slept but the phone awakened her. It was John Manley to tell her Danny James refused to apologize, at least in writing.

"But why? Why?"

John answered that he didn't know, he had only spoken to James' lawyer, but he'd follow it up, try to find out more.

Meanwhile, it was said that the President of the United States, himself, was secretly angry because of the incident and because James was good friends with the Vice President.

"This thing has all kinds of implications," said John Manley, then hung up.

When little Gladys came home from first grade she was crying.

"Mama, the boys called me a 'cunt.' They screamed it at me over and over: 'Cunt! Cunt! You're a cunt!' Mama, what's a 'cunt'?"

"Gladys, please, leave your mother alone. She's not feeling well!"

Gladys left the room. The phone rang again. Blanche picked it up. It was the man with the high voice again. "I can come six times in one night. Six times I can squirt that juice into your cunt. I can drive you mad. I can . . . ."

Blanche hung up.

It was a somber dinner that night, Blanche, Henry, Gladys and Blanche's mother. Blanche's mother had made the dinner: meatloaf, mashed potatoes, peas, tossed salad with olives, baked biscuits . . . . The conversation was general for some time, then Blanche's mother turned to Henry.

"Henry, what's a 'cunt'?"

"Oh, for God's sake, Grace!"

"I want to know: what's a 'cunt'? Why doesn't anybody tell me what a 'cunt' is?"

"Yes," said Gladys, "I want to know what a 'cunt' is too."

"Henry," said Blanche, "there have been some terrible phone calls, absolutely terrible!"

"Yes?"

"Obscene, terribly obscene . . . two men . . . one with a weak high voice, the other with a heavy slow voice . . . "

"Bastards!"

"I know. What can we do?"

"There must be something we can do. The phone company, the police, the FBI, somebody . . . ."

"Listen," said Blanche's mother, "I DEMAND TO KNOW WHAT A CUNT IS!"

"Oh, mother, please . . . ."

"Henry?"

"Yes?"

"Take her in the other room and tell her."

"What?"

"Take her in the other room and tell her."

"You mean it?"

"I mean it. I can't stand it any longer."

Henry and his mother-in-law walked into the kitchen.
He swung the door closed. They sat down, a vase of half-
wilted roses between them."

"Well?" said Grace.

"Well, mother, a 'cunt' is rather a vulgar term for something each woman possesses."

"Do I have one?"

"I'm sure you have. But I'm surprised you've never
heard the term."

"Henry, I was raised among God-fearing people."

"I see."

"Henry, where is my cunt?"

"Down there."

"Down where?"

"Between your legs."

"Down here?"

"There."

"Am I touching it?"

"Yes."

"But what's wrong with the 'cunt'? It's part of the
body."

"Of course."

"Then why is Blanche so upset?"

"The man inferred that she was a cheap $2.00 one, in
other words, a cheap prostitute."

"Henry?"

"Yes?"

"What's a 'prostitute'?"

"Oh my god, Grace . . . ."

"Why are you angry?"

Henry got up from the table, pushed the door open

and walked into the other room, sat in a chair. Blanche and Gladys were sitting on the couch.

"Did you tell her?"

"Yes."

"Then what's the matter? You look upset. I'm the one who ought to be upset, I've been getting those phone calls . . . ."

The door opened and Grace walked in.

"Listen, Blanche, I've got to know what a prostitute it. He won't tell me . . . ."

Henry stood up.

"Listen, I've got to get out of here for a while . . . ."

"Henry, don't you *dare* leave me in this crisis!"

Henry left anyhow. He got in his car and started driving south. He drove past a stop sign without stopping. The country was going to hell. First Watergate, and now this . . . .

Back at the house the phone rang. Blanche's mother got there first. It was a man's voice, about medium pitch.

"Hello," said Blanche's mother.

"Listen," came the voice, "I'll eat your entire cunt with my tongue. I'll chew your whole damned cunt to pieces. I'll drive you crazy, I'll suck your whole pussy right off of your body, I'll . . . ."

Blanche's mother held the phone in her hands but the receiver and mouthpiece had fallen off and were whirling and dangling in the air from the cord. When Blanche's mother finished the first scream, she started another one. And through the receiver of the phone, dangling down near the floor you could hear his voice:

"Ha, I've got ya hot, haven't I, baby? Got ya hot, haven't I? Hah, ha, ha . . . ."

Emil and Steve were the tough toughest guys in our grammar school, Hampton Road Grammar School, and Hampton Road was the toughest grammar school in town, and we were on the *west* side, which is unusual. It just happened that way. We grew up fast. Morrie Eddleman had more hair on his chest than any man I had ever seen. But most of the guys had grown up fast, and big. We all just happened to be in the same grade. It was an accident. Nelson Potter was hung like a horse and the girls stayed away from him but they talked about him and we talked about him.

Even when we were in the 4th grade our baseball team was beating the 6th graders and when we got to the 6th grade the boys from Templeton Jr. High used to come over after school and we'd beat them at baseball. Morrie Eddleman was a real home run hitter. He bounced them off the side of the school so much that they had to put up iron bars to keep the windows from getting broken. We all bought these blue baseball caps and we wore them when we played and we always won. We looked good in those blue baseball caps, those Jr. High School kids were really afraid of us but they tried to pretend not to be. I couldn't make the beginning lineup, I was a substitute, but I still got to wear the blue cap. Emil and Steve were the really tough guys though, Emil and Steve Yuriardi. They were even too tough to play baseball. Emil was in the 6th grade and his brother was in the 5th. But Steve was almost as tough as Emil. Those guys just stood behind the screen and watched. They wore these leather straps around their wrists and smoked cigarettes cupped in their hands and just watched us. And they looked at the girls as if they were nothing.

When we didn't have a baseball game after school, we had a fight, there was always a fight and the teachers were never around, nobody was around, and it wasn't Emil and Steve beating somebody up, sometimes it was somebody else doing it. They always got some sissy, some guy nicely dressed, and they beat on that sissy, really punched at him.

Whoever it was would get the sissy up against the fence
and we'd gather around and watch. I mean, the beatings
were good, but even the sissies at Hampton Road Grammar School were tough. They never cried, the blood coming
out of their noses and mouths, they stood up against the
chain link fence and did the best they could. I mean, you
just thought they were beat, their hands in front of their
faces trying to cover up from the blows and then suddenly they'd punch out and land one. They never begged or
asked for mercy. We had some tough school.

All of us were white guys except for Emil and Steve
and they weren't black or Mexican, but they did have this
darkness to their skin, a dark even brown, and it looked
rough, they were rough, and they never spoke to anybody
and they always traveled together, sneering at the girls and
sneering at us. They didn't get into too many fights because
they never said anything and they didn't bump into anybody and that's how things got started, by talking or bump-
ing. I don't know how they got into fights but when they
did it was damn near murder. They didn't get excited. They
just stood back and pumped them in and every swing hit.
They never missed a lot of punches like the rest of us. And
they weren't as tall as most of us but they were stocky and
they were mean. I really admired Steve. Even during a fight
sometimes he'd take time to look around at us; he'd give us
that same sneer and then the smallest of a smile, and when
he did that it meant: look, this can happen to *you*, too, and
then he'd land a very hard one. I would have given anything to be Steve.

I didn't know about Steve in class because he was one
grade behind, but Emil acted dumb in class. He wasn't
dumb, you could tell by his eyes and the way he sat, but he
acted dumb, he liked to act dumb. Miss Thompson would
ask him, "Now Emil, what is the capital of Peru?" and Emil
wouldn't answer, he'd just stare at Miss Thompson with
that stare. And Miss Thompson would say again, "Emil,
what is the capital of Peru?" and still Emil wouldn't answer. And he'd answer, "I don't know." It was the way he
said it, like he was insulting her.

"Emil, did you do your lessons last night?"

"No."

"Emil, go stand out in the hall."

Emil would get up in his certain way, slowly and easily, with this disgust and open the door and be gone.

"Henry, what are *you* sneering at?"

This always shocked me because I hadn't realized that I had been sneering.

"Henry, what is the capital of Peru?"

I knew that the capital of Peru was Bolivia, but I didn't want the guys to think I was a sissy.

"I don't know."

"Henry, did you study your lessons last night?"

"No, I didn't feel like studying my lessons."

The class giggled, mostly the girls giggled, and one or two of the guys laughed out loud.

"We'll have some silence here or everybody is going to lose recess."

Miss Thompson looked right at me, directly, she was around 32, wore very tight dresses but her hair at the back was done in a bun, and her eyes looked right into mine, and for a moment I couldn't help thinking as I looked back—I am in bed with you. Miss Thompson caught that immediately but ignored it.

"Now, Henry, what did you say about your lessons?"

She never pressed Emil like that and I wondered why. I guess it was because Emil was Emil. The class waited. I said, "I just didn't feel like doing my lessons. I'm not interested in the capital of Peru. I don't think it matters."

I'd heard a girl behind me say that and I thought that sounded clever. I looked at Miss Thompson and she was almost crying. I was surprised.

"Henry," she said, "that's what separates humans from animals, the ability to learn more intricate things and evolve ideas and feelings from them, don't you see?"

"There's nothing wrong with animals."

"Henry, I didn't say there was. Don't you understand?"

Miss Thompson brought out a small white handkerchief and poked the sharp corners at her eyes. Then she put her handkerchief back in her pocket. There were two pockets on either side of her skirt. She had a wonderful figure. She began to write upon a small square of paper. Then she folded it up and looked at me.

"Henry, I want you to take this to the principal's office."

The girl behind me who had said the capital of Peru didn't matter said to me, "Henry, you ought to apologize to Miss Thompson."

So when I went up to get the slip of folded paper for the principal's office, I said very quietly to Miss Thompson, "Miss Thompson, I apologize, I'm sorry."

"Just take that slip of paper to the principal's office, Henry."

When I went out the door there was Emil leaning against the wall near the water fountain. He looked very comfortable. I tried to get a look from him as I went toward the principal's office but he ignored me. I walked on down and opened the door. Mr. Waters was sitting behind his desk, looking very irritated. There was an iron sign on his desk: Martin W. Waters, Principal. I handed him the note and he unfolded it and read it. Then he looked at me:

"My boy, what makes you act like this?"

I didn't answer. Mr. Waters had on a pin-striped suit, grey and white, with a light blue necktie. All of him came down around that light blue necktie. I looked at the light blue necktie.

"My boy, we no longer use a ruler on the wrist for recalcitrant. That was abandoned last semester."

He let me stand there and he read the note again.

"Henry, what makes you act like this?"

I didn't answer.

"You refuse to answer?"

I didn't answer.

"Suppose your mother and father heard about this?"

I didn't answer.

Mr. Waters suddenly threw the note into the wastebasket. He looked at me. "You go stand in the phone booth until I tell you to come out."

I walked over to the phone booth, opened the door,

closed the door and stood there. It was hot in there. I looked down under the telephone. There were two magazines there. I tried to read them to pass the time. They were *Harper's Bazaar* and *The Ladies' Home Journal*. I closed the magazines and stood there. It was much worse than you can imagine. It was simply dark and stuffy and boring and dull, so dull, and I stood there and my legs ached and the minutes passed, I kept listening to the bells, and I thought, yes, that's the lunch bell and there's the afternoon recess bell, and there's the bell for back from recess, and now there's the fire alarm bell, they're all marching out into the yard and they're standing there and now there's the final bell, they're going home or they're going out to play or to fight, and then it seemed like another hour and the phone booth door opened. Mr. Waters was standing there still irritated and he said, "All right, Henry, you can go home now."

I went home because I didn't feel good about things and the next day in class there was Miss Thompson, she acted like nothing had happened, the whole class acted as if nothing had happened. There wasn't much that day except once Miss Thompson scraped the blackboard with the chalk like it happens and we made these sounds and Miss Thompson turned around and laughed. That was about all. Miss Thompson didn't ask me any questions and she didn't ask Emil any questions, she mostly asked the girls.

MY BOY, WHAT MAKES YOU ACT LIKE THIS?

After school we had another baseball game with the guys from Templeton Jr. High, and they knew it and we

knew it—that we would beat them but it was only a matter of how much and each time they came over we beat
them worse. I put on my blue cap and sat on the bench. We
were leading 7 to 3 at the end of the 4th inning when one of
their guys ticked one off the bat and it rolled up the netting
toward the back of the backstop. I was sitting on the end
of our bench and I stood up and ran over and as the ball
came on over the top of the backstop I was still running and
in full motion I caught the ball as it came down, strolled
out with it around the backstop and winged it back to our
pitcher, hard. But it wasn't accurate. It went far to his right,
took a hard bounce by our shortstop who made a rather
casual and effortless attempt to get it, then it rolled on out
to Morrie Eddleman who'd already homered and doubled,
and he got it neatly, winged it on back in on one bounce to
our pitcher, Clars Thurman. Thurman got it and whirled
a 3d strike past a guy 3 years older. We were going to win
another, easy.

It was then that I noticed Emil looking at me. He
kept his eyes on me. He was over behind the backstop. I
thought, well, here goes. I stood up and walked toward
him. His brother Steve was standing right beside him but
Steve was looking off elsewhere. I walked toward them.
I walked around the end of the backstop and moved toward them. They both had these leather straps around
their wrists. I walked up, Emil kept looking at me. I got
about 3 feet away from him and stopped. He gave me the
tiniest of a sneer and motioned me in. I stepped forward
another foot. He still kept staring the steady stare. Then
I stepped right up to him, although I think my eyes were
closed, almost closed. But I did see his hand quietly lift
from his side and his hand was cupped and it was his right
hand and under it was a cigarette, I could see the smoke
curling around , and he handed me the cigarette and there
was some screaming about something that had happened
in the baseball game and I felt the cigarette in my hand,
and I gloved it, I covered it, and almost without notice,
I'm sure nobody saw, I took a good drag, I sucked it in,
inhaled, held it, lifted the cigarette back to him out of sight

of all, then I stood and let the smoke out most quietly. Then I went back and sat at the end of the bench. I watched the rest of the game. We beat them good, 13 to 4, and they never came back again.

A Day in the Life of an Adult Bookstore Clerk

I t was the usual type of adult bookstore: tip sheets, the *Racing Form*, the daily papers . . . Further, it was divided into three sections—the legit section with the regular magazines and non-porno paperbacks; the section you entered through the swinging door where the porno bits are housed; and the section that led from the porno section to the arcade room where you could see a quick dirty flick for a quarter. It cost 50 cents to get into the porno section but you were given a silver token which was applicable to a purchase.

It was Marty's first day on the job and he had the day shift. He stood on the raised platform that gave him full view of the porno room. He couldn't see the arcade room.

Well, it seemed a better job than the furniture factory. It was clean and it was quiet. You could look at the boulevard and see the cars going by, you could see people walking by. The yellow cabstand was just outside.

It was 8:15 A.M. A guy around 35 in a yellow t-shirt and long sideburns walked in. Grey pants, long arms, black and white shoes, very pink clean face, large open blue eyes. He stood there and looked up at Marty.

"You got anything without hair on the box?"

"What?"

"Young girls, man."

"I don't know."

"You don't read the stuff?"

"I don't read it."

"I gotta pay 50 cents and take my chances?"

"That's right."

The guy put the 50 cents up and Marty gave him the token and he walked through the swinging doors. There were already two other guys in there. 30 minutes passed. The guy in the yellow t-shirt came out.

"You don't have shit in there, man. You oughta have some stuff without hair on the box."

Marty didn't answer.

"I saw something, though, in one of the glass cases. One of those masks. What do one of those masks go for?"

$6.95 plus tax."

"I'll take one."

Marty took one out from under the counter. It was a mask of a little girl crying. Her mouth was open. It was rubber and the entrance to the mouth was tube-shaped to fit the penis. Marty subtracted the 50 cent token from the purchase, put the boxed item in a brown paper bag, gave the man that and his change and he was gone.

Another guy came by, silently handed Marty his 50 cents, got his token and entered the porno room. Then a horseplayer came in.

"Give me number 4," he said.

"Number '4' what?"

"The fourth *Form* down from the top."

Marty counted 4 down, pulled it out and took the dollar.

"I'm going to bet the number 4 horse in the 4th race, plus any horses that go off at 4 to one."

Then he was gone.

Next one of the guys came out from the back. He gave the token back but Marty had seen him cut a photo from one of the magazines with a razorblade. He'd also been in the arcade room. Then a young guy, around 22, came through the swinging door, "Jesus Christ."

"What?" asked Marty.

"Jesus Christ, some of the guys came right over the coin slot of one of your machines back there. It's dripping with come."

Marty locked the register and walked back there. It was true. The coin slot of one of the machines was dripping with semen. Marty walked to the crapper, got a large handful of toilet paper and wiped the coin slot off. The title of the movie was, *A Girl's Best Friend: A Dog.*

Around 11:30 a guy came in and bought an inflatable doll. The doll went for $20.

"Listen," said the guy, "will you blow her up for me? I've got asthma."

"I've got emphysema," said Marty. "You'll have to take her to a gas station."

"All right," said the guy.

"How about some black lace panties for her?"

"Let me see them. Let me feel them."

Marty handed the guy the black lace panties. He felt them. "How much?"

"$6.95."

"O.K., I'll take them."

"How about some nice wigs? We've got blonde, black, brunette, red and grey."

"No, I think I've spent enough. Maybe later. I'll just take her and the panties."

You had to eat lunch at the counter. Marty locked the register and went down to the taco stand and ordered the enchilada lunch and a large coke. He took it back and ate it while sitting by the register.

About 1:00 P.M. a young girl came in. She might have been 21. Marty asked for her I.D. She was 21 according to her I.D. She wanted to see the dildoes. She wanted to see all the dildoes.

"Lay them all out," she said.

Marty laid them out on the counter. There were seven styles. The girl picked one of them up.

"What good is this thing?"

"What's wrong with it?"

"Look, " the girl ran her finger up the back of the dildo, "there's a ridge coming out here on the back. That's no good."

"Those plastic ones are the cheapest. Why don't you try one of the others?"

The girl handed the dildo back. "Don't you have any black dildoes?"

"No."

"You ought to have some black dildoes."

"I suppose we should."

The girl finally selected three dildoes. She seemed to prefer the one with the large protruding veins. Marty put the dildoes in a brown sack and then the girl was gone. Then Marty had to take a piss. He locked the register and walked through the porno room and into the arcade room. You had to go through the arcade room to get to the crapper. There was a guy looking into one of the machines and masturbating. Marty walked on, had his piss and as he walked by the guy was still masturbating.

When he got back to the register there was a guy waiting.

"I want the hands," said the guy. The hand was rubber and had little wires running through it. The wires allowed the hand to be fitted around the penis and then the hand was plugged into the wall and the fingers moved.

"The hands?" asked Marty.

"Yes. I want twenty hands."

"Twenty hands?"

"Yes, twenty hands."

Marty counted out twenty hands and the man paid for them. He went off with the hands in a large paper sack.

The phone rang. It was his boss, Herman. Herman had done 19 years for armed assault. Now he owned 22 adult bookstores. "How's it going? Any problems?"

"Fine. No problems."

"How much you takin' in?"

"Around 90 dollars."

"You'll hit 150 before your shift's up."

"I suppose so."

"Listen. I got a problem. I lost my man at the Hollywood shop. The fucking cops got him."

"What happened?"

"Well, he'd been going with the janitor's wife. He was sitting up with her one night and he got up and strangled her. Then he cut her body all up and buried her in Griffith Park. Then while he was asleep these two guys came and repossessed his car. When they opened the trunk they found two hands in there. He'd forgotten the hands. The cops came and got him. He was a good counter man. He'd been with me two years. He was honest. I never had to worry about him. It's hard to get a guy who doesn't rip you off."

"Yeah, I guess so."

"They're always ripping a man off. You give them a job and they rip you off."

"Yeah."

"You don't know a good honest man, do you? I need a man for the night shift."

"No, I don't know anybody honest, sorry."

"O.K., well, I'll find somebody."

"All right."

Herman hung up.

The afternoon went on. Around 4: 30 a guy came up out of the arcade room. "Those sons of bitches live back there," he told Marty. "It's dark and it stinks back there, they suck each other off."

Marty didn't answer. "That's not bad enough," said the guy, "but now somebody's shit back there!"

"What?"

"Yeah, a shit freak. You got a shit freak coming here. It happened last Tuesday too. There's a big stack of stinking shit back there right in the center of the floor!"

Marty walked back there with the guy and flicked on the lights. There was a guy at one of the machines, masturbating.

"Hey," said the guy, "cut the damned lights!"

There was the stack of shit right in the middle of the floor. It was an enormous stack and it stank, it stank very much.

"Did you shit on the floor?" Marty asked the guy at the machine. The guy had put his eyes back on the viewer and was still masturbating.

"Listen, I asked you if you shit on the floor."

"You're ruining my movie. I ought to get my quarter back."

"All right, I'll give you your quarter back. Did you shit on the floor?"

The guy at the machine pointed to the other guy, "No, he did it."

The other guy looked at Marty. "Listen, do you think I'd shit on the floor and then come and tell you about it?"

"He does it all the time," said the guy at the machine, he used to do it with the guy who worked here."

"You're a fucking liar," said the other guy.

"Who you calling a liar? I'll punch you out. I hate you shit freaks!"

The guy at the machine put his penis in his pants, zipped up and moved toward the other guy.

"All right," said Marty, "we'll have no fighting in here."

Marty found an old newspaper and picked up the shit with the old newspaper and took it back to the toilet. He was careful not to put the newspaper in the toilet. The main trouble, though, was that while he was back there some-body could be stealing something up front. He had to keep coming out of the arcade room to check the customers, then go back to carrying the shit.

When Marty was finished the guy at the machine asked for another quarter. Marty gave him the quarter. The guy put it in the machine, unzipped, got his penis in his hand and began watching. The other guy was gone. Marty walked back up front and sat down by the register.

When the night man came in, one Harry Wells, Harry asked him how he liked the job.

"Not bad," said Marty.

"It's got its drawbacks," said Harry, "but all in all, it's O.K."

"It beats the furniture factory," said Marty. He got his coat and walked out on the boulevard. Harry was right, all in all it was O.K. He was hungry and decided to celebrate his new job with a steak dinner at the *Sizzler*. He walked on down.

The place was high in the Hollywood Hills. It was a nice place. Three German Police dogs slept in the yard. The latest burglar alarm systems had been installed. But Herman couldn't sleep. He turned on his back; he turned on his side. That side. Then the other side. He tried the stomach. He went to the bathroom. There wasn't a sleeping pill in the house. It was hot. He sat in bed and smoked a cigarette. Then he stretched out. He tried his back. He tried both sides. He rolled and scratched and stared at the ceiling. Finally his wife said, "Herman, what the hell's the matter with you?"

"Joan, can I ask you something?"

"Sure."

"Do you read the papers?"

"Yes, I like to keep up with things in the Women's Liberation Movement."

"I know that. That's fine, but look, there are other problems too."

"I know, Herman. I'm no dumb wife. I'm an individual."

Joan read *Playgirl*, *Ms.*, *Woman*, and *California Girl*, among others.

"All right, I grant you that. You're an individual. We don't have any arguments there. Let's not get into a Buckley-Greer debate."

"A Greer-Buckley debate."

"O.K., a Greer-Buckley debate. Greer won. But Buckley isn't against Woman's Liberation, he's against some of the aspects of the Woman's Liberation movement."

Herman sat up in bed and lit another cigarette. "Listen," said Joan, "if this Woman's Lib thing bothers you so much, we better talk about it."

"I'm not even thinking about it."

"Then what is it?"

"Joan, I make my living doing these films and printing these books."

"I know that."

Herman put his cigarette out. "We've gone back to the

149

dark ages, we've been murdered. The Victorians are back in
button-top shoes. The churches are smiling from ear to ear,
from parish to collection box."

"What do you mean?"

"I mean today the U.S. Supreme Court passed a deci-
sion making the definition of obscenity a state matter."

"Which means?"

"Which means what is not obscene in Oakland can be
obscene in Twin Falls."

"That's impossible. What's obscene in one place is obscene in another."

"No, the Supreme Court says obscenity is a local
definition."

"So, you're in trouble?"

"Of course; I distribute nationally."

"That's what you get for your sexism."

"And what do you get for my sexism?"

"I'm your wife."

"You get a fine house in the hills; you drive a 1973 Caddy;
you belong to the best of women's clubs; you get maid service, a once-a-week shrink, the best of clothes and foods . . ."

"And I get you . . ."

"Well, yes, that's thrown in."

"Women as sex-objects. You just can't get away with it."

Herman walked to the bathroom, threw cold water on
his face and came back.

"Why don't you put on the air-conditioning?" asked
Joan.

"I always get a cold."

"Well, I don't."

Herman walked into the other room, put the switch to
on and came back. Then he was back in bed again. "We
might as well use the air-conditioning. We're gonna be
broke soon enough."

"Herman, we've got two hundred and ten thousand
dollars in the bank."

"You don't know how fast money can go when the con-
ditions revert. We're going to have to bribe local officials.
That won't be so bad. Most of them sell-out cheap. The

problem will be court costs. That's how they can bust us. We'll be in and out of court constantly."

"Look, Herman, I don't want to seem against you. I care for you. But you distribute sexism."

"I distribute crap. But some people need it. It makes them happy."

THAT'S WHAT YOU GET
FOR YOOR SEXISM.

"That doesn't make it right."

"It was Hemingway who said, 'No matter what you believe in, if it doesn't make you happy, you're wrong.'"

"Hemingway! That male pig! Attending bullfights, putting on boxing gloves, shooting animals . . . ! He was a little boy pretending to be a man. He was afraid of his impotency, of his homosexuality!"

"Oh shit," said Herman.

"I suppose you've got something against the gays?"

"Look, in my business 80 percent of the people I employ are fags."

"Gays."

"Gays, then."

"Herman, people are coming into their own. Wounded Knee. Marlon Brando says—"

"Please, Joan. You don't know what this Supreme Court ruling can do. It can not only kill off the crap I do, it can affect well-meant literature, painting, sculpture, movies . . . ."

"Movies? Like *Deep Throat* and *Last Tango in Paris*?"

"Those were good movies because they opened up the air . . . ."

"Would you like your child to see *Deep Throat?*"

"Joan, we don't have any children."

"If you had a child, would you like it to see *Deep Throat?*"

"That's a stupid question. It reminds me of the question they used to pop around the forties: 'Would you like your sister to sleep with a nigger?'"

"Herman, I'm talking about *deliberate* sexism, I'm talking about a *deliberate* obscenity . . . ."

"Arguing about obscenity is like arguing about God. Nobody knows."

"But we always manage to argue about something."

"O.K. We can't sleep. Let's try God."

"Herman, there *is* a God."

"Oh shit."

"Is that all you can say: 'oh shit'?"

"Shit yes."

"You pretend to be an intelligent man."

"I never said I was."

"I never said you did."

"Oh God!"

"See?" Joan laughed. "You're calling to Him."

"I'm going to Him."

Herman got up and walked to the kitchen. He found the scotch in the lower cupboard. He took three thimbles in a glass of water and drank it in two tries. Then he walked back to the bedroom and got back into bed.

"Why the hell don't you move around a little?" he asked

his wife. "You just stay stretched out there. It's not natural."

"Herman, people sleep at night. They don't get up and scratch themselves and walk around like you do."

"How do you know they don't? I'll bet half this town is up tonight walking around and scratching itself."

"Herman, get up and get me a drink, mix me a nice drink and light me a cigarette."

"And what are you going to do?"

"I'm going to get up and pee."

"You're going to get up and pee? Don't women ever piss?"

"Only people who stand up when they do it piss."

"That's discriminatory. I suppose if you drank some pee and drank some piss each would taste different."

"Of course. Women's glands . . . "

"Of course, women's glands. Now what do you want? Scotch? Whiskey? Gin? Vodka? Wine?"

"Two jolts of scotch in some soda."

"We don't have any damned soda."

"We have some damned soda. Just look in the refrigerator."

Herman got up and walked to the kitchen and looked in the refrigerator. She was right. There was soda. Score one for Greer. He mixed her drink and came back. He mixed two drinks and came back. He got into bed with his wife and they sat upright against the pillows with their drinks. He found the ashtray, the matches and the smokes on the headboard. He lit her a cigarette.

"Those birds," he said, "they sing all night. When do they sleep?"

"Those birds are happy. If you're not happy, you're wrong."

"Hemingway birds," he said.

"Hemingway birds," she said.

"They're gonna blow their brains out," he said.

"They're gonna blow their brains out," she said.

They sat there and listened to the birds. There were crickets too.

"This is ridiculous," Herman said. "210 thousand dollars in the bank and I can't sleep. Guys on skid row with a bottle of wine are sleeping like babies. I've got to be crazy."

"Why don't we take a couple of months off and go to Paris?" she asked.

"What? And come back and find the business vanished? I've got to stay on top of this thing. This Supreme Court ruling has me up against the wall."

"All right, Herman."

"Don't talk condescendingly to me, please."

"No, I meant it. Whatever you want to do. I guess I should worry more with you. I don't seem to contribute anything."

"You contribute."

"Thanks, if you mean it."

"I mean it. We're going to Paris. For two weeks."

"It'll do you good, Herman. It'll do me good."

"Shit, yes. Fuck the Supreme Court! Fuck the Supreme Court! Rosenbaum can handle affairs. Four weeks in Paris!"

"Rosenbaum can handle affairs. You'll stay in constant touch."

"I'll stay in constant touch. Six weeks in Paris!"

"Eight weeks in Paris!"

"Two months in Paris. Fuck the Supreme Court!"

"Three months in Paris! You can trust Rosenbaum."

"Two months in Paris. I can't trust Rosenbaum that much."

"All right, two months in Paris. Listen to the Hemingway birds!"

"Listen to the Hemingway birds. They're going to blow their brains out!"

They finished their drinks, made love and slept the remainder of the night.

Carl knocked three times and Billy opened the door. There was a big brunette on the couch (at least she looked big) with Billy in the room. Billy was a jock. "Who's this?" asked Carl.

"This is Joyce," said Billy.

"Can I make you some coffee?" Joyce asked Carl.

"No way," said Carl.

"Listen," said Billy, "you don't have to act nasty."

Billy walked over and sat next to Joyce on the couch.

"WHO'S THIS?" ASKED CARL.

"Act nasty?" said Carl. "Act nasty? Listen, I've been hustling you rides, I got you mounts with the best trainers in the game, even Harry Desditch, and what do you do?"

"Desditch? All he gives me are dogs. When his mounts get hot, the Shoe gets right on or Pinky. My stuff goes off at 80-1."

"All right, I get your *rides*, don't I? You get your fee. You get more for one ride than a lot of men get working all day. I get you out of the bullring, I get you up where you get a chance to cut some purses and what do you do? You go for a ride with a battery! Where'd you try to sting him? Maybe you should have had an instruction kit."

"I stung him on the bunghole," said Billy.

The brunette giggled. Billy grinned.

"Oh, it's funny, is it?" said Carl, walking up and down the floor. "You know how long you're gonna get set down?"

"Six months," said Billy, "I need a rest."

"They'll set you down for two years. You'll be lucky to exercise horses."

"Six months," said Billy, "I'll be able to do some eating."

"Two years," said Carl, "and if you eat up, you'll never come down. Your bone structure is too large. You'll be finished."

"He can eat me then," said Joyce.

"If he don't eat any better than he's been riding, you won't know he's there. Not unless he gets down there with his battery."

Billy stood up from the couch. He weighed 112. Carl was 218.

"Listen, you can't talk about my woman that way."

"Maybe you ought to sting her on the bunghole too."

Billy rushed Carl, swinging. Carl grabbed him by both wrists, then shouldered him back down on the couch.

"Bastard," said Billy, "I'll kill you!"

"You leave Billy alone," said Joyce.

Carl walked back and forth across the room. They sat on the couch watching him.

"A battery! Great Jesus, a battery! Why don't you use your brain? No matter what you do to a horse, burn him, tickle him or dope him, you can't improve him over two and one-half lengths at six furlongs, you can't get but three extra lengths out of him at a mile or over. If you're riding a goddamned pig that's eight lengths worse than the field, then what in the hell good are three lengths going to do you?"

"I didn't know how it worked," said Billy, "I didn't consider that."

Carl kept walking back and forth. "You didn't *consider* that! After I pull you out of those bullrings and get you one-half a rep, after I give you a chance to finally cut a good purse, you didn't *consider* that?"

"Well, if I had any brains, I'd be booking you."

"You'd be booking *me*? At 218 pounds? Where?"

"Well, maybe doorman at the Biltmore."

"Listen, I don't see how you can be so glib about this. You made this dumb-ass error and you act like it's a joke."

"I'm sorry, Carl, I really don't feel good about it."

"Listen, Billy, where we had you, all you had to do was do your job. The human greed thing can be a killer. The whole game is set up so there's enough for everybody, you don't have to squeeze it. In the fifties back east they tried to set one up. They fixed the horse, they even fixed the jocks. It was all set. They bet the house, the car, the baby's crib and grandma's life savings. But something ailed the horse. He wouldn't run. They backed up the pace and waited. Still he wouldn't show up. That race cost those boys millions. And they didn't need the money that bad. Everything was fixed and it still failed. And you got out there with a battery and a couple of wires and expect to conquer the world."

"I wish you'd shut up about that goddamned battery," said Billy.

"You got other boys to book," said Joyce, "you'll make it without booking Billy. You're the one who's greedy."

"Yeah," said Billy.

Carl stopped walking. He stood in front of the couch. "Well, maybe you're right. I am being greedy. But, Billy, let me tell you this. If you don't want to get barred for life, when you get up in front of that board, don't act *cute!* Don't crack wise. I think you got the makings of a damn good rider, I don't want to see you blow it.

"O.K., Carl, O.K."

"Billy, you were in this alone, weren't you?"

"Yeah, sure."

"You sure?"

"Sure I'm sure."

"I mean, I didn't notice any extra action on the board. When the books get an overload they dump it on the first flash. There wasn't any action showing."

"It was my idea."

"O.K, Billy. Well, I'll be going now. And remember, when you get in front of the board . . . "

"I'll remember," said Billy.

Carl walked to the door, opened it, closed it and was gone.

"Well," said Joyce, "he's gone. He feels bad."

"I feel bad, too. It was a dumb-ass trick."

"O.K., let's try to forget it. What'll we do today?"

"I dunno, Joyce, let's drive down to the beach."

"It's too cold to swim."

"I know. We can walk around. Eat something. Catch a drink. Look at the ocean. Relax."

"All right, it sounds good."

Joyce got up and walked to the bathroom and started combing her hair. Billy got up and walked to the window. The apartment was three floors up, facing toward the boulevard. Yeah, it had been a dumb-ass trick. But he had a bigger woman than any of them. Even Johnny. And when he put that 112 pounds on her he whipped her like a tiger.

When Joyce came out of the bathroom they went out of the apartment together. They waited for the elevator together. As the elevator came up Joyce said, "Don't worry, Billy, you'll make it."

"I know I will," he said.

They got on the elevator together, the door closed and they sank down toward the street.

Jimmy was walking up the right side of Alvarado Street about 8:30 p.m. that Wednesday night when the yellow late-model car slowed along the curbing beside him. There were three women in there. "Hey, kid," said one of them, "can you tell us where Avandale Terrace is?"

"What?" asked Jimmy walking over to the car.

Two of the women sat in the back, and the one dyed platinum with the excessive lipstick on, the one nearest the curbing, opened the door and pointed the .32 and said, "Get in, kid, and *now* . . . " Jimmy got in the back seat between them.

"Listen," he told the women, "I've only got $2 or $3 . . . "

"We don't want your money, kid," said the one who was driving. The one who was driving was the oldest; she had a very sad look on her face, a rather thick neck and wore very thick-rimmed glasses. The only attractive woman was the third, about 23, pale and sleepy-looking, but she lacked even fair breasts.

"What do you want with me then?" asked Jimmy. The platinum blonde kept the gun in his ribs.

"We want your cherry, kid," said the one who was driving.

The thin one giggled. The one with the gun twisted it a little into his side.

"We're takin' you to Sarah's apartment and that's where we're going to get your cherry. You still *got* your cherry, ain't you, kid?" asked the one who was driving.

"I haven't been laid, if that's what you mean."

"Oh, look how *uppity* he is! I like 'em *uppity*! Lots of spirit, it excites me!" said the platinum, continuing to twist the gun into his ribs. "But you ain't a fairy, are ya?"

"Fairy?"

"You know what I mean! Queer, fag . . . "

The car took a hard right throwing Jimmy against the platinum. She took the hand that wasn't holding the gun and pressed Jimmy's head towards hers, kissing him. "You

159

make me hot, you son of a bitch. I'm going to suck all the cream out of you, Virgin cream . . . "

"You women can't get away with this, I'll go to the police."

"You'll kiss my Aunt Minnie's ass too. A hell of a lot they're going to believe *your* story. We'll claim you raped us. It's our word against yours. Anyhow, you're going to *like* it, you're really going to like it."

Thick neck pulled under an apartment near the hills and they got out in the parking ramp and platinum poked Jimmy toward the elevator. "Just be cool, kid. I just got out of the Women's Jail, Marin County Civic Center, San Rafael, and I'm capable of going right back there if you pull any shit. So if you don't want to die with your cherry, cool it."

They stood there while the 23-year-old with the minor breasts pushed the elevator button. The elevator came down, the door opened, they got on. One of the women pushed the button and it began to rise.

"I'm sure glad," said thick neck, "that those Arabs are going to let us have a little oil for a couple of months. Man, it got so bad there I had to give my service station man some pussy for a mere tank of gas, an oil change and lube job and a small can of STP."

"It's all this greed," said the platinum, "it's this terrible immense greed that's ruining this country."

"O, come on, Dolly," said the minor breasts, "this country's been greedy for a long time."

"I mean," said Dolly, "that it's getting so much worse."

"The Lakers are playing the Warriors tonight," said platinum. "I'm taking the Lakers and giving 2 points."

"You're on," said thick neck, "five bucks."

"Five bucks," said platinum.

They got out of the elevator together, platinum pointing Jimmy down the hall with the .32 which she now held inside her purse. They stopped at 402, minor breasts got out the key, and then they were in the apartment, it was a nice apartment, wall-to-wall, and air-conditioning, vented heating, plenty of closet space.

"Sit down, kid," said platinum, "and make yourself at home. Drink?"

"No."

"You better have a drink. It'll loosen you up. You look a little nervous."

"No, nothing to drink, please."

"I believe you *will* have a little Grand-dad and water. Fix him a jolt, Sarah."

WE WANT YOUR CHERRY, KID

Sarah was the one with the minor breasts. She walked into the kitchen. The other two women stood looking at Jimmy who sat on the couch. "I do believe he's a real virgin," said thick neck, "look at him."

"You play with your pud, kid?" asked the platinum.

Jimmy didn't answer.

"You shouldn't play with your pud, kid, it's not natural, it affects the brain waves."

"Yeah," said thick neck.

Sarah came out with the drink. She handed it to Jimmy.

"Drink it down," said platinum, "it'll loosen your exhibitions."

Jimmy got it down in two tries, coughed a bit.

"Please, please . . . let me go," he said.

"Oh, shit," said Sarah, "Take off your clothes."

"Please . . . "

"The girl said take off your clothes, kid," platinum exclaimed, "now take 'em off!"

Jimmy stood up and unbuttoned his shirt, took it off, then sat down, took off his shoes, then got out of his pants.

"Oh, shit! Look at them skivvies!"

"He's *real* cherry!"

"Take them skivvies off, kid!"

"Oooh, look at that *cute* bum!"

"And look at his tiny . . . "

"Yeah, but it will get big . . . "

"Who gets him first?"

"We'll match, it's only fair . . . "

"O.K., hurry . . . Who's got some coins . . . ?"

"Here, I have three nickels . . . "

"O.K., odd woman gets . . . "

"One, two, three . . . flip . . . !"

"Whatcha got?"

"I got heads."

"I got tails."

"I got tails."

"O.K., he's mine . . . I got heads . . . I get head!"

Thick neck advanced across the wall-to-wall. The others watched. "Kid, I'm going to fuck you *good* . . . you're going to be calling for your mother . . . "

"Helen, can't I tongue his bunghole while you do it?"

"No, he's mine, all mine!"

She moved toward Jimmy, licking her lips slightly. Suddenly she grabbed him and tried to kiss him. He pulled his head away and Helen kissed him along the neck. He got a hand around and pushed her head away. "Oooh," said Helen, "I *like* this type! Real *feisty*!" Then she grabbed his head with both hands and kissed him long and hard on the lips, her tongue going in and out. Then she reached down and pulled his balls.

"Oh, Helen, look! HE'S GETTING HARD! HE CAN'T HELP HIMSELF! OH, HOW LOVELY!"

Helen already had her dress up and was working her

panties down at the same time trying to hold Jimmy in reach. Sarah walked into the kitchen and poured herself a Grand-dad, drank it down. Dolly put on a Frank Sinatra record. Then they both stood there and watched as Helen forced Jimmy back on the couch and climbed on top of him, pulling her dress back out of the way.

He was sitting up at his place one night. He hadn't had a woman in three or four years. He engaged in masturbation, drinking, and a grim yet comfortable isolation. He had often thought of being a writer and had bought a second-hand typewriter, but no writing had come of it. He was drinking wine and looking at the typewriter. He got up, walked over to it, sat down and typed:

I wish I had a woman. I wish a woman would knock on my door.

Then he got up, turned on the radio and poured another glass of wine. It was an early evening in July. Both of his parents had died within the last five years, plus his last girlfriend. He was in middle-age, tired, without hope, even without anger or resentment. He felt that the world was mostly for other people; what remained for him were merely matters of eating, sleeping, working, and waiting for death. He sat down on the sofa and waited.

There was a knock on the door. He got up and opened it. It was a woman in her mid-30s. Her eyes were very blue, almost frighteningly so. Her hair was a light red, a bit straggly; she was in a short black dress with red stripes revolving about the dress in barberpole fashion. She seemed neat, but casual. "Come in," he said, "and sit down."

He motioned her to the couch, went into the kitchen and poured her a glass of wine.

"Thank you. My name is Ms. Evans."

"Thank you. My name is Fantoconni. Samuel Fantoconni."

"Yes, we know, Mr. Fantoconni. We received your application and we're here to ask you some questions."

Ms. Evans crossed her legs and he could see flashes of upper thighs. He quickly memorized the upper thighs so that he could use them in his masturbation fantasies. Ms. Evans examined the piece of paper she held in front of her.

"Now, Mr. Fantoconni, how long have you been on your present job, the one with *Carploa and Sons?*"

"Twenty-two years."

"How long were you married?" Ms. Evans crossed her legs again.

"Thirteen years."

"Did you like your marriage?"

"I don't know."

"You don't know?"

"Yes, I don't know."

"You *do* know that you were divorced?"

"Do you need the bathroom?"

"What do you mean?"

"I mean, if you need the bathroom you go right through that door there."

"I don't need the bathroom, Mr. Fantoconni. Who divorced who?"

"She divorced me."

"I see."

He took her glass into the kitchen and refilled and refilled his own and brought them both out.

"Thank you," she said taking her drink. "Now why didn't your marriage work, Mr. Fantoconni?"

"Just call me Sam."

"Mr. Fantoconni, why didn't your marriage work?"

"Don't be an asshole."

"*Please!* But what do you mean?"

"I mean that the structural relationship of marriage within our society is impossible."

"Why?"

"Why? Because I don't have the time."

"You don't have the time? Why?"

"You've just answered my question."

Ms. Evans lifted her drink and looked at him over her drink with her too-extremely blue eyes. "I don't understand you."

"I'm sorry. But you ask these questions."

"We must query our prospective clients, Mr. Fantoconni."

"Query, then."

"Are you bashful?"

"Oh, Christ . . ."

"Answer, please."

"Yes."

"Have you been hurt by women?"

"Yes."

"Do you think women are hurt by men?"

"Yes."

"What's to be done?"

"Nothing."

Ms. Evans finished her drink. "May I have another?"

"Of course." He walked into the kitchen and poured two drinks. When he walked out again her skirt was hiked very high; the form of her haunches was unbelievably beautiful, much like magic. He felt frightened, yet pleased. She drank her drink immediately. "How old is your car?"

"Eleven years."

"Eleven years?"

"Yes."

"Why don't you get another one?"

"I don't know. Inertia, I suppose."

"Inertia. I believe you." She laughed: it was a lovely lilting laugh. "How long has it been since you've had a woman?"

"Four years."

"Four years? Why?"

"I'm afraid of what will follow."

"Why don't you get a whore?"

"Because I don't know what a whore is."

"Get a *Webster*."

"You're right. That's a whore."

"College?"

"No."

"Where do you get your edge?"

"Despair."

"What?"

"Deluge."

He finished his drink, took her empty glass and walked back into the kitchen. He opened another bottle of wine, poured two drinks, brought them back and sat on the couch next to her. He handed her a glass, kept the other.

"I fascinate you," he said, "because I'm not on the make."

"You're on the make but in a totally different way."

"Being able to care but ready to give it up without a qualm."

"Ultimate cynicism."

"Ultimate training."

"Both," she said.

"We sound like a cheap Noel Coward bit."

"You liked him?"

"There's no way to like him or dislike him. He was just a semidelightful inefficiency. A tossed salad: Oscar Wilde mixed with a Jeanette MacDonald-Nelson Eddy duet with George Gershwin at the piano."

"You're starting to talk too much, you're getting pompous and snide. The wine is getting to you," said Ms. Evans.

"I was born," he said, "in West Kansas City in 1922 . . . "

"I don't want to hear it." She switched her legs again, this time a bit nervously.

"You remember Alf Landon?"

"No."

He walked into the kitchen, refilled the drinks, came back. "I don't have any cigarettes. Do you have any cigarettes?"

"Yes." She opened her purse and brought out a package, a light green package of cigarettes. It was a fresh pack. She undid the cellophane, tapped out two. He lit them. "What went wrong with your marriage?"

"Oh," she said, inhaling, "the usual shit."

"Like?"

"He played around, I played around. I forgot who started it. His dirty shorts next to my dirty panties. It's impossible to carry on a high-pitched day-by-day relationship."

"I know."

"You know what?"

"It's this country: we're the spoiled children of the universe—love out front, dangling in searchlights—Liz and Burton."

"You're drunk."

"I liked Burton's face. Liz reminds me of a specimen in a lab, only perfect for what it is. Then, plop."

"Plop."

He reached over and kissed her. She pushed away from him a moment, then gave. When they broke she said, "I'm here to check your credentials."

"I'm sure."

She pushed him away. Her fingers were long and narrow, he noticed them as she pushed him away.

"You suck," he said.

She had her cigarette in her right hand and he got the palm of her left hand across his face, it caught part of his nose. His cigarette shot out of his mouth—sparks, fireworks—it broke, his hand catching part of it—there were these tiny sparks and spilling, and dark ash, and then white paper and unburnt brown tobacco.

"Care for another drink?" he asked.

Ms. Evans had both a briefcase and a purse and she gathered them about herself as she got up. As she stood up the dress dropped back over her flanks. She made a motion to straighten out some wrinkles in her dress, then gave off. "You're nothing but a goddamned cowboy like the rest."

"Right. The world may not exactly radiate over its continuous fucks but it certainly carries on."

"That's supposed to be clever?"

"Supposed to be accurate."

She walked toward the door and the walk was magic; he let his eyes fall into each fold of her wrinkled dress, and each fold was an intimacy, a warmness and a sadness, and then his mind quickly laughed at his softness, and then he focused upon her behind, the twin circles, watching what the circles did. He wanted to say, come back, come back, we've been hasty.

The door closed. He had one more drink. Then he went to bed. He didn't masturbate. He slept.

Within two weeks he got a letter in the mail informing him that he was not acceptable for automobile insurance from the main company but that there was a subsidiary branch out of St. Louis which would most possibly accept his application at nominal but slightly higher rates if he would fill out and mail the enclosed forms, postage-free. It seemed quite simple. There were just little squares to check after the questions.

He checked the questions, made the appropriate markings within the squares and dropped the prepaid envelope into a corner mailbox two or three days later.

Her name was Minnie Budweisser, yes, just like the beer, and Minnie might drag you back to 1932, but she was hardly that, sitting in my office that hot July afternoon, just in slacks, not trying to show too much, not much of it was even tight-fitting, but you could see all that woman in there, the almighty woman that one woman in a million possessed. There she was: Minnie Budweisser, but she'd had sense enough to change her name to Nina Contralto for box office purposes. I looked at her, she was it, the tits weren't silicone and the ass was real, and the movements and the flow and the eyes and the gestures. She was there. She had the damnedest eyes I'd ever seen—they kept shading: first they were blue, then green, then brown, they kept shading, changing, she was a witch, and yet I knew she probably ate peanut butter sandwiches and snored a little in her sleep and even farted and belched once in a while.

"Yes? I asked.

"I'm down from Vegas."

"Trouble?"

"No trouble. Just sick of it."

"Come down to learn Spanish at Berlitz? Become an ambassador?"

"Fuck you."

"Anytime. We pay 5 bucks an hour. You'll get tips from the sicks. If you really want to make it, you'll trick on the side. Ninety-three percent do. If you give head you can bank 23 thousand a year, only 6 grand tax-deductible."

"Fuck you."

"No, fuck you. You've only got five good working years. After that you're down at *Norm's* with a sweaty ass. You score now or you'll never score again. The body's all you got, and it just won't last."

"When do I start?"

"Six p.m., tomorrow night."

Nina was ready at 6 but Helen was still on. I sat at a table and brought Nina a double Scotch. Helen was on but Helen was just dumb. She'd gotten a silicone job but one of the tits had come out about one-half size larger than the other and she couldn't dance, she just moved one leg and then moved the other. She was just like a sleepwalker. The boys played pool and turned their backs to her at the bar.

Then Nina got up there. "No music, please," she said. And then she began making these movements: it was more a prayer than a dance; it was as if she were looking into the sky for salvation, but it was *hot*, don't worry—she had on these tall silver spikes and she had on these pink lace panties and her buttocks whirled in heat to some unsolvable god. Actually—with *another* woman—you might think it corny—she had on these long black gloves that ran halfway up between the elbows and the shoulders, and all these rings were on the fingers of the gloves; her long stockings had the word "LOVE" embroidered into them near the tops. She had the mascara, the long false eyelashes, even pearls about the neck, but it was the movement, the movements—and in silence—that did it. Her body was the magnificent gift but it wasn't that—there was something searching inside of her and she couldn't find it, the man, the way, the city, the country, the out. She was totally alone, without help, although many thought they could help her. As the final act in her dance she took the small red rose that was in her hair and she bit into the stem with her teeth and voluted up at the ceiling, whirling, moving, almost beyond meaning. Then she stopped, stiffened, and walked off coming down the steps at the side.

I raised her to $10 an hour right then. I told her about it. "Thanks, daddy," she said, "but I need some coke now or at least I want to sniff some h. Let's go someplace and score."

"All right," I said. So I took her down to Vanilla Jack's in the Canyon and we sat over his coffee table and he spread it on the mirror and we tried some. I didn't get any results but Nina said it was straight stuff. I gave it the two-on-one (double-nostril suck). Nothing happened. "I'm crazy," I said, "but I don't think it's there—it's spread, no backbone."

Nina tried it again and said it was there. Jack weighed it all in a little silver scale made in Munich, and I paid him, thinking there's no chance for any of us: we just *think* we're circling the vultures.

I got to my place, got her to my place, we got out the mirror and spread it. I had gotten a good bottle of French wine, vintage way back and I put some Shostakovich on the Frisbee. She was as beautiful as ever. With some women their beauty can vanish in one half-hour, or even sooner— as soon as they begin to speak, then their tricks and cons, having vanished, there are no cards left and no light left— well, one card, let's fuck for the sake of fuck and hope for the best. Nina held, she remained total.

I suppose Jack's stuff was good. I began to feel it, even though I mistrusted that Munich scale. "I'll marry you," I told Nina, "I'll give you half of my money."

"You don't understand," she said.

"Understand what?"

"You don't know what love is."

"I love you."

"You just love the *idea* of me. It's all shadow and light and form."

"But I love that. Christ, give me a chance."

"Suppose I were 66 years old? With one eye missing and my shit running out of a sack taped to my side?"

"I don't know."

"You know. Spread some more of that shit on the mirror."

We got higher and higher and then finally went to bed together. I didn't try. I didn't want to try. The world ran through the top of my head and down my back and out the window.

I didn't try with Nina again. She kept coming to work and making it with her silent dance and she had 75 guys in love with her. I found out from a pretty good source that she wasn't making it with anybody after her show. All that body, untouched. There were crimes against mankind and that was certainly one of them.

She worked the 6 p.m. to 2 a.m. shift. That Wednesday afternoon somebody stole all the clothes out of her locker: the silver spikes, the long black sleeves, the long stockings embroidered "LOVE" near the tops. All the other gear. She came down and began banging lockers and screaming. She was in an old white T-shirt and bluejeans and she looked more beautiful than the sun, raving and wobbling and insane. I told her fuck, forget it, I'd pay her night's wages, all she had to do was to go around and serve an occasional drink to the boys. It wasn't a bad night: Nina was better serving drinks than the other girls were on the wood. I drove her to her apartment that night and she was laughing.

It was strange the next day. She was on at 6 and she came on down the street toward my place at 4:30 in the afternoon moving toward my place. She was all over the sidewalk with that great body and everybody looking, and she was in this mini-skirt, runners all over her stockings, she was rocking back and forth, the newsboys and the ordinaries watching—they'd beat off for a month to the memory of it and then she hit up against the frontglass of *Billy's Half-Hard Club* hard, hit that hard, and it didn't break, and she had on this red wig, this big red wig and it fell off of her head and she didn't know it and just kept moving toward my place—out of it—and somebody picked up her wig and followed her. It was more than snow. She stepped in and started really doing a dead-ass dance in mockery of the girl on the wood then. It irritated me.

"Listen, " I said, "you're an hour and a half early."

"So what?" she asked.

"So," I said, "fuck you, you're fired."

"Fuck you," she said, and walked out.

I think of her sometimes now but I get the idea that somehow she's not in this town or in any town near here. Now here I am calling L.A. a town. It's a city, isn't it? But I finally found out who stole her gear. It was the one with the silicone who got one breast bigger than the other. She wears it now, the tall/silver spikes, the pearls, the long black gloves with all the rings, 17 rings, and the "LOVE" stockings, all of it. She's even learned to dance a bit, but it just doesn't work.

Barry, who I hadn't seen for two years, phoned and asked if I wanted to fuck his wife's mother. I said all right, got the directions to where they were living, got in my car and drove out. It was somewhere off the San Berdo freeway, quite a ways out. I found the street, the house, parked the car, got out. Barry was sitting on the front steps drinking a beer. I had four six-packs. We went into the house and Barry started putting the beer in the refrigerator. "The mother has a pussy just like the daughter. I've fucked them both. There's no difference."

"If there's no difference, I'll take the daughter."

"Fuck off," said Barry. "Come on, they're in back."

We took some beer out into the backyard. I knew Barry's wife, Sarah. He introduced me to the mother, Irene. She flashed me an enormous smile. "Oh, Mr. Bukowski, I've read your books and I think you're a wonderful writer!" Both of the ladies were in short pants and blouses, wore sandals. Irene had nice legs but they had very many blue veins upon them.

"We're going to bake some weenies," said Barry.

"I just love hot weenies," said Irene.

Barry took me over and showed me his new motorcycle. "Want a ride?" he asked me.

"No thanks, kid, bad for the hemorrhoids."

"Oh Barry," said Irene, I'll go!"

Irene climbed on the back and they spun out of the yard and into the street. I finished my beer and opened another. I sat down next to Sarah. "Irene thinks you're the greatest thing since Hemingway," she said.

"I'm closer to Thurber mixed with Mickey Spillane."

"That doesn't sound so good."

"It isn't."

"Mother is very lonely. She has trouble meeting people."

"I'm scared."

"Don't be."

Barry had only cycled around the block. They came in with a whirl of dust. Irene slid off. "WHEEEEE!"

"Come on," Barry said to me, "help me get some wood."

I walked around behind the garage with him. "She's really horny," he said. "I think she got it off on the bike. My god, she's hot!"

"Barry, I don't know what to do."

"Just relax. It will happen."

"Yeah."

We both came round the side of the garage with the wood. "Hurry," said Irene, "I could eat one of those things raw!"

"Now, Irene," I said, "you wouldn't want to do that."

"Oh, isn't he *funny*!" she said. "I've always said he was one of the few writers around with a sense of humor." She drained her beer can and tossed it into the bushes, cracked open another one. Sarah spread mustard and relish on the bun and Irene watched the weenies.

"Oh, I want the *big* one!" she said.

"You're very funny too, Irene," I said and opened another beer. I tossed my old can into the bushes next to hers. "Our cans side by side."

"Oooh," went Irene, "ha, ha, ha, ha!"

"I think we're going to move to Mexico," said Barry, "a good writer needs isolation."

"A good writer needs money," I said.

"I've sold nine novels this year," said Barry. Barry wrote a novel a month, all on incest. I'd met him right after he'd come out of the madhouse. He used to be a baby sitter before he cracked the incest market.

We finished the weenies and sat about in the chairs drinking beer and watching the sun go down. Barry got up and came out with two six-packs and carried them into this shack in the back. "That's where you and Irene are going to sleep," he told me. I looked at Irene. She was lighting a cigarette. Her fingernails were lacquered purple.

Suddenly both Barry and Sarah stood up and walked into their house. I was alone with Irene. "Oh," she said, "I just love sunsets, don't you?"

"No, not really."

"You're a cynic, aren't you?"

"I suppose I would be if I said I loved sunsets when I didn't."

"Oh no, that would be a hypocrite."

"You're a smart girl, aren't you?"

"I've been around."

THEY SPUN OUT OF THE YARD.

"Vassar?"

"What's that?"

"The name of the Frenchman who invented the hydraulic water pump."

"Oh, shit. Let's get in there and get it on."

I followed Irene into the shack. There was a bed and a chair, a lamp and a nightstand. She threw herself on the bed. I sat on the chair and opened a beer for her and a beer for me. We sat there drinking the beers and looking at each other. The screen door pushed open and a little black kitten walked in. I picked him up. "Ain't he sweet?" I asked.

"Yeah," she said.

I petted the kitten. "They're so innocent. Look at the eyes. Look at the eyes, will you, Irene?"

Irene got off the bed, took the kitten, flung open the

screen door and threw him into space. Then she came back and threw herself upon the bed again.

"I need another beer," I said. "Look, we hardly know each other. Where were you born? Italy?"

"Denver."

"Look. Why don't you get on some high heels? Nylons? Gadgets. I like ear rings."

"I've got some on."

"Oh."

Irene got up and walked out. She was gone a long time. She was gone so long that I got onto the bed with my beer. Jesus Christ, I thought, did D.H. Lawrence have to go through this? What did a man have to do in order to become an immortal writer?

Irene walked in. Strictly from *Frederick's*: spiked heels, ankle bracelet, peek-through panties, a bra that pushed the nipples out like burning cigar ends. She wobbled to the bed and fell down beside me.

"Oh, shit!" I said, "too much! It's so great that I have to have one more beer. Just one more beer, Irene!"

"All right."

I drank the beer and stared at her spiked shoes, her calves, her ankles, her nipples. It would soon be mine, all mine. I finished the beer and threw my arms around her. Our lips met. An enormous fat tongue slashed through my teeth and into my throat. I sucked on her tongue. It was very wet. Then I bit into it and she pulled it out. I undid her brassiere and the breasts fell flat. As I sucked on one nipple I played with the other with my fingers. Valentino must have done this at his best, I thought, but I'm not going the entire route. I pulled her panties off and mounted.

I must have drunk 15 or 16 beers. I pumped. I pumped and I pumped and I pumped. It wasn't bad. I pumped for 15 minutes. She'd left her shoes on. I looked back and looked at her spiked shoes on her feet. I pumped 15 minutes more. I couldn't climax. I pumped, hit, rotated, changed rhythms, used a part of it, used all of it and the springs sounded and sounded and Irene was under me and I looked at her and her eyes were rolled back into her head, she was showing me the backs of her eyes, no pupils no color. I gave it one last grand surge and charge. No good, no climax. I rolled off.

"I'm sorry, Irene." The lights were out. She got up and climbed over me.

"I'll be back."

She walked out. I heard her walking down the path and into the back door of the main house. I got dressed. Then I walked out, down the driveway, got into my car and drove home.

Barry phone me the next day. "I'm sorry, man," I said, "couldn't make it."

"Wait. She loved it. She wants to see you again."

"What?"

"I'm serious . . . ."

Next thing I knew I got a letter from Barry. They were in Mexico. Marvelous maid service. Marvelous. Cleaned the house and did everything. Young girl. Sarah is jealous. Irene is horny. Just sold another novel. Marvelous fishing off the coast.

I don't know how many months went by. Somehow, as such things happen, I found myself living with a grey-haired woman, one Lila. Lila was of good body, and sometimes of excellent mind and other times no mind at all. Her front teeth were crooked and yellow and when she screamed at me the lips parted and she showed me all these teeth, quite frightening, but she was good in bed, well read, and kept her fingernails clean. The body was nice, as I said, but one of her weaknesses was going to all these meetings, Communist party meetings, poetry readings, and one day she came back all dressed in black, she said she was going to wear black until the Vietnam War ended, it was her way of protest and she covered that good body with all this black throwaway material purchased from the Goodwill, thriftshops, and elsewhere, she just flopped on all this black and it was very scruffy because when you protest you don't do it in a slick black gown with the tits hanging, you suffer. So we both suffered and the Vietnam War had been going on for 40 years and it would go another 40. So I rather gave up on her but went on living with her, as one does . . .

Then one day the doorbell rang. It was Barry and Irene. They'd come up out of Mexico. Barry was to edit a nudey mag in North Hollywood. Sarah was shopping in Van Nuys. Sarah was also working in watercolors. Not bad. Everybody sat down and I went in and broke out the beer. Irene crossed her legs high. She had on long spiked heels. And nylons held with blue ruffled garters. I'd never realized that her legs were so long. Irene looked at Lila. "Oh, aren't you *proud* to be living with a great writer like Bukowski?"

Lila stiffened her back and didn't answer.

I tried to keep from looking at Irene's legs. They were glorious. She knew I was looking but refused to pull her dress down. "What are you wearing black for?" she asked Lila.

"So many lives are wasted in useless causes," said Lila.

"You ain't shittin', honey," answered Irene.

Barry said they had to go but I insisted upon another round of beers. Irene hiked her dress higher. We were *all* looking at Irene's legs. "You people all come out and see us now," said Irene. Then they got up and left.

I told Lila that I was going to take a bath. I went in there and locked the door. I hadn't used soap in years. I mean, that way. Pink Lady Godiva.

This time I climaxed.

"**H**alf of what you make goes to the house, the other half to you," said Marty. It was the third girl he had interviewed that morning. The ad had stated that the job paid from $500 to a grand a week. This one was about 23, quite stately, even clean-looking, blonde, with pale blue eyes that stared and stared. She was dressed in a white blouse and black slacks.

"You give head?" he asked the girl.

"What?"

"You gotta give head, are you any good at it?"

"I guess."

"Most of the guys who come in here want head."

"I see."

"You better see. You work here, you produce. We're one doughnut shop that does it well. We get few complaints. We take care of the cops and we take care of the customers. Once in a while we get a guy who complains. For that we take ALL of his money instead of part of it. Then we kick his ass a bit and set him back out on the street. Take your clothes off."

"What?"

"Take your clothes off. Do you shave your box?"

Marty lit his cigar and waited. She had on light green panties.

"The panties too. Take off the panties. Put everything on that chair."

The girl stood there, naked.

"Not too much breast but what the hell. And you ought to scrub your teeth more, they're stained. You been to college?"

"One year."

"One year. That's nice. Where?"

"Claremont."

"Claremont. That's nice. Turn around. You got a black boy hustling you?"

"No."

"It's all right if you do, just keep him out of here. You got a wart on your ass."

"That's a mole."

"Oh. Now all right, did I tell you to start getting dressed?"

"No, sir."

"Don't. I'm getting a hard. I think that wart did it."

"Mole."

"Mole. You'll get the 6 p.m. to 2 a.m. shift. Can you piss?"

"Of course."

"I mean, in a man's mouth and on his chest, his legs, his balls and over his toes. Can you do that?"

"Yes, sir."

"You're a nice girl. Class. I like that one year of college. I got a daughter in college myself. How about shit?"

"What's that?"

"You know what it is. We get lots of shitfreaks in here. Can you let a guy suck a turd out of your ass?"

"I think so."

"You sure as hell better know ahead of time. You married?"

"No."

"You live alone?"

"I live with my mother."

"You and your mother, what are you hooked on, coke or H?"

"We don't take dope."

"You will. Look, I still got this hard. It's busting out of my pants. You see it?"

"I see it."

"You believe in God?"

"Yes."

"I thought so. Nice girl."

"Can I get dressed now?"

"Just leave your fucking clothes OFF! It's not costing you anything, is it?"

"No."

"We got an operation going here that nothing around Hollywood and Western can touch. We got something going for any type alive. We got guys who just like to come in here and watch television with a girl. We got a special room for that. Then we got two or three days shackjobs going. We got special apartments for that: stoves, bathtubs, the works. They even go shopping together at *Ralphs*. We got two floors here and we use them all. We're an institution here and we treat our help better than *Mark C. Bloome*. Sometimes you gotta slash a guy's ass with something like this."

TAKE OFF THE PANTIES.

Marty reached into the desk drawer and pulled out the leather whip. He handed the whip to the girl. "That son of a bitch cost us 80 dollars and it has already brought joy to over two hundred men and boys. Let me see if you can handle that thing. Work out."

The girl raised the whip.

"Hey! Not on ME, you cunt! Lay it into that chair over there."

She slashed the whip at the chair.

"No, you flick the END. Try it again! Now that chair

is a guy's ass bent over. See him there? Bent over? See his bunghole? His balls are dangling. Flick his cheeks good! Enjoy it!"

The girl flicked the whip at the chair.

"That's better. But we're going to have to train you. You got to beat them until they're bloody. They'll beg you to stop but they don't mean it. You'll know when to stop. You'll stop when they come. Most of them whack off but the real pros can come without touching their dicks."

The girl lashed at the chair again.

"All right, that's enough. We haven't finished paying for the furniture yet. What's your social security number?"

"651-90-2010"

"Phone number?"

"614-8965"

"Address?"

"4049 Fountain."

"Name?"

"Helen Masterson."

"Helen, touch my dick."

"What?"

"Just come over here and touch my dick. I won't take it out from under the cloth. Just come on over here and touch it with one of your fingers. That's all you've got to do."

Helen walked over, reached down and touched Marty's penis.

"O.K. you're hired. Get dressed. You start tomorrow evening."

Helen got dressed and went to the door, opened it. There was another girl sitting out there. Marty saw her. "Come on in, dear, and close the door behind you."

Helen walked outside and she was on Hollywood Boulevard. She walked down to Western, crossed the street, and found a telephone near the taco stand. She dialed the number 614-8965.

"Ma?"

"Yes?"

"It's Helen. Ma, I got the job."

"Oh Helen, I'm glad. And I think I got a job too. I filled out an application for *The House of Pies*."

"Great, Ma."

Helen hung up. Then she walked over to the taco stand and ordered a chili burrito and a large coke.

Lucille was not a bad sort, I mean compared to most who had lived with me. Like the others she drank, lied, cheated, stole and exaggerated, but as a man goes on he stops looking for the whole cloth, he'll settle for a piece of rag. And then he'll pass that on to the next while scratching his ear.

But, generally, while things are working just a little, a wise man will tend to accept the moment because if you don't you just get a bag with you in it and when you shake it you only hear one sound. Boy, you've got to poop up some guts now and then to find out where the sun lays it down.

Lucille would tell little stories about the south. Well, not the real south but the south of Arizona and New Mexico, Midwest south. We'd sit up in bed drinking our wine and she'd talk: "My god, it was terrible. That convent. Those bitches. We were all little girls and they'd starve us. The richest church in the world, the Catholic Church, and they'd starve us."

"I like the Catholic Church, they give a good show, all those robes, that Latin, drinking the blood of Christ . . . "

"We were so hungry, so very very hungry. We'd climb out the windows at night and go into the garden and dig up these radishes, they'd be surrounded with dirt and mud, and we'd eat it all, the dirt, the mud, the radishes . . . we were so hungry. And when we got caught we were punished terribly . . . Those bitches in their black hoods and dresses . . . "

"Don't spill the wine on the sheets, it's harder to get off than beet juice."

Lucille, like the rest of them, had come out of a long and unhappy marriage. They all told me stories of their long and unhappy marriages and I'd lay there next to them thinking, "Now what am I supposed to do?"

It was never quite clear to me so I drank very much with them and fucked them often and listened to their speeches but I don't think I did much for them. I gave them an ear and a cock, I *did* listen and I did fuck, whereas most men only *pretended* to listen. I guess I had an ace but I had to listen to an awful lot of shit and then weigh and measure it, and when I got through with that, the substance I had left could be blown away with one nostril pinched off. But I was a kind man. They all admitted that: I was a very kind man.

"Those radishes tasted *so* good, mud, sand and all . . . "

"Put your hand on my cock. Rub my balls."

"Are you still Catholic?"

"No way. You got a hair caught in your ring. You're killing me. I hate women who wear rings, especially turquoise. It proves they're in with the devil, that they're witches . . . Touch the head of my cock."

"You've got the biggest balls of any man I've ever met."

"I could say something about you, too, but I don't think I will . . . "

Outside of that, Lucille had a minor weakness. She'd get drunk on the wine and spread herself across the bed while I was sitting on a chair and she'd start in: "You're a fag, a shoe-tree, a pimpernel . . . you murdered the Frogs at Verdun, you shaved the hairs off of Joan of Arc's pussy and stuck them into your ears like flowers . . . You eat your own shit like your American heritage . . . you think Beethoven is a wart out of lower Seville . . . your mother made you smear her panties with beeswax while she had her hysterectomy . . . "

She kept it on and on, this certain night I'm talking about. I dropped to my knees: "Lucille, my love, you know that I'm a kind man, you've admitted as much. I'm begging you upon my knees to please shut up. Please, I *beg* you! There are certain truths in your wallfly buzzings; there are also certain minor exaggerations. I beg you to cease, little buttercup!"

"You sucked off Henry VIII and smeared buttermilk up his ass. You drew the loop around the Louisiana French. You hate Henry Fonda!"

"Don't say that about Fonda or I'll smash your teeth in!"

"You murdered the golden-haired children of the Valencia of my dreams!"

"No, no, that was your husband!"

"It was *both* of you! Bring me more wine!"

"Yes, my love."

This particular night Lucille went on and on. I am a kind man but you must understand voice *intonation* to understand anything. There is this particular poisonous sound that can be vent loose, it is a sound that itches and scratches and bullies and pukes and mewks. It continues in this same relentless and never-ending tonality, and no matter what one says to it or how one attempts to appease it, it goes on and on and on. Sometimes babies can do this to you, or women, or sometimes men.

The hours went on and Lucille went on. I don't know how many times I asked mercy or how many warnings I gave. But it does happen, finally. I walked toward the bed and I told her as I approached: "All right, buttercup, this is it."

But Lucille continued to wail away, on her back, belly distended with cheap wine, a one-inch ash on her cigarette, the neon signs of central L.A. turning her white, then pink, then yellow, then blue . . . I picked up the end of the bed and closed her into the wall and sat back down. I poured a drink, lit a fresh cigarette and crossed my legs.

Lucille was gone. There was nothing in front of me but brown paneled woodwork. Cliché or not, I had to admit to a definite sense of peace. I remembered Lucille when I had first met her legs, her eyes, her lips, her very round ears, and her slurred tongue. Not knowing a person at all was much better, always, than knowing all of them. One might at least endow them with magics that could never exist, and then, after living with them, blame them for the magics that had never arrived.

I drank my drink and began to hear sounds behind the woodwork: "God o mighty, please help me! Help me!"

"You'll be all right, baby. Relax. I can see the Goodyear blimp from here. It's flashing lights. Let me read you the message . . . "

"Let me out, I BEG YOU! I'M DYING!"

"Oh, fuck," I said and walked over and pulled the bed down. There she was. My flower.

"Oh, shit, I think my arm's broken!"

"Now don't give me a goddamned bunch of trouble. Let me pour you a wine. Care for a cigar?"

"I tell you my arm's broken. It's broken!"

"For Christ's sake, be a man! Here's a drink! Drink up."

"It hurts, it hurts, o my god how it hurts!"

"Stop your goddamned yollering or I'll put you right back into that wall next to your asshole!"

Nothing seemed to frighten her. It was disgusting. I took another big hit of Tokay and took the elevator down. I walked down the street a bit and found the back of a super-market. There were some wooden crates stacked up against the side of the building. I took a piss in the moonlight then walked over to the wooden crates. I began ripping boards off, slats. A curved nail came up and caught the inside of my wrist as I was ripping a board off. A little trickle of blood ran down my arm. I cursed. Shit, what a man wouldn't do for a whore.

I got back upstairs with my bundle of shit. First we had some Tokay and cigarettes. Then I got up and took off the top bedsheet and like some large lion of anger, cheap cigar rolling in the center of my mouth, I ripped that bedsheet up, and then cracking boards across my knee for correct size. I got that arm all wrapped up like Dr. Keene. Then I sat down and turned on the radio. Shostakovich's 5th. Great. I had always been a lover of the masses. I drank down one-third a bottle of Tokay and looked for the Goodyear blimp.

"O, my god," said Lucille.

"Shut up. I told you to shut up. I'm not going to tell you to shut up much longer."

I just don't know. She just kept yallering and yallering about her arm being broken. I finally said all right and I took her down to the elevator and we got in the car and the car started and I drove her toward the General Hospital . . . .

I drove the old hack right into *Emergency* instead of *Ad-missions*, knowing that the difference was at least 72 hours. We lucked it. Knowing that Lucille had a broken arm they rushed her into x-ray and had her chest x-rayed. Then they sat her on a little cart with a white sheet over it and there was a lineup; people from car crashes with blood running out of them like good Arabian oil and coming down the floorway where healthy young black interns skipped over it all, talking about their luck at the racetrack that day or how Lucille Ball ought to give it up before her fanny dropped below her kneecaps.

I got bored and started bumming cigarettes all over from blood death cases, bloodsuckers, and underwater octopi. Lucille was rolled in one door and walked out another. She was neatly bound. A broken arm bit. She looked cute. Like she'd been kissing the doctor.

I got her down to the car and we got in. We had time, just before closing, to get some port and muscatel from a store, four bottles in all. The moon was high that night and we drove on slowly, nipping . . .

It was in all the bars afterwards, hearing about it weeks afterward: "I'm the only woman in the world who has ever been folded into the wall on a folding bed and had her arm broken," she kept telling everybody. I guess it was unique. Of course, it was mathematically possible that the same thing had happened to another woman.

The strangest thing was that she loved me more after I broke her arm than before it was broken. Anyhow, we got thrown out of the place of the folding bed because of one reason or another, and we got a place right across the street, the rent was cheaper, they weren't as nosey or as sensitive to noise and unemployed people, and the bed was right down there on the floor, just no place else to go just like beds should be.

Harry called from his place three or four times after getting in from the track. Two hours went by, he had a New York steak at the *Sizzler*, then drove on over. Lilly was kneeling on the floor wrapping Christmas presents. Her children were over at her ex-husband's. "Well," she said, "how'd you do? You lost, didn't you?"

"No, I lucked it. I won $94. I've been phoning you. I told you I'd come over after the track."

"You said it'd take a long time."

"It does. But they don't run them in the dark. This was the shortest day of the year."

Lilly didn't answer.

"Look, I guess I'll get Nadia her present."

"Sure. And, O.K., get me some wrapping paper, gift-paper, and some cat food. And listen, you got a hammer in your car?"

"Yeah."

"Bring the hammer, too."

Harry walked out, got in his car and drove down to the store. A toy for a 6-year-old girl. He walked around the store. It was all cellophane and plastic and cheap paint and unfair. He gave up and got 6 or 8 small things: a compass, a toy wrist watch, a makeup set, a fingernail set, balloons, a puzzle, trick soap bubbles, a purse and a set of ornaments. Variety in shit was better than just solid shit. Harry got the other things, plus a 6-pack of Diet Rite and a large jar of mixed nuts. When he parked he lifted the hood of the Volks and got the hammer out. Then he found that the hood wouldn't shut again. He stood out there banging the hood trying to make it shut. He stood out there 10 minutes banging the hood.

Lilly stepped out on the porch. "What the hell's going on out there?"

"I took the hammer out of the hood and now it won't shut. It's the addition this guy put on the bumper. It gets in the way. I didn't notice it when I bought the car."

Lilly went back in without saying anything. Harry kept banging the hood. It was foggy and the steel was wet and his hands slipped and he ripped some skin off of one knuckle. Lilly came back out on the porch. "Did you get the hammer?"

"Yes. I took it out of the hood. That's how all this happened."

Lilly walked down the steps. "I need the hammer." She walked up to the car and lifted the hood.

"Look," said Harry, "I told you I took it *out* of the hood."

"Oh."

He took the hammer off the top of the car and handed it to her. She took it and walked up the steps and into the house. Harry slammed the hood a few more times, then quit. $1299 for a '67 Volks and the hood won't shut.

When he got in with the stuff she was watching *Geronimo* on TV, played by Chuck Connors. Chuck Connors was the worst actor in a Hollywood full of bad actors. He showed her the presents he had gotten Nadia. Lilly didn't comment.

"Want a Diet Rite?"

"No, I've got some tea on."

"How about some nuts? Good for the soul." He screwed the cap off the jar.

"No, I don't want any."

They sat and watched *Geronimo*. It was hard for Harry to believe that Indians never smiled. They had to, especially when things went bad.

Lilly reached over and got some nuts. They watched the TV together. Then the news came on. The fog had jammed up the airport and all the Christmas people wanting to fly out to meet relatives were going liquid-paper-silly.

"People overemphasize bloodlines. Just because you're related to somebody doesn't make them any more important than anybody else."

"Oh, yes it does."

"Why?"

Lilly didn't answer. Harry threw in a mouthful of nuts as President Ford's economic advisers walked up to the Capitol building with their briefcases.

The news ended and they walked into the bedroom. She went to the bathroom first and Harry climbed into bed and looked over the day's racing program. He'd really lucked it that day. Next trip they'd probably have him on the cross. If one could only find a pattern? But what happened was that everything kept alternating. They'd show you one kind of play in one race and then in the next you'd get the opposite. If a man were brilliant enough he could figure on the movement of the tides . . . Everybody needed some kind of poison to keep them clean. Horse-poison was his cleanser. Some had art or crossword puzzles or stealing ashtrays out of bars and cafés.

Lilly came in and climbed into bed, turned her back on him and began reading a book about a man who specialized on leaving his body and floating into space. Harry got up, went into the bathroom and brushed his teeth. Then he came back and climbed on in. He read *London Magazine* awhile, found his name and where a critic called him an "immensely successful writer." Ta, ta. He put the book back on the headboard, turned and closed his eyes.

"I went into this shop," he heard her voice, "and I met this girl who runs this shop and she said we might go into business together. She does these things with metal and I can do my heads."

"There's a depression," said Harry, "you've got to be careful. Do you think the stuff will sell?"

"I don't know. But you've got to try."

"I suppose so. But be careful; some of these places have leases. You've got to lease for 6 months or a year and if things don't move you're still stuck with the rent."

"She does some awfully good stuff. I like it."

"Good stuff and what people buy are often different things."

"I might try it, though. I'm sick of waiting on those drunks in the bar. They all want me to save them."

"That's just a line. They're already saved when they lift that drink."

"You ought to know."

"Well, if you open that shop you could give poetry readings."

"There you go! Every time I talk about opening a place you say I can give poetry readings! That's a putdown! You're relegating me to the status of a Vangelisti! Admit it's a putdown!"

Harry thought a while. "All right, maybe it is a putdown. But you ought to make your shop known. Put on a fucking puppet show, anything."

Lilly turned out the light. Then he heard her: "You know, I have a greater potential than you have. I really have. I tell it like it is. My sisters tell it like it is. We'll become known. You can't get away with your lies."

"Please be kind. Let's call it fiction."

"They're getting on to you."

"O.K., they're getting on to me."

"You always have this *superior* attitude!" Lilly sat straight up in bed and screamed: "Jesus Christ. We All Know You're Harry Dubinski The Great Writer!"

Then she fell back on the pillow. "My sister, Sarah, she hasn't been published yet but she has *drive*, she's 47 and when I go up there that typewriter is *going all the time*, she's got drive and spunk. Those novels keep coming back and yet she drives out another one. She's got it. I don't know when *you* write. You're either asleep or drunk or at the racetrack."

"Wallace Stevens had a saying: 'Success as a result of industry is a peasant's ideal.'"

"I can *talk* to my sister! We Get To The Source, We Get Down To Where Things Are Really Happening! We Discuss Things! We Get To The Root!"

"O.K., fine then. Tell me something that you've found out."

Lilly rolled in the bed. "Oh, shit, you disgust me! You just don't understand anything—love, feelings, any of it! My sisters have more life in their little fingers than you have in your fat whale body!"

"Some of the girls don't seem to mind my whale body."

"Your whores, the readers of your poems!"

"I play you fair when we're not split."

"But we manage to split, don't we?"

"Yes, keep it in the plural."

"My sisters have ambition, *real* ambition, you don't realize that, you just don't!"

"Ambition without talent is useless unless you have a damned good publicity agent."

"You keep mouthing these things, you won't *talk* to me. You just mouth off slogans like some damned John Thomas."

Harry moaned.

"Talk to me!" she said. "Talk to me!"

"A horse usually wins when he comes down from his last odds."

"I need to sculpture new heads, that's my problem. I need new heads to sculpture! I think I'm going to do naked men, eight feet tall! You wouldn't like it if I had naked men in here modeling for me, would you? You wouldn't like it, would you?"

"I don't know."

"I need rope, lots of rope!"

Harry didn't answer.

"I need a boot in the ass," she said, "I need people to *drive* me. I need new things, different things! All we do is sleep! Sleep! Sleep *depresses* me! I used to sleep for three weeks at a time when I was a little girl! I hate it! You just loll around! You're YEARS OLDER THAN I am! We need different things! We ought to try something different!"

"Look, Lilly, you just need a different type of guy . . . "

"Oh, you men *always* say that! You never ADJUST! You never sit down and say, well, look, maybe we ought to try this or try that or try *something!* You always just say, 'Well, if you don't like me the way I am I'll just LEAVE, I'll just LEAVE!' Every time we get into this you leave! And we've been together four years! We used to have these *violent* arguments when we first met and then we'd make up and have a marvelous reunion! Now you just come back. You used to accuse me of things, you used to protest! Now you just come back and take off your shoes and read a newspaper! You've got no bounce!"

"Things change. I used to think you were somebody

else but it was just the somebody else I had put up there in my mind. The error was mine. Now I don't expect what I expected. Hell, we're growing, don't you see? There's not all this constant need for a bunch of fucking fuss. The sights are on target, we can relax."

"You're not even jealous anymore of what I do with other men!"

"You told me that you hated my jealousy, that true love meant trusting another person."

"O.K., what *is* true love?"

"Two cats fucking in the courtyard at 2 a.m."

Lilly became silent for 3 or 4 minutes, then she spoke again: "I believe in that psychic I went to see. He told me that you would never become a truly great writer. And I believe him. You have all these large *dead* spots in all your stories, large large large *dead* spots! You'll never make it!"

"I'm not particularly interested in making it. Ambition makes me vomit."

Two or three minutes passed. Then Lilly leaped out of bed and raised both arms over her head and screamed: "I'm Going To Do Great Things! Nobody Can Realize How Great I'm Going To Be!"

"O.K.," said Harry, "you be great. I'm leaving."

"You're *leaving*! You're *leaving*! . . . You don't *realize* how much you've held me back! You've STOPPED MY SCULPTING, YOU'VE STOPPED EVERYTHING IN ME! LEAVE, LEAVE, LEAVE!"

Lilly began running through her house screaming. "LEAVE, LEAVE, LEAVE! That's all you *know*: LEAVE!"

She screamed a long scream, then pulled the Christmas tree down, smashing the ornaments and the lights. There were other sounds as she ran about the house. The earthquake of the Thirties lost by at least half a length. Harry had seen it before at his place, hers. Glass doors smashed, mirrors, everything.

She ran into the room charging him and he remembered the other times, all the other times. "Don't," he said, "or I'll really belt you. I *mean* it!"

Lilly backed off. Then she ran into the other room and

he heard the sounds and the screams: "Leaving. Always Leaving! Well, Leave Then; Leave, Leave Leave!"

Harry grabbed his glasses, the latest issue of *London Magazine*, the last two chapters of his novel-in-progress, and evacuated in coat and pants and shoes without shorts or shirt or stockings or the day's racing program. He got out the door and made it down to the car in the driveway while she screamed: "I Hate Christmas. I Hate This House. I Hate You . . . I . . . "

I hate Christmas, too, he thought, trying to work the key into the door and he had the wrong key but he found the right one and got the door open and got in and pressed down the button just as she got there as he was trying to start the car and tried to open the door.

"I'll kill this beautiful car, I'll murder this car, I'll kill *you!*" And she started beating against the front window.

He put it in reverse and got it on out as she ripped the mailbox from the front of her house, a huge iron contraption that almost did in the windshield glass, and then she found a rock, and it hit, too, but only against the useless hood, and then Harry was driving down the little neighborhood streets, and the fog was in, immensely, and he flipped the wipers of his newly bought '67 Volks and the wipers didn't work and he rolled down the left window and tried to see into the night.

It got worse until he got to the main boulevard and then he opened it up all the way to the liquor store on Western just above Hollywood Boulevard, and he parked it, Harry did, and walked in, and he had on the old coat and no shirt and he tried to button the coat across his chest and gut, but he'd gained weight, whale-boy Harry, and he gave it up, went to the rack and pulled out one six-pack of Heineken (light) and two of Michelob in the bottle and walked back to the counter.

The guy at the counter took his money and made change and while making change asked, "Smokes?"

"No smokes," said Harry.

Harry walked out and found his blue Volks, got his keys mixed up again, had to sit the beer on the roof while he found the door key and there were 3 girls sitting in a car across from him and the car had all the doors open, there weren't any men in it and they were just sitting there and one of the girls said, "Hey, hey, look at that!"

And they started laughing in this slow, subdued laughter, and Harry found the right key, got the door open, threw the beer from the roof into the far seat, right front, some of the bottles dropping out and onto the floorboard, and then he looked at the girls, gave a slow evil wink, bowed like a quiet and holy man, got in, started it, and drove off.

He drove over to Carlton Way, parked it, locked it, packed the sixes to the door, got the key on in, and then the phone rang.

I suppose one of the most amazing and startling acts in the sports world happened in the opening professional football game of the regular season between the New York Razors and the L.A. Wolfhounds in 1977. I was covering the game for one of the local papers, and as the Wolfhounds lined up to receive the kickoff the whole stadium became a babble of incoherent voices as the deep and only receiving back, unknown, became noticed. He appeared to be a good 8 feet tall and was close to 450 pounds. He was announced as Graham Winston. The kick floated down to him and Graham began to move. And he moved quickly and with grace and with that total size New York Razor tacklers hit against him and fell off as if he were a tank. Several actually shied away from contact and Graham Winston crossed over the goal line for a touchdown. The remainder of the game was similar. The Wolfhounds just handed the ball to Graham and he ran up and down the field. At times he was tackled but it usually took three or four men and they had to gang him at once. The final score was L.A. Wolfhounds 84, New York Razors 7.

The reporters had some questions after that one as Graham Winston sat on a rubbing table sucking at quart bottles of beer. Chubby Daniels, the coach, stood beside him rubbing his neck and smiling.

"Where'd you find this?" I asked the same question all the other reporters were wondering about.

"We found him working a rundown farm in the Midwest."

"Just like that?"

"Yes, one of our scouts happened to be passing through on his way to check out a prospect when he saw all this hunk of size behind a plow."

"Give me another fucking bottle of beer," said Graham.

"He's even pretty. The movies might get him."

"We got him signed, ironclad."

"As fast and big as he is he could probably whip the heavyweight champ."

LOSER EAT CANDY SHIT.

"We got him signed, ironclad."

"You like football?" one of the reporters asked Graham.

"Shit, yes. All those people screaming, it makes me feel good. Hey, this is Hollywood, isn't it?"

"Yes, I mean we're near it."

"Well, I wanna get fucked. I wanna fuck a starlet."

"Take it easy, Graham," said Chubby Daniels. "You've just been discovered today. You're invincible, it'll all come to you."

"I wanna get fucked tonight. And gimme another bottle of beer. This one's warm."

"How they gonna stop this guy, Chubby?"

"That's their problem."

"It might ruin their whole game."

"The game was ruined long ago," said Chubby. "Professional football is like society: win and win any way you can and as big as you can. And let the losers eat candy shit. Now I'm going to ask you boys to leave so my man here can catch a little rest. Also, I've got to make some phone calls."

It was said that that night with two of his bodyguards watching that Graham Winston mounted Mona St. Claire, the rising starlet in her very own apartment bedroom. That Graham did not slice her apart was the very wonder. Yet it was said that two days later she was up and walking around and eating yoghurt, sour cream, and Winchell's Donuts . . .

The Wolfhounds beat the Bluebirds 94 to 14 and the Mounties 112 to 21. Graham Winston's photo was on the cover of almost everything and there were stories about his life, his wants, his philosophy in scores of magazines. He was seen with Elizabeth Taylor, Liza Minnelli, and Henry Kissinger. He ran automobiles off of bridges and into rivers drowning his women. He was caught with dope, he was caught molesting a 7-year-old girl, but he remained free and he ran up and down the football fields, breaking tackles and tacklers . . .

Halfway through the season he announced that he was quitting football and going into "acting." The Wolfhounds began court action and the cameras rolled. They got him on a television series: *Big Cowboy Heart*. He was the good, good tough boy. He straightened out every mess in the prairie and a few in the cities too. Meanwhile professional football returned to normal, which meant that the murderous abilities of the teams were just about equal. Graham Winston was seen on all the commercials. The superman of every man's and woman's imagination had actually come down to earth and inherited it. It was the closest thing to the second coming of Christ imaginable, although nobody ever put it that way: he was less sacred and therefore more interesting, more apt to err, and he had the $6 Million Man beat by 46 million. In fact, that's what they began to call him: the $50 Million Man. They began calling him that with my help, that is. I lucked it and became his press agent. So it helps me tell this story . . .

I was sitting with him one night in his New York City penthouse. He was caught up, ahead on his series *Big Cowboy Heart* and was having a party. Graham loved parties. He loved to dance and sing and get drunk. So there we were sitting this particular night. Graham was at the piano, he had just beaten it bloody. He was drinking Scotch, vodka, beer and wine and smoking $5 cigars. He was a little bored.

"Oh, everbody's here, Graham. There's Truman Capote, John Wayne, Sammy Davis Jr., Cal Worthington, Billy Graham, Liz Taylor, Liza Minnelli, Henry Kissinger, Richard Burton, Cher, Charo, Earl Wilson, Nick the Greek, Linda Lovelace, Marlon Brando, and some Indians."

"No shit?"

"No shit."

"I'm bored with all this, Charlie."

"I've got a saying, Graham. 'Only boring people get bored.'"

"Shit, that don't help me none."

Graham got up from the piano. He walked over to this very lovely slim blonde dressed in this long glittering white dress. He took out his pecker and began pissing all over her dress. It put her in a state of shock and Graham just stood there spraying her, up and down and over. Finally the girl screamed and ran off. Graham put his pecker back in and zipped up. He walked to the bar and poured his own drink, Scotch mixed with port wine. Then he turned around and screamed at the crowd: "I HATE YOU ALL! YOU'RE AS PHONY AS I AM!"

All the talking stopped and people sat and stood grinning, sipping at their drinks. "Phoniness is the state of the universe," said Truman Capote. "We are just the more excellent of the phonies."

"Why don't you suck shit through a straw?" asked Graham.

He walked back to the bar and poured himself another special. Then he looked at his audience again: "I often wondered what the top of the world looked like. Now I'm here and I wish I were back behind a plow following a mule's bunghole."

"You can take a boy away from the bunghole but you can't take the bunghole away from the boy," said a young Jewish comedian who was working his way up in Vegas nightclubs.

Graham Winston downed his drink and walked over to Billy Graham. "Hey, hey, your first name is just like my last name!"

"God bless us," said Billy.

"Why should God bless us?"

"We do not demand his blessing we only ask them."

"It's all so drab. You're just saying words."

"God's words of love."

"How come you're not drinking?"

"I abstain."

"My friends drink with me. You're gonna drink with me, else you're my enemy."

"The only enemy is the devil and evil."

"You stand around here eating my olives and chickens legs and looking at all these women's asses and tits and legs and eyes and movements and you're not going to *drink* with me?"

"No, my son."

"Well, shit," said Graham Winston, "I guess that's the way it goes."

He picked up Billy Graham and holding him high above his head he walked between Joe Namath and Norman Mailer, and then he kept walking until he came up against this window overlooking the street. We were 40 floors up. He threw Billy Graham through the glass and Billy Graham dropped down. Graham Winston walked back to the piano, sat down, and tried to beat out a tune.

"I never could play the piano," he told me.

Graham Winston got life. And I was looking for another job. It was in the exercise yard one day. Graham wouldn't join the groups. Some didn't, most had to. But it was one day the White Supremacy and the Black Supremacy and the Brown and the Yellow Supremacy groups got in a fight in the exercise yard, and men in prison who can't get knives somehow find them or make them, and Graham Winston was big enough to get in the way. Nobody knew who got him, which group. But there he was in the sunlight, 8 feet tall and 452 pounds dying, the blood coming out of three holes in his belly. Then the $50 Million Man was dead. But I'll remember him best as taking that football down the field, especially after the kickoff, and seeing him go. It was wondrous beyond all wonder. It made me feel great inside as if there were really chances for miracles in a world over-extended and finally flat and tired. I should have known better. And like I said, now I'm looking for a job, but so are a lot of other people.

He came into town one night dressed all in black. His horse was black and the stars weren't even out. He wore a gun and a straggly beard. He walked into the bar and ordered a whiskey. He drank it down and ordered another. Everybody became very quiet. One of the girls walked by and he grabbed her by the wrist. "How much, honey? My horn's standing tall."

"You don't carry that much money," said Minnie.

"I got a dollar, baby."

She pulled away. "You probably got the clap anyhow," he said, finishing the second whiskey.

"Where's the head?" he asked the crowd. Nobody answered.

"So you won't tell me where the head is, huh?"

There was no answer. He took out his cock and pissed on the barroom floor.

"We don't rightly like that, stranger," said the bartender.

"Well, next time I ask, I expect an answer. I rightly feel a bowel movement coming on."

"What's your name, stranger?" asked the bartender.

"Put and Tame. Fuck the first Dame."

"You're looking for trouble?"

"Yeah, well, pussy's trouble. Any man knows that."

The stranger walked over to the poker game at the far table, drew up a chair, and sat down.

"Did we ask you to sit?" asked one of the boys.

"Piss on your dead mother's tits," said the stranger. "Deal me in."

"All right. Ante."

The cards went around. The stranger held three, asked for two. Billy Culp held four, asked for one. The others dropped out. Culp and the stranger kept raising. The pot got to 75 cents and Culp called. Then the cards were laid down. The stranger kicked the table over and knocked Billy Culp to the floor. "There's only one ace of hearts in a deck, son of a bitch!" The stranger had his gun out. "Son of a bitch,

207

I've a good mind to connect your bellybutton up to your asshole!"

"Listen, stranger, I swear I'll never cheat again! Take all my money but spare my life."

"O.K, shitass," said the stranger and he gathered up all the money and walked back to the bar.

"I'm buying a bottle," he told the bartender. The stranger stood there swigging from the bottle. He took a mouthful and spit it on the bartender's shirt. "This seems a goddamn dull town," the stranger said, "don't seem to be a man in the carload of you all. But," he winked, "lots of women." And as Stardust Lil walked by he reached out and ripped the top of her dress and her tits spilled out.

"Lovely," he said, "lovely."

A cowboy in a red shirt stood across the room. "That's my woman, stranger."

"Kid," said the stranger, "no man owns a woman. Some women own men, yet there are some men who can never be owned. Women have hearts like rattlesnakes. They'll tear your guts out and then squat over you and piss right into them."

"You're saying that men are better than women?"

"No different than."

"I don't appreciate your showing my woman's breasts to the whole bar."

"Christ, kid, learn the female. That bit made her happier than anything that's happened to her for years."

"I ought to blow your balls off!"

"O.K., fine. Wait until my dick gets hard."

The kid reached. The stranger reached. Then the kid had extra red in his red shirt and Stardust Lil had lost her 17th lover. She wept over him, then let out a little fart, and ran to the back room.

"Son of a bitchin' male chauv pig," breathed a tiny voice from somewhere in the room.

"By god," said the stranger, "by god, that gits it!" He picked up the whisky bottle and drained one quarter of it. "What the hell do you people do for entertainment, fall back into your dull limpness? If God created you, He was sure as hell in need of better instruction."

The doors swung open and there was the sheriff. "My name's Billy Budd and I'm the sheriff of this here god-damned town and I draw me a salary to maintain law and order. My father ran away when I was 6 and my mother became the town whore but I grew up righteous and I believe in right and I hear what you been doing ain't exactly right, so one of us is going to have to leave town. I'm calling your card, stranger, I'm calling your whole god-damned hand!"

"You got any next of kin?" asked the stranger.

"None."

"That's good. I ain't a man who likes to spread extra heartbreak. The world's so cold now. If people would only leave me alone I wouldn't have to do what I have to keep doing."

The stranger took another good hit from his bottle, put it down and walked over to the sheriff. He reached for the badge and unhooked it from the sheriff's shirt.

"Open your mouth."

"What?"

"Do you need a motherfuckin' hearing aid? I said, 'Open your mouth!'"

"What for?"

"Because you're going to chew on this badge until your teeth ache. And if you don't hurry up and git to it I might make you swallow it."

The sheriff opened up his mouth and the stranger dropped the badge in. "Now come on, bite it! I said, BITE IT!"

The stranger stepped back and pulled out his gun. He fired some shots at the sheriff's feet. "BITE IT!"

The sheriff began to bite the badge. The blood started coming out of his mouth. "BITE IT!" screamed the stranger. "BITE IT HARDER!" He fired some more shots at the lawman's feet.

"O.K.," said the stranger, "now take that badge out of

your mouth, pin it on your shirt and walk the hell out of here!"

The sheriff did just that and was gone just as Stardust Lil walked down the stairway in a new dress, a sexier and prettier dress than the one before.

"Baby," said the stranger looking up from the bar, "you finally met yourself a man."

Stardust Lil just kept walking down the stairway, smiling.

"Goddamn, baby, that dress really fits you, it's like you were born into it, shimmering and sliding and slithering. I think I'm going to take you with that dress on. I don't want you to take it off. Of course, we may have to lift the hem a bit."

god, a woman could get bored

Stardust Lil walked up to the stranger and put one hip up against him. "Pour me a drink, killer."

"You like me, don't you?"

"Sure."

"Women like winners, I'm a winner, I know how."

"Sure, stranger, I like winners."

"I suck too. Titties and pussy. I give the long ride."

"All the guys say that."

"How many do it?"

"About one man out of 30 really knows how to make love."

"That's rough."

"It's disgusting. I've been finger-fucking myself for the last three years. I'd rather go to bed with a woman because a woman knows what a woman wants."

"You a lez?"

"No, but what's a woman supposed to do when most men are just apes with stinky crotches and no imagination."

"Have another drink, baby."

"Yeah."

"I can send you way beyond the heavens, baby."

"What happened to your other women?"

"I've left 50 broken hearts behind me."

"Why?"

"Oh, they just into such dumb things, like trying to correct your spelling and how you hold your shoulders."

"Let's go upstairs to my place, stranger, if you're man enough."

"Man enough I am," he said.

They mounted the long stairway together with every eye in the bar on them. Lil sparkled in her dress and her movements. There wasn't a man in the bar who wouldn't give up five years of his life to be with her up there.

They waited. Five minutes went by, then 15, then 20. Then the door opened and Stardust Lil walked out. She looked about the same, only her hair was a bit awry and tossed. She walked slowly down the long stairway. Halfway down she gave a little laugh and said, "All right, boys, go on up there and get him, boys."

Nobody moved and Lil kept walking down the stairway.

"Nobody can make our sheriff bite his badge," she said. She really looked lovely and redeeming coming down toward the light of the bar. "Go get him, boys," she repeated.

Nobody moved. Lil reached the bottom of the stairway. "Oh hell, you dogs, I already got him!" She had a brown paper bag in her hand. She threw it. It whisked across the floor. Then the contents rolled out. It was white and weenieshaped and one end was gnashed raw. The blood began to milk out across the floor. And just as it did some drunk in the church tower began to ring the bell. And Mrs. McConnell's bitch dog whelped a litter of 7.5 female, 2 male. And Stardust Lil walked back to the bar and finished the last of the stranger's bottle, sticking it into her lips and draining it. It had been a better night than most, she thought. Really better than most. God, a woman could really get bored.

I awakened at 8:30 a.m. Meg had the radio on to Brahms. She had the radio on very loud. Meg not only had false teeth but she was a dry fuck. There was no way to get her to lubricating. It was like sticking your cock into a roll of sandpaper: it ground and scraped and burned tire skin.

"Turn that radio down! I'm trying to sleep!"

"This is the only way to listen to symphony music."

I got out of bed and walked into the kitchen and turned the radio down. "I live here, after all," I told her. Meg was sitting on the couch having her second glass of Scotch and her fourth cigarette. She had the morning paper. "I want to read you Jack Smith."

"I don't like Jack Smith."

Meg proceeded to read me the Jack Smith column. It was very clever and journalistic and comfortable. I listened until she finished. "Jack Smith is a fine writer," she said. "I like Jack Smith."

"All right, like him."

"I like the *New Yorker* too. I've got a right to like the *New Yorker*. In the old days Thurber and the editor used to have long arguments about the use of the comma. They used to live on ham sandwiches and coffee getting that thing out."

"Yes, poor fellows, while the rest of the country stood in soup lines."

"I still like the *New Yorker*."

"Listen, I'm going to take a shit."

When I came back out she had the radio on loud again and was on her third Scotch. "Have you ever heard a live concert?"

"Yes."

"How'd you like it?"

"It was very stiff and they sat me behind a pillar."

"You don't like very many things, do you?"

"Hardly."

"Well, there's some of your writing I don't like."

"There's some of my writing I don't like either."

"Have you done it yet?"

"Done what?"

"Fucked my sisters."

"No."

"You will."

I walked into the kitchen and got a beer. When I came back out she was on her fourth Scotch. "Listen, I was going to go home today but I'm too drunk to drive now. I'll go tomorrow."

"Listen, you've been here a week."

"I promise I'll go tomorrow."

"You said that yesterday. I can't get my goddamned writing done."

"You can write while I'm here. I won't mind."

"Thanks."

"We *do* have things in common."

"Like?"

"Like we both like Knut Hamsun and Celine."

"I'm going to the fucking racetrack."

"This early?"

"This early."

When I got back at 7 p.m. she was still sitting on the same spot on the couch, still smoking and drinking and the radio was still on to the classical music station. Mozart was on. "How'd you do?"

"I lost."

"Some woman phoned while you were out."

"What was her name?"

"She didn't leave a name."

"What'd she want?"

"She didn't say."

I walked into the bathroom and let the bathtub water run. I came out and got a beer.

"Listen. I want to know something," she said.

"What?"

"Have you fucked my sisters yet?"

"No."

"You will."

Meg got up and turned out all the lights. Then she lit

the four big candles she had purchased. She had brought along the holders in a large paper bag along with a copy of *The Heart is a Lonely Hunter*. I walked into the other room, undressed and got into the tub. She walked in holding a candle. "You've got the body of a young boy. You're an amazing man."

"Don't forget, Meg, you promised to leave tomorrow."

"Oh, I will. There are *other* men."

She walked out holding the candle high.

When I came out again she was sitting in the same area of the couch. Suddenly a large flame arose beside her. It must have been two feet tall. She didn't see it.

"Meg, for Christ's sake, get up!"

"What is it?"

"The fucking apartment's on fire!"

She stood up and I ran into the kitchen and came out with a pot of water. I pulled the cushion aside and poured the water into the hole. Meg had dropped a lit cigarette into the couch. I came out and poured more water into the hole.

"We're going to have to babysit this thing all night. They can flare up in a moment."

So we sat there for two hours drinking and pouring water into the couch and listening to classical music on the radio. Meg talked throughout the two hours about her ex-husband, about her trip to Greece, she talked about D.H. Lawrence and A. Huxley, she talked about her sisters. Then she blew out all the candles but one and we went to bed. She brought her bottle and her glass with her and her cigarettes and she sat them on the nightstand beside her. She poured a drink, lit a cigarette, and sat up in bed. I stretched out and closed my eyes.

"Let me suck you," she said.

"What?"

"I want to suck you."

"No."

"Why not?"

"I'm tired from the horses and I'm about to puke."

I turned on my stomach and tried to sleep. She sat there

drinking and smoking her cigarettes. "I'll make you eggs Benedict for breakfast," she said.

In the morning she was back on the couch, the radio was on, and she was smoking. I got dressed and walked out there.

"O.K. Meg, this is the morning and you're leaving."

"When will we get together again?"

"I don't know. We'll figure something out."

Meg had this gigantic purse and she started stuffing everything into it.

"There's this cowboy. I met him in a bar. I went home with him. He's got this big house. His children have left. He has this big house and he wants me to stay with him."

"Why don't you give it a try?"

"Why don't you bite your own dick off?"

"That's pretty hard to do."

"I'm leaving."

And she was gone like that, door closed, and off down the walk. I walked into the bedroom and noticed that she had burned a hole in the bed lampshade with her candle. I turned the hole in the shade toward the wall. There was a knock on the door. I walked over and opened it. It was Meg.

"My car isn't running right." She had a Mercedes.

"Oh shit, now wait."

"It's true, it hardly runs. I can't drive it that way. It'll never make Claremont. It won't make the freeway."

I walked out and checked the motor, the wiring, and so forth. Then I drove it around the block. It stalled and wouldn't go over 10 miles an hour.

"There's a Mercedes place right around the corner," said Meg. "I've seen it. Drive it on in."

The mechanics were sitting around drinking beer. A girl came out with her breasts hanging out and had Meg sign a worksheet. "We'll check it out and give you a ring," said one of the mechanics waving his beercan at us.

We went back to my place and turned on the radio. I poured myself a Scotch out of Meg's bottle.

"Go ahead and write," she said, "it won't bother me."

I sat there and drank Scotch with beer chasers and we waited for the phone to ring. It did.

When Meg finished talking she came out. "It's going to cost me $400," she said, "good thing I brought my checkbook."

"When will it be ready?

"Maybe Thursday, Friday for sure."

That meant Saturday.

"What day's this?" I asked.

"Wednesday."

Meg sat down at her favorite place on the couch. "There's nothing I can do," she said. "They're crooks but I need my car."

"Sure."

"My oldest sister owns her own horse and has nice legs. You like nice legs, don't you?"

"Yes."

"I want you to promise never to fuck either of my sisters."

"I promise."

Meg stood up, walked into the kitchen with her drink, and said, "I'll make us some eggs Benedict."

Then she turned up the radio louder. It was Brahms again.

Gary picked up the phone. It was Joan.

"Listen, I'm worried," she said, "she won't be back, will she?"

"Who?"

"Diane."

"I told you, Diane went to Nevada. She was going to get herself a 'Summer Man.' I'm supposed to be her 'Winter Man.' This is July 7. You are my 'Summer Woman'."

"I've heard about Diane."

"All nice things, I suppose?"

"No."

"Listen, she lives in her place, and I live in mine. She's in Nevada with her Summer Man or her Summer Men."

"I don't want to be attacked by any roller derby queen."

"She's in Nevada."

"I heard about the time she . . . "

"Don't believe it. You know how people talk. Make us some fried shrimp and coleslaw."

"All right."

Gary hung up.

The intercom buzzed, he hit the button, and Marie came through:

"A Mr. Charles K. Strunk to see you."

"And he's from where?"

"He won't say."

"All right, let him in."

The door opened. The man had on a skintight purple outfit with a crude circle on front: Mars behind a flash of lightning. He had on a thick wide belt with spikes sticking out of it. His face was very red. He looked like a wino.

"Strunk," he said, "Charles K. Strunk."

"Gary Matton," Gary said.

They shook hands and Gary told him to sit down.

"We need to," said Strunk, "build these runways so the flying saucers can land. That is their problem. They are unable to land because they need special runways. They have been attempting to land since 1923."

"Do you think the function of a modern art museum is to build runways for flying saucers?"

"I can't find sympathy for my plan anywhere else."

"We all have problems. I once had a lady friend who hated food and only weighed 80 pounds who wanted to climb this 8,000-foot mountain in high heels."

The phone rang. It was Joan again: "Do you want french fries?"

"I love french fries. Yes, make plenty of them. Are you all right?"

"I'm all right," she said and hung up.

"Did your lady friend climb the 8,000-foot mountain?" asked Strunk.

"I don't know. She ran off one night in the rain and never returned after we drank three or four bottles of cold duck."

"This runway must be made entirely of zinc."

"Where can I reach you if we get something going?"

"Don't be funny."

"You mean you . . . "

"Yes."

"But if you landed, why can't they?"

"The strip must be made entirely of zinc."

"And you look like us."

"No, you look like us."

"What's the difference?"

"Us."

"Like what?"

"Well, for one: sexual powers."

"Such as?"

"We can copulate for 12 hours."

"And?"

"We have no need for food, water, sleep, or war."

"Then what do you want down here?"

"We want to try some of your women."

"You mean, you've been trying to land since 1923, flying around since 1923 in those saucers just because you want to try some of our women?"

"Yes."

"You realize that we have mostly pathogenic orgasms?"

"Yep. And we've got to have zinc runways."

Charles Strunk stood up. They shook hands again. "You'll hear from me."

Then he was gone.

When Gary got home—which was a middle court in a courtyard just off the edge of the massage parlors—Joan had the shit ready and was in her miniskirt, and Gary boiled himself in hot bathwater, drinking vodka 7s with beer chasers, lighting an occasional Salem or Mary Jane, and when he got out he put on some fresh shorts for decency and told Joan he wasn't hungry, and she sat on the couch and he could just see her white legs tickling out, and she was unhappy but durable and Gary kept drinking in bed, and then the phone rang and it was Diane back from Nevada and she said, "I know you're with another woman but that doesn't matter to me. I want you to come get your stuff."

"What stuff?"

"I mean your bathrobe, your photo albums, and that $2 cane you purchased at K-Mart when you twisted your ankle trying to dance to that Greek music."

"I mean," Gary said, "why don't you burn all that stuff or trash it? It doesn't interest me."

"I INSIST," she said. "I INSIST you come get that stuff out of here! That's all I ask. I don't ask any more."

"Look, didn't you hear me, just burn it or trash it. It really doesn't matter."

"No, I INSIST, I INSIST, I INSIST."

"All right."

Gary began to get dressed Joan noticed.

"Where you going?"

"I'm going over there."

"Where?"

"Diane's."

"You're going to fuck her."

"Hell, no."

"Yes, you are."

"Wait. You don't understand women."

"Only women understand women," she said.

"That could be the problem," Gary said.

When he got there Diane didn't give him the bathrobe, the photo album or the $2 K-Mart cane. She simply began to beat upon him. Gary pushed her to the floor and began to walk away. She reached up and grabbed the arm of his coat, ripping it completely off. A ring of spittle was about her mouth.

"We can copulate for 12 hours."

"You can't get away with this!" she screamed. "You'll never get away with this! Never, never, NEVER!"

"All I want to do is to get away from you." Gary walked toward the door. Diane was up and upon him, fists beating upon his ears, his neck, his eyes, his mouth . . . "

"Goddamn you," he said, "just keep it up and I'll give you a goddamned good one, I'll show you up FAST!"

"I DON'T CARE! I DON'T CARE! HIT ME, HIT ME! KILL ME, I DON'T CARE!"

Then there was this long insane wail. The neighbors would think he was murdering her. Gary opened the door and walked out. She was upon him, upon his back, upon his sides, beating and wailing. In one sense he was frightened, in another sense he was immune to all of it because he felt it was unfair: a cheap-shot action. The world was not always a propitious place.

"RUN FROM MY HOUSE!," she screamed. "RUN FROM MY HOUSE! I DEMAND THAT YOU RUN FROM MY HOUSE!"

Gary opened the door and began walking down the long steep cement stairway to the street. Diane kept beating upon him, balance was almost impossible. He struck back. He landed a good right hook to the rib cage. She stood stunned for a moment in a corner of the stairway under a dripping ivy plant. Before she recovered and got herself down in the street, Gary had the car door unlocked and he was inside driving away with her fists beating against the glass.

Gary was back in his shorts, they'd be drinking a couple of hours and he was coming out of the bathroom toward the bedroom when Joan asked, "Shall I get it?"

"Get what?"

"Somebody's at the door."

"O.K."

He sat on the edge of the bed and worked at his drink. Then he heard Diane's voice: "Hello, I just came to check on my rival. I want to see what you look like."

There was no answer.

Oh, thought Gary, this is O.K. This is real humane and reasonable. I'll pour them both a drink. Then they can both agree that I'm a fine sort. Gary stood up. Then Diane said, "You're a pretty little thing, aren't you?"

There was a screaming. And a whirling of bodies. Gary got up to separate them, fell across the end of a barbell he never used, and wrenched his knee. When he got up hobbling in his shorts he heard the screams from central hell. The women ran out the door and down the courtyard. He rushed forward, fell again, then got up. He looked down at his belly. It was very white. Then the screams stopped. Diane walked in and sat in a chair near the door. Gary closed the door and got a beer and sat down and waited. The police arrived.

"Open up. Open the door."

"No," said Gary, "you've got no rights to enter."

"Ask them if they've got a search warrant," said Diane.

"You got a search warrant?"

"We don't need one. We have to know if there's somebody being murdered in there."

"There isn't. It's just a family argument."

"Is that woman your wife?"

"Only under the law of the jungle."

A period passed. Then the police got a key from the landlady and opened the door. "I refuse to allow you the right to enter," said Gary.

"Shut up, buddy," said the cop with the short blonde eyebrows. But both of the cops just put the edges of their shoes into the room. Then the cop with the short blonde eyebrows looked at Diane.

"Did you attack that other woman?"

"Attack?" she asked. "Who attacked who? Look at my blouse!"

Diane's blouse was torn, one arm of it almost ripped off.

"What's your relationship to the man?" the cop asked.

"Look, Diane," Gary said, "you don't have to answer that question."

The cop moved one foot further in and bent his body forward.

"All right, sir, if you interrupt me one more time I'm going to have to arrest you under code #82a-9b17 which means direct and malicious interference against the stability of mathematical fact-finding . . . "

"All right," said Gary, "I'll keep quiet."

The cop with the short blonde eyebrows and Diane kept interchanging questions and answers.

"All right, sir," said the cop, finally turning toward Gary, "which of these women do you want?"

"I'll take that one," said Gary, pointing to the woman in the chair near the door.

"All right, sir," said the cop and he closed the door. Gary heard them both walking down the center of the courtyard. "That fellow," he heard one of them say to the other, "seems to know what he is doing."

That made Gary feel better and he stood up and walked

to the kitchen and poured himself another drink from the rum and pear juice. When he came out he looked at Diane and said "Why don't you take a bath? Somehow you've managed to piss all over yourself."

And it was true her clothing was darkened with urine. Maybe, he thought, that's where the expression "pissed-off" came from. Diane walked into the bathroom. He heard the water running, pulled back the covers of bed, and crawled in there. He stayed in there listening to the water run. Then the phone rang. Gary picked it up.

"It's Strunk, Charles K. Strunk. Are you going to give us that zinc runway?"

"Yes, I've decided to. I do believe that there is a way to manipulate the Modern Museum of the Arts funds."

"May I suggest areas of landing and completion?"

"All right. Keep in touch. We'll work it out."

"O.K," said Strunk and hung up.

A few moments later, Diane walked out of the bathroom toweling her beautiful body.

"I heard you on the phone. It was that bitch again, wasn't it?"

"No."

"Who was it?"

"I'm going to build a zinc landing strip for the men from outer space."

"Really?"

"I don't know. Maybe."

Diane got under the sheets and blankets and they were back together again, once more.

Outside of La Paz, about an hour and a half, there is this jungle and it's a strange jungle; there are no reptiles or animals, just birds, very odd birds, all beaks or all tail, and they lived off the fruits of the trees and shit all the time—as did the natives. The natives lived almost forever, especially the men, they'd walk by brown and bent and thin and with these rags around their waists but the rags did very little good (I thought) because their balls and cocks flopped out and hung down, and the men looked at you and knew that they would still be there—in that jungle—long after you were gone. The women seemed to sit more, doing things with their hands—masturbating—but for it all, they looked sadder and died earlier, which is a complete reversal, say, of a city like Santa Monica, Calif. Anyhow, I was with the Peace Corps teaching rehabilitated alcoholic paraplegic once-thieves the rudiments of geometry and algebra. The Peace Corps people kept coming back from that place with gooney-bird eyes and so they finally sent me to try to bring it together, me and my wife, Angela.

Angela and I were rifting, it was definitely winding down, but like many other people we wanted to make sure we knew it was finally finished because it's quite an over-load on the wires to go out and search a replacement that might end up in the same fix. So we were in a state of slowly falling away from each other. There was an inflexible grim-ness to it all, and yet we had to pass through the grimness, we needed it, somehow, like we had once needed the love.

So there we were in the jungle—falling apart—among a people who seemed able to endure without either grim-ness or love, and the birds wandered and half-flew about and shit and shit. Help was needed. There was an old white guy called Jamproof Albert. I don't know what he was do-ing there, but he ran errands between the jungle and the city, and so I told him, "Jam, here's some scratch. I need relief. The numbers here don't balance and the silence . . . well, bring me something, let's see, yes, bring me back a monkey."

Jamproof was gone two or three days and when he came back he had this monkey and he handed it to me and said, "Here, take this fucking thing!" And then he was gone. I looked at the monkey and he looked just like a guy who had once wanted to run for president and had gotten lucky and died, so I called him "Dewey." Or maybe he had run for president and died.

I tried to pet Dewey and he bit my finger. Then he leaped off my lap and while looking at me he took his hose and pissed all over himself and then he took his hands and rubbed the piss into his fur. The problem with pets in that country was that people didn't look at them as possessions, but as forms of direct competition for food and lodging. So most of the people beat their pets instead of petting them. Also, Dewey was a full-grown monkey and his habits were ingrown. Dewey also had a lot of penis for his size and it always seemed to be in some state of turmoil, a very red part poking out, it looked like a bright red pencil, only it was wet and it seemed to drip. I was sitting noticing this when Angela walked up. She looked at Dewey and smiled for the first time in weeks.

"Glad to see you're feeling better," I told her.

"Fuck off," she said and walked into the hut. Dewey followed her in. When I walked in he was sitting in her lap.

"That's my monkey," I said.

"You don't understand animals or women," she said, "fuck off."

"I'm going to give that bastard a bath," I said, "he's pissed himself."

"What his name?"

"Dewey."

Angela looked down at the monkey: "Oh, Dewey, Blu-ey, Youee, Youee . . . "

The monkey looked up at her and ran his tongue rapidly in and out of his mouth.

"Give me that bastard," I said. I reached for him and grabbed him. As I did he got one of my fingers in his teeth and wouldn't let go. The pain was incisive. He hung from my finger in midair and with my free hand I got him about the throat and began to strangle him.

"You fiend," screamed Angela, "you're hurting little Dewey!"

"I sure as shit hope so!"

I kept the pressure on. Suddenly the teeth on my finger loosened. Blood spurted. Dewey fell to the floor and was motionless.

"You *killed* him! You KILLED him, just as surely as you killed everything that was ever decent within me!" screamed Angela.

I bent over him, felt his pulse. There was none. I listened for a heartbeat. There was none. I walked over and poured a drink. "Sorry, Angela, we'll have to give him a decent funeral. Catholic priest, sticks of incense, all . . . "

"You've always been so full of this HATE," said Angela. "Of all the men on earth I had to come across a shit like you . . . "

Dewey leaped up and ran toward the door. "Hey, fucker!" I screamed and ran after him. I never expected to catch him. Old Dewey, for a monkey, just wasn't very fast. Maybe it was all that hose he carried. Anyway, it delighted me that I could outrun him. I caught him after a 25-yard run. I took him to the tin washtub we all bathed in. I pumped the water in and dropped in the soap chips. Then I dropped Dewey in. It was probably his first meeting with water—outside—and his first introduction to soap. It was better than any fight since Dempsey-Firpo. I got him good, though. I even cleaned out his bunghole. Then as I began to wash him behind the ears he became very quiet. It worried me. I pulled him out and took himself and placed him on the floor. He had kept his mouth open during the washing and had swallowed mouthfuls of soapwater. His belly was immensely bloated. Angela just looked at me.

"I can't even hate you anymore. You're just something like a centipede, like a roach . . . like a tick . . . like a snail . . . like bugshit . . . You're a disgusting imbecilic slug . . . "

"I'm sorry, Angela . . . I think he's dying . . . poor little cocksucker . . . he swallowed all that soapwater . . . I repent . . . fuck . . . I'm shit . . . "

Then Dewey moaned. He turned his head and puked up two coffeepots worth of soapwater. Then he got to his feet and held himself upright against a bedpost. Then he turned and slowly walked toward the doorway. I let him go.

"He's free," I said.

"He's more a man than you'll ever be," said Angela.

"It was my parental upbringing," I said, "it's insurmountable . . . "

He was not to be seen for days. I feared him dead. But we had this compound, shaped somewhat like the observatory in the hills behind Los Angeles and in it the natives had stored supplies of grains and foodstuffs that the U.S. government had sent down there for them to eat but the natives after a bite or two had gone back to the more natural things that grew up in the air and out of the ground, but they had stored these packs of foodstuffs into the compound and Dewey had gone into there and holed-up and found a sustaining rebound within the darkness and the U.S. dollar war against the Red Menace. Meanwhile, I had broken my leg . . .

The first day I saw Dewey out of the compound he noticed the cast on my leg but he didn't quite know what it meant. I had always been able to catch him and he knew it. As I moved toward him he made his usual futile effort to run, looking back. Then he noticed that I wasn't gaining. He stopped and let me get near him and then ran off. Somehow it came to him that I could no longer catch him. He ran up close, screamed something at me, then ran off. He did it again. "You bastard," I said, "I'll get you, I'll out-think you!"

Dewey stood there and looked at me. Then he pissed all over himself and rubbed it into the fur. Then he ran off bogging his bunghole up and down at me . . .

I knew he slept in the compound and I got up that night to get him. The moon was full and even the shit-birds slept. I crept into the compound. Dewey was asleep on a shelf near a small window at the back of the compound. He was bloated with U.S. foodstuffs. I moved toward him. He snored a most nasty snore. I stood two feet from him and moved out one hand. He did a double movement: one bound to his feet and the next bound out the window . . .

That noon while Dewey was in the house with my wife I went in and boarded up the little window in the compound. That night I again crept into the compound. Dewey was asleep on the shelf, the snore nastier than ever. I got nearer. I was right over him. "The white American male," I whispered to him, "rules the universe." He made the first bound to his feet, then noticed the boarded window for the first time. His little hands beat upon it and I had him. I carried him back into the house and sat on a chair and pulled his ears and blew cigarette smoke into his eyes. He didn't resist. He just looked at me like a monkey looking at a man. Then Angela awakened. "You just let Dewey go! He's mine!" When he heard her voice his red pencil came out.

"The *hell* he's yours. I paid 40 American dollars for him."

"I tell you, he's mine! There are things money can't buy!"

"Like what?"

"Just let him go or I'll kill you."

"Ta, ta. Now I mean, baby, just what's been going on between you two?"

"You're so suspicious, you're so jealous . . . even of a *monkey!*" You're the most jealous man I ever met. You know what that means?"

"Uh-huh."

"It means a basic insecurity, a lack of faith in yourself, a lack of faith in the one you love."

"Yeah, I worry."

"You overreact."

"Yeah." I took Dewey's head and twisted it toward me. I blew a mouthful of cigarette smoke into both of his eyes. Angela leaped up. She screamed. Then she rushed at me with a Coleman lantern in one hand and a candlestick in the other. I let go of Dewey and I caught Angela coming in and got her with a left to the solar plexus. She dropped and Dewey ran out the door.

"Yes," said Angela laying on the floor, "you'd hit a *woman* but you wouldn't hit a *man*, would you?"

"Hell, no, I wouldn't hit a man, you think I'm crazy? What the hell's that got to do with anything?"

"You're so disgusting," she said, "you are so *utterly* disgusting!"

"That I know," I told her. "Now how about a weather report?" . . .

Dewey stayed away from both of us after that. He knew that Angela and I were rifting but he didn't care to hang around for the broken coffee cups, the accusations and counter-accusations. He didn't report back to the compound and, of course, I still had the cast on my leg . . .

It was a week and a half later when I saw him for any length of time. I was sitting under a tree with a hangover while Angela was in the house ripping pictures and paintings from frames, tearing up photo albums, my shirts and underwear, my books, my love letters . . . Dewey was standing on the roof of the compound, the sun a little bit behind him, lighting him up like a miniature god. He caught my eye, screamed something at me, then pissed all over himself and rubbed it into his fur. A group of children passed. Children always passed in groups of 12, 14, 17, so forth, going somewhere . . . without adult guidance. Most of them had never seen a monkey except perhaps via photo or word. When they saw Dewey they began to scream, "MONO! MONO! MONO!" Dewey heard them and reacted. He was a show-off. He leaped from the compound and passed blithely through the air and caught his hands on a clothesline and swung back and forth. "MONO! MONO! MONO!" They stopped and watched him. Dewey dropped from the clothesline and ran along the ground. He made for one of the makeshift combos of boards and tree limbs nailed together that held up the wiring, the electric wiring, that came all the way from La Paz . . . in its fashion . . . we never got our electricity when it rained or in a windstorm, and sometimes it just stopped, seemingly, out of whim, but it always started up again when one had completely given up. Dewey made for our jungle phonepole. "MONO! MONO! MONO!"

The difference, though, between Los Angeles and where we were was that the wiring had no insulation—it was simply bare wiring. Dewey climbed up our phonepole toward the top. I couldn't speak. He neared the top. Then he hung there at the top and looked over at the wire. I knew what he was going to do. It was just another clothesline to him.

"DEWEY, DON'T DO IT!" I screamed.

"MONO! MONO! MONO!" screamed the children.

Dewey leaped out and grabbed the wire with both hands. He hung there and you could see the jolts bouncing his body. He couldn't let go. Sparks shot off of his fur. I could smell burnt hair and flesh. Then he was still and he hung in the air like a design. The children stood for two or three minutes ingesting and digesting the sight. Then, wise in the ways of the world, they marched off together.

The pole was too weak to climb, it wouldn't bear my weight. I went into the storage shed behind the house, unlocked the green tin container and got out the ax. I always kept those accessories a secret from Angela. I got out the ax. I came back and cracked down our jungle phonepole. It came down like a giraffe's neck shot in the belly. The problem was that the other poles only allowed the wire—where Dewey hung—to fall within five feet of the ground. Dewey hung there in front of me at about my chest. I walked back and sat down under the tree again and looked at him. He was only an ornament. And I knew nothing about women—or electricity. I got up from under the tree and walked up to Dewey. I took the fingers of one of his hands and one by one uncurled them from the wire. The hand let go. Then I did the same with the other hand and Dewey dropped to the ground.

Of course, then—running out of things to break and tear—Angela came out of the house.

"Oh, what have you done to him? WHAT HAVE YOU DONE TO HIM?" She crouched over Dewey and I didn't answer. A thin rain began to fall. Angela looked quite lovely. I almost forgave her for being a woman. She looked at me: "You beast, you stink, you stink-rot deadwood of soul! The devil could shit in hell and the stink of that would seem like five-dollar-an-ounce perfume compared to you!"

Then she picked up Dewey, she lifted him up off the ground and as she did one of his eyes opened—the left eye. Angela began to laugh.

Then the right eye opened. Angela began to laugh and to cry. She carried him slowly to the house. She opened the door, closed it, and they were inside. I walked back and sat under the tree.

An Affair of Very Little Importance

I met her like this, something like this: I was giving a poetry reading down in Venice, some flea-dive on the shore, but I packed them in and I read it out; and I was drunk during the reading and much drunker afterward, I got my money and then got in my car, and drove all through Venice at a high rate of speed with 3 or 4 carloads of people chasing me. There was to be a party, but I told them, "First I need a little fresh-air drive." And off I went with them after me.

On the last roll-around I took my car and drove it onto a residential sidewalk and pushed the gas pedal down. They followed in the street, honking and hollering. Where the police were, I don't know. Then I backed up into the street and followed the other cars to the party. She was driving one of the cars and her name was Mercedes, but she wasn't driving one.

The party wasn't exceptional; even meeting Mercedes wasn't exceptional. There were more interesting women there. She was about 28, dressed in a green miniskirt, fair body, fair legs, a blond about 5'5", a blue-eyed blond; her hair was long, though, slightly wavy, and she smoked continuously. At the party she seemed almost always at my side, but she spoke very little, and when she did speak, it seemed bland, even dull, and her laugh was too loud and too false.

I didn't particularly like Mercedes, but I liked the party less. She was able to guess about the party.

"Let's get out of here and go to my place," she said to me.

"I'll follow your car."

I told the people I was going. We walked out the door.

"Fuck her good, Chinaski!"

"Eat her cunt!"

It wasn't too long a drive. Mercedes lived in an apartment off the Venice boardwalk. I followed her up. As she unlocked the door, I said, "Hey, what about drinks? We need something to drink."

"I have something."

I followed her in. It was a large apartment. There was a piano and some bongo drums. Mercedes had a jug of Red Mountain wine. I followed her into the kitchen as she got ready to pour the drinks.

I grabbed her from behind, turned her around and kissed her—a long, slow kiss. I pulled her head back by the hair and held one hand there and put the other on her ass. I moved my mouth slowly around hers, tasting her, dominating. She gave me the slightest tongue flick. I hardened and pushed against her, then broke off.

We took our drinks into the other room. I sat down at the piano and began pounding the keys. I don't know how to play the piano. I played it then like a percussion instrument, searching for the beat. I stayed way up on the right-hand side, getting the icy, high sounds. Mercedes put the bongos between her thighs and we got it off together. Not bad.

Then we sat down on her sleeping bag, our backs to the wall, and drank the wine. Mercedes got the jug out of the refrigerator and brought it back to the sleeping bag. She had some joints already rolled and lit one for us. I could hear the ocean out there, but Venice was depressing to me.

It had gone from the Timothy Leary dropout syndrome to free love to drugs. The Timothy Learys had grown old or OD'd. The dream had drowned. Religion came along and picked up what was left in and out of the madhouses, on the park benches and in the tiny rooms.

Mercedes and I kissed again. She kissed well. I felt her breasts: fair. She lit another joint, and we had some more to drink.

"I work for a marriage-counseling outfit," she said. "We're all divorced."

"What do you tell them?"

"We go by the book. It's funniest when they both come in together."

"Human relationships don't work," I said. "There's nothing you can tell them."

"I know it."

"Why do you live down here?"

"I like it. We've got a group. I've got a guitar."

"You have!"

"Yes, it's in the closet. We get together sometimes on a Friday or Saturday night in front of this guy's house, in his yard, and we play. People come by and listen. We get some good crowds."

I pulled Mercedes down on the sleeping bag, rolled on top of her, grabbed her head with both hands, got inside her lips with mine; mashed them open and crushed her with a kiss, getting down on her teeth, her mouth ripped open like a flower. I held inside of her; her tongue came up, and I sucked on it, then flicked mine underneath hers. I hardened again and rubbed my cock at her center. Then I pulled off, sat up; we had another joint, and we sat there and finished the jug.

I awakened in the morning, sick, without having had sex. Mercedes was in the bathroom. I stood up, straightened my clothes and put my shoes on. She came out.

"Good morning," she said.

"Good morning. I'm sick"

"I don't feel too well either."

"I've got to get back to L.A."

I went to the bathroom to clean up. When I came out, she handed me a slip of paper. It was her phone number. I kissed her with a very light kiss.

Outside it was hot. The flies whirled around the garbage cans that were up against the apartment-house walls. I got in my car and drove off, deciding not to see her again.

The phone rang on a Thursday night at my place. I answered. It was Mercedes. "I see that your number is listed . . . ."

"Yes."

"Well, listen, I work right in your neighborhood. I thought I might come by to see you."

"All right."

Twenty minutes later she was there. She had on another miniskirt, but this time she looked a little better. She had on high-heeled shoes, a low-cut blouse, and small blue earrings.

"You got any grass?"

"Sure." I brought out the grass and the papers, and she started rolling some joints. I broke out the beer, and we sat on the couch and smoked and drank. With beer you had a chance. I sat there and drank and kissed her and played with her legs. We didn't talk much. But we drank and smoked quite a long time.

We undressed and went to bed, first Mercedes, then me. We began kissing, and I rubbed her cunt, then her clit. She grabbed my cock. Finally, I mounted. Mercedes guided it in. It entered and forced forward, my mouth on hers as it did. She had a good grip, she wasn't loose, and I began.

After a few strokes I teased her awhile, pulling it out almost all the way out and just moving the head back and forth at the very opening of the cunt. Then I slid it in a few strokes, slowly, in lazy fashion. Then suddenly I rammed her 4 or 5 times, brutally. Her head rocked: "Arrrgggg. . . ." She made a sound. Then I relented and stroked, then I rotated, side to side, swinging it, then straightened and rammed.

It was a very hot night, and we both sweated. Mercedes had gotten quite high on the beer and joints. I decided to finish her off. I blasted it in and out, in and out; I ripped her with kisses; and her head rocked under the thrusts. I pumped on and on, 10 minutes, 15 minutes more. I was hard, I couldn't climax. The fucking beer, too much fucking beer.

"Make it," she said, "oh, *make* it, baby!"

I rolled off. Christ, it was a hot night. I took the sheet and wiped the sweat off. I could hear my heart as I lay there. My cock went down. Mercedes turned her head to me. I kissed her. My cock began to rise again.

I rolled on top of her, kissing her as if it were my last time on earth to do so. My cock slid in. I began again, but this time I knew I was going to make it. I could feel the mounting miracle of it moving toward the final point. I was going to come inside of her cunt, the bitch. I was going to pour the juices into her, and there was nothing she could do, the cunt. She was mine. I was the conquering army, I was the rapist, I was dominance, I was death.

She was helpless under me, her head rolling, rocking, as she made sounds: "Arrrggghh! . . . uggg! . . . oh . . . oh . . . oofff! . . . ooooh!" My cock sensed it all, fed on it. I made a strange sound, then I spurted. I spurted right into her center, and she took it, all of it. I rolled off.

I wiped off on the sheet. In 5 minutes she was snoring. I too was soon asleep.

In the morning we both showered and dressed. "I'll take you to breakfast."

"All right," Mercedes said. "By the way, did we fuck last night?"

"My God, don't you remember? We must have fucked for 45 minutes!"

"I *do* feel like I've been fucked."

We went out to a place around the corner. I ordered eggs over easy with bacon and coffee, what toast. Mercedes ordered hotcakes and ham, coffee. We sat by the window and watched the traffic and drank our coffee. The waitress brought our orders. I took a bite of egg. Mercedes poured syrup over her hotcakes.

"My God," she said, "you must have *really* fucked me! I can feel the semen running down my leg."

I decided not to see her again.

She phoned me 2 or 3 weeks later. "I got married," she said, "to Little Jack. You met him at the party. He has a short, fat dick. I like his short, fat dick. And he's a nice guy and he's got money. We're moving to the Valley."

"All right, Mercedes. Luck with all."

A couple of weeks later it was Mercedes on the phone again: "I miss those nights of drinking and talking with you; suppose I come over tonight?"

"All right."

She was there in 15 minutes, rolling joints and drinking beer. "Little Jack is a nice guy. We're happy together."

I sucked at my beer.

"I don't want to fuck," she went on. "I'm tired of abortions. I'm really tired of abortions."

"We'll figure something out."

"I just want to smoke and talk and drink."

"That's not enough for me."

"All you guys want to do is fuck."

"I like it."

"Well, I can't fuck. I don't want to fuck."

"Relax."

We sat on the couch. We didn't kiss. Mercedes was not a good conversationalist, and her laugh was still coarse and high and not true. But she had her legs and her ass and her hair. I had found some interesting women, God knows, but Mercedes just wasn't one. I had intended to write a dirty story for one of the magazines that night, and here she was fucking up my night, or *not* fucking it up.

The beer kept coming and the joints went around. She still had the same job. She was having trouble with her car. Little Jack was going to buy her a new one, or maybe she'd get a Yamaha. Little Jack had a short, fat dick. She was reading *Grapefruit* by Yoko Ono. She was still tired of abortions. The Valley was nice, but she missed Venice, the group. And she used to ride her bicycle along the walk.

I don't know how long we talked or *she* talked, but much beer went down, and she said she was too drunk to drive home.

"Take your clothes off and go to bed," I told her.

"But no fucking," she said.

"I won't use your cunt."

She undressed and went to bed. I undressed and went into the bathroom. She saw me come walking out with a jar of Vaseline.

"What are you going to do?"

"Just take it easy, baby, take it easy."

I took the Vaseline out and rubbed it over my cock. Then I turned out the light and got into bed.

"Turn your back to me," I said.

I reached one arm under her and played with her bottom breast, and with my top hand I played with the top breast. It felt good with my face in her hair. I hardened and slipped it into her ass. I grabbed her around the waist and pulled her ass in toward me, sliding it in.

"Ooooooh . . . ," she moaned.

I began working. I dug it in deeper and slammed and slammed. The cheeks of her ass were very big and soft; they felt like pillows full of air. I ripped and ripped and began to sweat. Then I rolled her onto her stomach and sunk it deeper. It was getting tighter. I got into the end of her colon, and she screamed.

"Shut up, goddamn you. You want the cops?"

It was tight in the colon. I slipped it in farther. The grip was enormous. I felt as if I were fucking the inside of a rubber hose; the friction was immense. I rammed it in and in, got a hitch in my side, a burning pain, but continued. I was slicing her in half, right up the backbone. I roared it in like a madman, and then I began to climax. I pumped the juices into her intestine; they kept coming. Then I lay there. She was crying.

"Goddammit," I told her, "I didn't use your cunt. I told you I wouldn't use your cunt." I rolled off.

In the morning Mercedes said very little, got dressed, and left for work. *This*, I thought, *is* it.

It was a good 6 to 8 weeks when I answered the phone and it was Mercedes: "Hank, I'd like to come by. But just for talk and beer and a few joints. Nothing else."

"Come by if you wish."

Mercedes was there in 15 minutes. She looked very good. I'd never seen a miniskirt that short, and her legs looked fine. I kissed her a long one right off. She broke off.

"I couldn't walk for two days after that last one. Don't rip my butt open again."

"All right, honest Injun, I won't."

It was about the same. We sat on the couch with the radio on, talked, drank beer, smoked. I kissed her again and again. I couldn't stop. She looked steaming that night, yet she insisted that she couldn't. Little Jack loved her; love meant a lot in this world.

"It sure does," I said.

"You don't love me."

"You're a married woman."

"I don't love Little Jack, but I care for him very much, and he loves me."

"It sounds fine to me."

"Have you ever been in love?"

"Yes, a couple of times."

"Where are they tonight?"

"I don't know. Probably with other men. I don't care."

We talked a long time that night and drank a long time and smoked any number of joints. Around 2 a.m. Mercedes said, "I'm too high to drive home. I'll total the car."

"Take your clothes off and go to bed."

"All right, but I've got an idea."

"Like what?"

"I want to watch you beat that thing off. I want to watch it squirt *juice*!"

"All right, that's fair enough. It's a deal."

Mercedes undressed and went to bed. I undressed and stood at the side of the bed. "Sit up so you can see better."

Mercedes sat up on the edge of the bed. I spit on my palm and began to rub my cock."

"Oh, look, it's growing!"

"Uh, huh . . . "

"It's getting *big*!"

"Uh, huh . . . ."

"Oh, it's all *purple* with big *veins*! It's *throbbing*! It's *ugly*!"

"Yeah."

I kept beating my cock, and I moved it near her face. She watched it. Just as I was about to climax, I stopped.

"Oh," she said.

"Look, I've got a better idea."

"What?"

"You beat it off."

"All right."

She started in. "Am I doing it right?"

"A little harder. And get most of it, rub most of it, not just up near the head."

"All right . . . Oh, God, *look* at it . . . I want to see it squirt *juice!*"

"Keep going! Oh, my God!"

I was just about to come, and I ripped it out of her hand.

"Oh, damn you!" Mercedes cried.

Then she swiftly reached out and put it in her mouth. She began sucking and bobbing, running her tongue along the back of my cock while it was in her mouth.

"Oh, you *bitch!*"

Then she pulled her mouth off my throbbing shaft.

"Go ahead! Go ahead! Finish me off!"

"No!"

"Well, Goddammit then!"

I pushed her over backwards on the bed and leaped upon her. I kissed her viciously and drove my cock on in. I worked violently, pumping and pumping; I reached near to it quickly; I moaned and then it began spurting; I pumped it full into her, feeling it enter, feeling it steam into her center.

I rolled off.

When I awoke in the morning, Mercedes was gone. There was no note; she was simply gone. I got up and too a shower and an Alka Seltzer, two Alka Seltzers. I pissed. I brushed my teeth. Then I went back to bed and slept until noon.

It has been 4 months now, and she has not phoned. She will not phone. I will never see Mercedes again, and neither of us will miss the other. What it meant, I have no idea.

There is a new one down from Berkeley. She has buck teeth and a little baby's voice. She fucks me while sitting on my lap and facing me. She's 22 and doesn't have any breasts. I have no idea what she wants. Her name is Diane. She gets up early in the morning and starts drinking whiskey.

I sometimes drive past the building that Mercedes works in. That's as close as I'll ever get to seeing her again. It's that way for many people all over America. We do things without knowing why, and later we don't care why we did them. But I wish Diane had tits; breasts, I mean.

Break-In

t was one of the outer rooms of the first floor. I stumbled on something—I think it was a footstool—and I almost went down. I banged into a table to hold myself up.

"That's right," said Harry, "wake up the whole fucking household."

"Look," I said, "what are we going to get here?"

"Keep your fucking voice down!"

"Harry, do you have to keep saying *fucking*?"

"What are you, a fucking linguist? We're here for cash and jewels."

I didn't like it. It seemed like total insanity. Harry was crazy; he'd been in and out of madhouses. Between that and doing time he'd spent three-quarters of his adult life in lockup. He'd talked me into the thing. I didn't have much resistance.

"This damn country," he said. "There are too many rich pricks having it too easy." Then Harry banged into something. "Shit!" he said.

"Hello? What is it?" We heard a man's voice coming from upstairs.

"We're in trouble," I said. I could feel the sweat dripping down from my armpits.

"No," said Harry, "*he's* in trouble."

"Hello," said the man upstairs. "Who's down there?"

"Come on," Harry told me.

He began walking up the stairway. I followed him. There was a hallway, and there was a light coming from one of the rooms. Harry moved quickly and silently. Then he ran into the room. I was behind him. It was a bedroom. A man and a woman were in separate beds.

Harry pointed his .38 Magnum at the man. "All right, buddy, if you don't want your balls blown off, you'll keep it quiet. I don't play."

The man was about 45, with a strong and imperial face. You could see he had had it his own way for a long time.

His wife was about 25, blond, long hair, truly beautiful. She looked like an ad for something or other.

"Get the hell out of my house!" the man said.

"Hey," Harry said to me, "you know who this is?"

"No."

"It's Tom Maxson, the famous news broadcaster, Channel 7. Hello, Tom—"

"Get out of here! NOW!" Maxson barked.

He reached out and picked up the phone. "Operator—"

Harry ran up and slammed him across the temple with the butt of his .38. Maxson fell across the bed. Harry put the phone back on the hook.

"You bastards, you hurt him!" cried the blond. "You cheap, cowardly bastards!"

She was dressed in a light-green negligee. Harry walked around and broke one of the shoulder straps. He grabbed one of the woman's breasts and pulled it out. "Nice, ain't it?" he said to me. Then he slapped her across the face, hard.

"You address me with respect, whore!" Harry said. Then he walked around and sat Tom Maxson back up.

"And you: I told you I don't play."

Maxson revived. "You've got the gun; that's all you've got."

"You fool. That's all I need. Now I'm gonna get some cooperation from you and your whore or it's going to get worse."

"You cheap punk!" Maxson said.

"Just keep it up, keep it up. You'll see," said Harry.

"You think I'm afraid of a couple of cheap hoods?"

"If you're not, you ought to be."

"Who's your friend? What does he do?"

"He does what I tell him."

"Like what?"

"Like, Eddie, go kiss that blond!"

"Listen, you leave my wife out of this!"

"And if she screams, I put a bullet in your gut. I don't play. Go on, Eddie, kiss the blond—"

"The blond was trying to hold up the broken shoulder strap with one hand. "No," she said, "please—"

"I'm sorry, lady, I gotta do what Harry tells me."

I grabbed her by the hair and got my lips on hers. She pushed against me, but she wasn't very strong. I'd never kissed a woman that beautiful before.

"All right, Eddie, that's enough."

I pulled away. I walked around and stood next to Harry. "Why, Eddie," he said, "what's that big *thing* sticking out in front of you?"

I didn't answer.

"Look, Maxson," said Harry, "your wife gave my man a hard-on! How the hell are we supposed to get any work done around here? We came for cash and jewelry."

"You wise-ass punks make me sick. You're no better than maggots."

"And what have *you* got? The six o'clock news. What's so big about that? Political pull and an asshole public. Anybody can read the news. I *make* the news."

"*You* make the news? Like *what*? What can *you* do?"

"Any amount of numbers. Ah, let me think. How about, TV newscaster drinks burglar's piss? How's that sound to you?"

"I'd die first."

"You won't. Eddie, go get me a glass. There's one there on the nightstand. Bring me that."

"Look," said the blond, "please take our money. Take our jewels. Just go away. What's the need for all this?"

"It's your loudmouthed, spoiled husband, lady. He's getting on my fucking nerves."

I brought Harry the glass, and he unzipped his pants and began to piss into it. It was a tall glass, but he filled it to the brim. Then he zipped up and moved toward Maxson.

"Now you're gonna drink my piss, Mr. Maxson."

"No way, bastard, I'd die first."

"You won't die. You'll drink my piss—all of it!"

"Never, punk!"

"Eddie," Harry nodded to me, "see that cigar on the dresser mantle?"

"Yeah."

"Get it. Light it. There's a lighter there."

I got the lighter and lit the cigar. It was a good one. I puffed on it. My best cigar. Never had anything like it.

"You like the cigar, Eddie?" Harry asked me.

"It's great, Harry."

"OK. Now you walk over to the whore and get that breast out from under the broken shoulder strap. Pull it out. I'm gonna hand this jerk-off this glass full of my piss. You hold that cigar next to the nipple of the lady's breast. And if this jerk-off doesn't drink all of this piss down to the very last drop, I want you to burn that nipple off with that cigar. Understand?"

I got it. I walked around and pulled out Mrs. Maxson's breast. I felt dizzy looking at it—never had I seen anything like that.

Harry handed Tom Maxson the glass of piss. Maxson looked over at his wife and tilted the glass and began to drink. The blond was trembling all over. It felt so good to hold her breast. The yellow piss was going down the newscaster's throat. He stopped a moment at about the halfway mark. He looked sick.

"All of it," said Harry. "Go ahead, it's good to the last drop."

Maxson put the glass to his lips and drained the remainder. The glass fell from his hand.

"I still think you're a couple of cheap punks," gasped Maxson.

I was still standing there holding the blond's breast. She yanked it away.

"Tom," said the blond, "will you please stop antagonizing these men? You're doing the most foolish thing possible!"

"Oh, playing the *winners*, eh? Is that why you married me? Because I was a winner?"

"Of course that's why she married you, asshole," said Harry. "Look at that fat gut on you. Did you think it was for your body?"

"I've got something," said Maxson. "That's why I'm Number One in newscasting. You don't do that on luck."

"But if she hadn't married Number One," said Harry, "she would have married Number Two."

"Don't listen to him, Tom," said the blond.

"It's all right," said Maxson, "I know you love me."

"Thank you, Daddy," said the blond.

"It's all right, Nana."

"'Nana,'" said Harry. "I like that name, 'Nana.' That's class. Class and ass. That's what the rich get while we get the scrubwomen."

"Why don't you join the Communist Party?" asked Maxson.

"Man, I don't care to wait centuries for something that might not finally work. I want it now."

"Look, Harry," I said, "all we're doing is standing around and holding conversations with these people. That doesn't get us anything. I don't care what they think. Let's get the loot and split. The longer we stay, the sooner we draw the heat."

"Now, Eddie," he answered, "that's the first good bit of sense I've heard you speak in five or six years."

"I don't care," said Maxson. "You're just the weak feeding off the strong. If I weren't here, you'd hardly exist. You remind me of people who go around assassinating political and spiritual leaders. It's the worst kind of cowardice; it's the easiest thing to do with the least talent available. It comes from hatred and envy; it comes from rancor and bitterness and ultimate stupidity; it comes from the lowest scale of the human ladder; it stinks and it reeks and it makes me ashamed to belong to the same tribe."

"Boy," said Harry, "that was some speech. Even piss can't stop your flow of bullshit. You're one spoiled turd. You realize how many people out there are on this earth without a chance? Because of where and how they were born? Because they had no education? Because they never had anything and never will have and nobody gives a fuck, and you marry the best body you can find, your age be damned?"

"Take your loot and go," said Maxson. "All you bastards who never make it have some alibi."

"Oh, wait," said Harry, "everything counts. *"We're* making it *now*. You don't quite understand."

"Tom," said the blond, "just give them the money, the jewelry . . . let them go . . . please get off Channel 7."

"It's not Channel 7, Nana. It's letting them *know*. I've got to let them know."

"Eddie," said Harry," check the bathroom. Bring back some adhesive tape."

I walked down the hall and found the bathroom. In the medicine cabinet was a wide roll of adhesive. Harry made me nervous. I never knew what he was going to do. I brought the tape back into the bedroom. Harry was yanking the phone cord out of the wall. "OK," he told me, "shut off Channel 7."

I got it. I taped his mouth good.

"Now, the hands, the hands in the back," said Harry.

He walked over to Nana, pulled out both of her breasts and looked at them. Then he spit in her face. She wiped it off with the bedsheet.

"OK," he said, "now this one. Get the mouth, but leave the hands loose. I like a little fight."

I fixed her up.

Harry got Tom Maxson turned on his side in his bed; he had her facing Nana.

He walked over and got one of Maxson's cigars and lit it. "I guess Maxson's right," said Harry. "We *are* the suckerfish. We *are* the maggots. We *are* the slime, and maybe the cowards."

He took a good pull on the cigar.

"It's yours, Eddie."

"Harry, I can't."

"You can. You don't know how. You've never been taught how. No education. I'm your teacher. She's yours. It's simple."

"You do it, Harry."

"No. She'll mean more to you."

"Why?"

"Because you're such a simple asshole."

I walked over to her bed. She was so beautiful and I

was so ugly I felt as if my whole body was smeared with a layer of shit.

"Go on," said Harry, "get it on, asshole."

"Harry, I'm scared. It's not right; she's not mine."

"She's yours."

"Why?"

"Look at it like a war. We won this war. We've killed all their machos, all their big-timers, all their heroes. There's nothing left but women and children. We kill the children and sent the old women up the road. We are the conquering army. All that's left is their women. And the most beautiful woman is all ours . . . is yours. She's helpless. Take her."

I walked up and pulled back the covers. It was as if I had died and was suddenly in heaven, and there was this magical creature in front of me. I took her negligee and ripped it completely off.

"Fuck her, Eddie!"

All the curves were absolutely where they were supposed to be. They were there and beyond. It was like beautiful skies; it was like beautiful rivers flowing. I just wanted to look. I was afraid. I stood there, this horn of a thing in front of me. I had no rights.

"Go ahead," said Harry. "Fuck her! She's the same as any other woman. She plays games, tells lies. She'll be an old woman someday, and other young girls will replace her. She'll even die. Fuck her while she's still there!"

I pulled at the shoulders, trying to gather her to me. She had gotten strength from somewhere. She pushed against me, pulling her head back. She was completely repulsed.

"Listen, Nana, I really don't want to do this . . . but I do. I'm sorry. I don't know what to do. I want you and I'm ashamed."

She made a sound through the adhesive on her mouth and pushed against me. She was so beautiful. I didn't deserve that. Her eyes looked into mine. They said what I was thinking. I had no human right.

"Go ahead," said Harry, "slam it to her! She'll love it."

"I can't do it, Harry."

"All right," he said, "you watch Channel 7 then."

I walked over and sat next to Tom Maxson. We sat side-by-side on his bed. He was making small sounds through the adhesive. Harry walked over to the other bed. "All right, whore, I guess I'll have to impregnate you."

Nana leaped out of bed and ran toward the door. Harry caught her by the hair, spun her and slapped her hard across the face. She fell against the wall and slid down. Harry pulled her up by the hair and hit her again. Maxson made a louder sound through his adhesive and leaped up. He ran over and butted Harry with his head. Harry gave him a chop along the back of the neck, and Maxson dropped.

"Tape the hero's ankles," he told me.

I bound Maxson's feet and shoved him onto his bed.

"Sit him up," said Harry. "I want him to watch."

"Look, Harry," I said, "let's get out of here. The longer we stay—"

"Shut up!"

Harry dragged the blond back to the bed. She still had on a pair of panties. He ripped them off and threw them at Maxson. The panties fell at his feet. Maxson moaned and began to struggle. I punched him a hard one, deep into the belly.

Harry took off his pants and undershorts.

"Whore," he said to the blond, "I'm gonna sink this thing deep into you and you're going to feel it and there's nothing you can do. You'll take all of it! And I'm going to cream deep inside of you!"

He had her on her back; she was still struggling. He hit her again, hard. Her head fell back. He spread her legs. He tried to work his cock in. He was having trouble.

"Loosen up, bitch; I know you want it! Lift your legs!"

He hit her hard, twice. The legs rose.

"That's better, whore!"

Harry poked and poked. Finally, he penetrated. He moved it in and out, slowly.

Maxson began moaning and moving again. I sank another one into his belly.

Harry began to get up a rhythm. The blond groaned as if in pain.

"You like it, don't you, whore? It's better turkeyneck than your old man ever gave you, ain't it? Feel it growing?"

I couldn't stand it. I stood up, took out my cock and began masturbating.

Harry was ramming the blond so hard that her head was bouncing. Then he slapped her and pulled out.

"Not yet, whore. I'm taking my time."

He walked over to where Tom Maxson was sitting.

"Look at the SIZE of that thing! And I'm going to put it back into her now and come right inside her, Tommy boy! You'll never be able to make love to your Nana without thinking of me! Without thinking of this!"

Harry put his cock right into Maxson's face. "And I may have her suck me off after I'm finished!"

Then he turned, went back to the other bed and mounted the blond. He slapped her again and began pumping wildly.

"You cheap, stinking whore, I'm going to come!"

Then: "Oh, shit! OH, MY GOD! Oh, oh, oh!"

He fell down against Nana and lay there. After a moment he pulled out. Then he looked over at me. "Sure you don't want some?"

"No thanks, Harry."

Harry began to laugh. "Look at you, fool, you've whacked off!" Harry got back into his pants, laughing.

"All right," he said, "tape up her hands and ankles. We're getting out of here."

I walked over and taped her up.

"But, Harry, how about the money and jewels?"

"We'll take his wallet. I want to get out of here. I'm nervous."

"But, Harry, let's take it all."

"No," he said, "just the wallet. Check his trousers. Just take the money."

I found the wallet.

"There's only $83 here, Harry."

"We'll take it and we leave. I'm nervous. I feel something in the air. We have to go."

"Shit, Harry, that's no haul. We can really clean them out!"

"I told you: I'm nervous. I feel trouble coming. You can stay. I'm leaving."

I followed him down the stairway.

"That son of a bitch will think twice before he insults anybody again," said Harry.

We found the window we had jimmied open and left the same way. We walked through the garden and out the iron gate.

"All right," said Harry, " we walk at a casual gait. Light a cigarette. Try to look normal."

"Why are you so nervous, Harry?"

"Shut up!"

We walked four blocks. The car was still there. Harry took the wheel and we drove off.

"Where are we going?" I asked.

"The Guild Theatre?"

"What's playing?"

"*Black Silk Stockings*, with Annette Haven."

The place was down on Lankershim. We parked and got out. Harry bought the tickets. We walked in.

"Popcorn?" I asked Harry.

"No."

"I want some."

"Get it."

Harry waited until I got the popcorn, large. We found some seats near the back. We were in luck. The feature was just beginning.

Flying is the Safest Way to Travel

ddie and Vince, they sat in two seats at the back of the airliner. They were in their early forties. They were dressed in cheap suits, no neckties, wash-and-wear shirts, unshined shoes.

"That stewardess, Vince, the short one with the great legs, I'd like to have that one. Just look at her *ass*!"

"Naw," said Vince, "I like the tall one. I like her nose and her lips, her stringy uncombed hair. She reminds me of a drunken slut who doesn't know where she's at."

"She doesn't have any breasts, man."

"I don't care."

The plane ran through a bank of clouds and they watched the white threads, smoky, rolling around out there. Then they were back in the sunlight.

"Eddie, are we going to do it?"

"Why not?"

Vince finished his drink and sat it on the seat tray in front of him. "It's dumb."

"All right. Forget it. I'll do it alone."

"I think it's dumb, Eddie. Let's not do it."

"Vince, you don't have the guts of a rabbit." Eddie finished his drink, put the empty container on Vince's seat tray, folded his tray and locked it into the back of the seat in front of him. Then he stood up, stepped into the aisle, pulled at the handle of the overhead compartment and extracted a very fat briefcase. He closed the compartment and sat down again with the briefcase on his lap.

"All right, Vince. You with me or not?"

"Look, Eddie, think it over . . . "

"You with me or not?"

"All right, all right . . . "

Eddie reached down by the seat arm, pressed the little button with the design of the stewardess upon it and waited.

"Eddie, don't do it. Let's just order a couple of drinks."

It took three or four minutes but the stewardess arrived. It was the one with the great legs.

"Yes, sir, did you ring?"

"What's your name, stewardess?"

"Vivian."

"Vivian, I want you to lean forward because I want to whisper something to you that the other passengers shouldn't hear."

"Sir, I'm *very* busy . . . "

"I'd suggest you do as I say. It's very important."

The stewardess leaned forward.

"Now, Vivian," Eddie whispered, "this briefcase you see sitting here on my lap has enough TNT in it to blow your goddamned legs off and your goddamned ass off, plus all your other parts . . . "

The stewardess just stared at Eddie.

"And, there's enough here to blow off all my precious parts and also all the parts of everybody on this plane. You will now escort me and my friend up to your Flight Captain and his co-pilot."

"Yes, sir," said the stewardess.

"Come on, buddy," Eddie said to Vince.

The stewardess walked up the aisle and the men followed her. They walked through first class and then entered the flight compartment. The three of them stood behind the pilots.

"Captain Henderson . . . " the stewardess began.

"Captain Henderson," said Eddie, "you will not send out any radio calls nor will you answer any radio calls."

"Take control, Marty," Henderson said to the co-pilot.

Then he turned. "Now, what the hell . . . "

"Well, look at the Captain," said Eddie. "He's *fat*, isn't he?"

"Sure is," said Vince.

"Hey, boy," Eddie spoke to the Captain, "you're a little bit fat, aren't you?"

Captain Henderson didn't answer. He looked at Eddie with the briefcase. Eddie's right hand was under the upper flap.

"Now, Captain, I asked you a *question*!"

"Well, I might be ten or fifteen pounds overweight."

"Looks more like twenty. Drink a lot of beer?"

"Look, what the hell is this?"

"How much beer do you drink, fat boy?"

"When I'm off duty, five or six bottles."

"It might be a pleasure to blow some of that lard off of you. Now, you, co-pilot, what's your name?"

"Marty. Marty Parsons."

"You just keep this thing on course for New York City, you hear me?"

"I hear."

"Now my friend here, Vince, he doesn't say much. I'm the leader and he's the crazy one. He has the old suicide complex. It runs in the family. Hey, Vince, tell them about your brother."

"Eddie, these people don't want to hear about that."

"Go on, tell them. I want them to know how it runs in the family."

"What is this?" asked Vivian. "Do we have to listen to little stories up here?"

"Shut up, bitch! Now go ahead and tell the story, Eddie."

"Well, I had this brother. His name was Dan. He wasn't very happy . . . "

"Look," asked Captain Henderson, "what do you people want anyhow?"

"We'll get to that soon enough. I want to hear the story. Go ahead, Eddie . . . "

"Well, my brother wasn't very happy. He decided to kill himself. He jumped out of a second story window. He wanted to land on the sidewalk but he didn't . . . "

"O.k. Where did he land, Vince?"

"Well, he didn't hit the sidewalk. He landed on an old iron-spiked fence, on his side . . . "

"Go ahead, Vince . . . "

"The ambulance crew got there and he was stuck on his side with fourteen iron pickets in his side. So the one attendant said, 'We have to get him off of there right away.' But the other attendant said, 'No, that will kill him for sure.' Nobody knew what to do . . . "

"All right, Vince . . . Then . . . ?"

"Well, there was all this blood coming out. So they just held my brother up to keep the pickets from going in deeper. And they waited for help . . . "

"We could have dynamited him off . . . So then?"

"My brother was crying and screaming. Finally, a big-shot doctor pulled up and said, 'What we've got to do is get a welder or somebody to come and cut those spikes off. Then we can take him to a hospital and pull them out one at a time.'"

"Listen," said Captain Henderson, "I don't understand this whole thing . . . "

"Go ahead, Vince."

"So they called in an iron-worker and he cut the spikes from the fence. They took my brother to the hospital and kept him there for the next fourteen months. They would take one spike out, bandage the hole, wait a few weeks before taking out the next one and then they'd pull that one. Finally, after more than a year of yanking the spikes out they put him in this place and held him for therapy . . . "

"Psychological therapy," said Eddie. "Then what happened?"

"They let him go. Two weeks later he killed himself with a shotgun."

There was silence. The plane went on toward New York City.

Then Eddie spoke. "What we are going to do here is to rape ourselves a stewardess a piece. We like your stewardesses."

"You can't get away with such a thing," said Captain Henderson.

"Either we do or we all die."

"Then what? Then what's your plan?"

"We've got a plan. Don't worry about that."

"Look, you can get laid on the ground, you can get laid anywhere for 50 bucks."

"We don't want those. We want your girls."

"You're attempting a dangerously foolish thing."

"Let us worry about that. By the way, I've got the

old suicide complex too. That's why I've teamed up with Vince."

"Well," said Vivian, "I'm not cooperating. You can blow us all to hell!"

Eddie handed Vince the briefcase. "Careful . . . Don't drop it! Stick your hand under the flap. Easy. Do you feel the switch, Vince?"

"Yes."

"Don't press down on that thing unless you feel that we've been crossed . . . "

"Do I wait until you tell me, Eddie?"

"No, use your judgment." Eddie turned toward Vivian.

"To hell with you," she said, "you don't scare me, you goddamned freak!"

Eddie punched her quickly in the belly and as she doubled over he punched her in the face. Vivian fell in the corner of the flight deck behind Captain Henderson's seat. She was gasping and trembling. She began weeping in a hysterical fashion. Eddie rushed to her and pushed his handkerchief into her mouth.

"Either of those guys move a move, Vince, you hit the trigger!"

"O.K., Eddie . . . "

Eddie bent over Vivian and pulled her skirt up around her waist. She had on pantyhose and tried to turn on her side. Eddie pulled her straight.

"Oh," said Vince, "you're right, Eddie, she's got *beautiful* legs! I'm scared, I'm really scared but I'm getting a hard!"

It was true, her legs were beautiful and full, packed, like ripe figs on a tree, culminated, perfect, almost to the point of bursting in the tight pantyhose. Vivian reached up and clawed and raked Eddie's face with the fingernails of each hand. He hit her again, hard across the face, and her hands dropped. He unzipped and the thing was before him, mad and untended. He bent over her, grabbed her ass and pulled at it. Her eyes stared at him. They were wide and a deep brown. He remembered the old Marlon Brando movie and he reached down and tore her pantyhose in front, in between the legs. "I'm going to squirt it inside of you, you bitch!" He poked futilely, then reached his hand down and forced the head of it in. She was trembling and wiggling, a snake creature. Then it entered a bit more. And then he plunged it in, totally. He began to ram wildly, watching her head bob and bounce against the floor. There was no holding it back. He could feel the climax arriving and he thrust it wildly and deeply in, then it came. It seemed as if he had endless semen, it came out and out as he stared at her wide brown eyes. Then he was still. Eddie slowly got up, stood a moment transfixed, looking down at her. Then he put it back in, zipped up and turned to Vince.

"O.k., your turn now. I'll go get your stewardess."

"You guys can't get away with this!" said Henderson.

"You think not?"

"How are you going to get away with it? How are you going to get out of here?"

"Let us worry about that. Meanwhile, shut up a while!"

Vivian rose from the floor, her skirt falling back into place, although rumpled. She swayed, and pulled the handkerchief out of her mouth.

"How'd you like it, baby?" Eddie asked her.

"You low-life swine," she said, "you stank! If I could kill you, I would!"

The flight door opened and the other stewardess entered, the tall one with the awry hair. "What's going on here?" she asked. "I've been serving drinks out there all alone and *everybody's* thirsty!"

"Get out of here, Karen!" said Captain Henderson.

"Just stay where you are, Karen!" said Eddie. He walked over and took the briefcase from Vince and slid his hand under the upper flap.

"Vince, lock that door. We've got all the company we need."

Vince locked the flight door. Karen looked at Vivian. "Oh . . . what happened to you?"

"I've just been raped . . . "

"And now it's your turn, Karen," said Eddie.

"He's got dynamite in the briefcase, Karen," said Henderson.

"What? That doesn't mean I submit to this type of thing," said Karen.

"Karen, you're next. My friend desires you. We have the TNT and we are prepared to use it. Remember you are to protect the plane, the crew, and the passengers in all moments of duress. I had a friend who worked in baggage once. He told me about the rule."

"To hell with the rule," said Karen, "nobody's raping me!"

"Captain Henderson," said Eddie, "are you ready to say our last prayers?"

"Look, Karen," said Henderson, "I believe these guys are crazy enough to do it."

"Captain Henderson," said Marty the co-pilot, "Karen is my girlfriend."

"Think of the passengers," said Henderson, "think of the aircraft."

"You're just thinking of your own ass, Henderson."

"Go ahead, Vince," said Eddie, "take her! I can tell that none of these want to die! Go ahead, take her!" Eddie slipped his hand deeper under the upper flap of the briefcase. He was beginning to sweat below the hairline, little beads forming on his forehead.

Vince began to move toward Karen. "Captain, please take the controls," said Marty. Henderson took the controls. Marty turned and looked at Vince. "Stay away from her, son of a bitch!"

"Go ahead, Vince," said Eddie, "*take* her! One move out of anybody and I'm blowing us all to shit! I mean it!"

"O.K., Eddie . . . "

Eddie looked at Karen and he could then see why Vince wanted her. It was that wild uncombed hair, the pointed nose, and the lips, the way they pouted, slightly idiotic. Vince moved to Karen, grabbed her. His mouth was on hers and her hands pushed against his chest, weakly. She seemed stricken, numbed . . .

"You got the best one, Vince," said Eddie, "you son of a bitch, you lucked it!"

Then while still kissing Karen, Vince held her with one hand around the waist and lifted her skirt with the other. Her legs were long and slim and glorious. Her pantyhose were dark. Vince held her about the waist still kissing her, bending her backwards, and with his free hand he mauled her ass.

Marty got up from his seat. "Stop it, you bastard! I'm telling you, stop it!"

"Just stay out of this, Marty," said Eddie, the sweat now running awkwardly down his face, "just stay out of this Marty, I'm telling you! I wanna *watch* this one!"

Then Vince reached down and grabbed her between the legs. He kissed her under the throat shoving her head back. Marty charged from his seat and leaped at Vince, and then there was the mark of the sun and the fuselage and the wings separated and the engines shook loose from the wings and dropped and the fuselage dropped, spinning nose-down whirling like a very large dart and losing its tail section as the engines fell through the sky. It was over a small town in Midwest America and not much damage was done except for part of a tail fin which sheared through a roof and sliced off a right arm to the shoulder of a seven-year-old girl working on her history lesson.

Fly the Friendly Skies

I t was 12:35 p.m, lunch had been served, drinks had been served, and the jetliner steadied through midair and the movie came on: *The Dream of the Dancer*, a nice slight plot of a film featuring a junket of third-rate actors. It was a Miami to L.A. flight, #654 on a Thursday in March, almost clear skies, not much doing. The biggest problem was a backup at the restrooms, small lines forming, but that was standard after lunch and drinks. The passengers were an admixture of male and female, none of them exceptional, unusual or desperate except for three: Kikid, Nurmo, and Dak. They had three seats, right, side, middle. They had been observing the others and speaking quietly. Then as a stewardess walked by, Kikid nodded and Dak jumped up with the length of wrapping twine which was formed into a noose. He trailed behind her, then dropped the twine over her head and tightened it, held her there.

"Quiet, bitch, or you die!"

Most of the passengers were aware of the proceedings but they just stared like cows or they acted as if they were watching a movie which had nothing to do with them.

Nurmo and Kikid jumped up. They were all small young men, dark, thin, nervous.

"Take her up to the captain and begin proceedings," Kikid said to Dak.

The passengers watched as Dak pushed the stewardess toward the pilot's compartment. A heavy-set young man further up the aisle from Kikid and Nurmo turned on his seat and said to them, "Listen, you'd better change your minds about this thing; this is a very serious thing."

"Listen, man," Kikid said, "you stay out of this!"

"Yeah, man," said Nurmo, "you stay the fuck out of this!"

The heavy-set young man, who might have been a football player, continued: "I'm just warning you for your own good."

"Listen, man, I'll give the warnings around here!" Kikid responded.

"I just want to repeat," continued the young man, "that . . . ."

"Goddamn you! What did I tell you? What the god-damn hell did I tell you?"

Kikid ran up to where the young man was sitting. The young man saw him coming and started to rise but he had to undo his seatbelt first. It cost him. Kikid grabbed him by the collar, then something flashed in his hand—it was a metal can opener. He gouged the pointed end into one of the young man's eyes and twisted. The scream of pain almost shook the aircraft. The young man held both of his hands to his head where the eye had been. The eye was on the floor. Kikid looked down, saw it, stepped on it with his shoe, crushing it like a snail.

"Now," he said, "you want to keep your other eye, you keep your fucking face shut!"

Just then the captain's voice came on over the intercom: "THIS IS CAPTAIN EVANS. I'M SORRY TO INFORM YOU BUT THIS PLANE HAS BEEN HIJACKED. WE HAVE NOW CHANGED COURSE TO HAVANA, CUBA. PLEASE COOPERATE WITH THE HIJACKERS. DO NOTHING TO CAUSE HARM TO YOURSELF OR ANY OF THE OTHER PASSENGERS. THANK YOU."

"All right," said Kikid, "now I want everybody to stay in your seats."

"Yeah," said Nurmo, "stay in your seats."

A stewardess rushed up from the rear of the jet. She had a first-aid kit and she began administering aid to the blood-ied young man who had lost his eye.

"Well, well," said Kikid, "we've got these neat little dolls all over the place! Nothin' like lots of gash!"

He watched her bending over the young man. She had a beautiful behind, so full and young, a truly maddening rump. He reached out and grabbed her ass, hard, then let go. The stewardess straightened up and faced Kikid. She had a little girl's face, freckles, heavy lips, long red-brown hair.

"Keep your hands off me, you pig!"

"Attend your patient and feel lucky that's all I might do!" Kikid told her.

"You just hijack your plane. Let me try to save this man's life!"

She turned back to her job.

Nurmo who was standing behind Kikid said, "We're not hijackers! We're FREEDOM FIGHTERS!"

"All the way," said Kikid.

He kept looking at the stewardess' ass. He had never seen an ass quite that marvelous and he'd seen and studied many, many asses. It just kept making those movements at him. He reached over again and grabbed a cheek of that ass, hard.

The stewardess whirled and faced Kikid again.

"I am trying to stop the flow of blood here! Otherwise, this man will die!"

"Is that right?" Kikid asked.

He pulled the wrapping twine from his pocket. Just like Dak's. It was formed into a noose. Then in a swift motion it was about the stewardess' throat. He tightened it and drew that little girl's face with all that ass toward him. He pulled it in close, then, kissed her viciously. Then he let her go, looked at her.

"Oh my," he said, "I do believe I'm getting hard!"

Kikid kept holding the stewardess close to him by the twine. She looked good to him, all flushed and fearful. The other passengers watched, terrified.

"Hey, man," Nurmo objected, "we're trying to hijack a plane here! What's all this bullshit with the broad?"

Kikid turned to Nurmo, still holding the stewardess with the twine. "Listen, man, I'm running this show! Now, you go up front and check on Dak, see that everything's okay up there!"

Then he looked back at the girl. "I like you baby. I like you very much! Now you're going to kiss me off! Right in front of all these nice people here!"

"No," said the girl, "I'll die first!"

"Well, baby," Kikid smiled, "that's up to you."

Tightening the twine just a bit about the girl's throat, Kikid reached down and unzipped his fly. He pulled his penis out. It hung there, limp and ugly. Meanwhile, the wounded man had slumped in his seat, his lifeblood dripping into the aisle. Kikid pulled the girl's face closer to his, smiled at her: "Baby, you're going to kiss me off, NOW!"

"I'll die first!" she screamed.

Kikid smiled again, tightened the twine. The girl stood there, her face darkening. Kikid tightened the twine again. The girl's head began to move down.

"That's it, baby! Just a little lower! There, there . . . you're gonna like this and I'm gonna like this and maybe all the people watching are gonna like this!"

The girl's head was down there.

"NOW GET IT, WHORE, OR SO HELP ME, I'LL KILL YOU!"

"My God, can't somebody do something?" an old woman in a rear seat croaked out.

"Somebody is doing something, grandma," said Kikid, "and she's doing real well, just like a pro. Just like a goddamned pro! Oh oooooh, shit, I can't stand it! I love you, you cunt! Oh, get it, get it ALL! Swallow it, you bitch, get it all!"

Then Kikid pulled away, shoved the stewardess to the floor, said "That's the quickest head-job I've ever had. You lick and suck at the same time and this FREEDOM FIGHTER wishes to thank you."

Then he pointed to the dying man: "Okay, see if you can patch this asshole up! He's messing up the floor with his blood!"

The movie, *The Dream of the Dancer*, ended just then, though it was doubtful that any had watched it. Kikid zipped up just as Nurmo returned from the captain's cabin.

"How's it going up there?" Kikid asked him.

"It's okay, Dak still has the girl hostage and we're on course to Havana."

"Fine," Kikid stated, "as FREEDOM FIGHTERS our mission is about accomplished."

"What'll we do now?" asked Nurmo.

"Just wait," Kikid answered.

It was 1:43 p.m., approaching the Gulf of Florida, the stewardess showing great courage in attempting to stop the flow of blood from the dying man. It all seemed a matter of waiting, one way or the other. Kikid and Nurmo just stood there watching over the passengers.

"All right, you people, you know what your captain advised you. Don't cause any trouble. We have the girl as hostage up front. You try anything funny back here, the girl dies," Kikid told them.

Suddenly a flash of silver light leaped into the cabin.

"What the hell was that?" Kikid asked.

"Geez, I dunno . . . " Nurmo said.

Kikid ran to the window, leaning across some passengers. "Look! That's where the flash came from! See that thing out there?"

Nurmo leaned across and looked out of the window.

"I see it! Look, it's silver and round and glittering!"

"It's a fucking flying saucer!" yelled Kikid.

"Hey, it's gone!"

"Where'd it go?"

They ran to the opposite windows. There was nothing in sight. They stood back in the center aisle.

"It's weird," said Kikid, "a flying saucer."

"I can feel it right over us!" said Nurmo. "And I can feel that something strange is going to happen!"

"I know what it is!" said the old woman who had spoken before, "it's God! God has come to save us from being hijacked to Havana!"

Kikid whirled on the old lady and said, "Grandma, you're full of shit!"

"The Lord has come to save us!" she screamed.

Then there was a flash of purple light, a purple light as never seen upon the earth before, and then before them appeared a creature quite globular, almost all head with eyes as bright as 500-watt electric bulbs. Everything about the Thing was tiny except for the head: tiny ears, legs, mouth. It must have weighed 300 pounds and its skin had a metallic texture. How it managed to stand on its tiny legs was unbelievable. But the total effect the thing gave off was one of awesome power and an uninhibited and splendid intelligence. It stood, consuming the scene.

"Oh God!" wailed the old woman. "I had no idea you'd look like this!"

"Quiet, you gooney harridan," the Thing spoke to her.

After a moment the Thing spoke again.

"Why is this craft headed for Havana? I intuit its original course as LAX. Hmmm . . . I see . . . "

The Thing turned toward Kikid and Nurmo.

"Listen, man," Kikid said, "maybe we can make a deal?"

"I don't deal," the Thing answered.

And with that, a beam shot out from one of the Thing's 500-watt eyes.

Kikid slowly began to melt and then he was gone, left a stink similar to that of burning rubber.

The Thing turned toward Nurmo.

"Listen, man," said Nurmo, "anything you say! I'm on your side! I'll be your slave for life! I'll work for six cents an hour and give half my salary to charity! What do you say?"

The answer came from the other 500-watt eye as Nurmo slowly melted down to the smell of burning rubber.

"God, you've saved us!" exclaimed the old woman, "but there's one more up front!"

"Shut up, old woman. I know about up front. I'll take care of that at my leisure."

"Thank you, God," said the old woman.

"Thank you, God," said a man.

"Yes, thank you, God," somebody else said.

The Thing turned to the stewardess who was still working on the dying man. She stood up. She had made a valiant effort and her uniform was blood-smeared. The passengers watched.

"What work do you want me to do?" she asked.

"You're going to suck me off!" the Thing said.

"No! Never!"

"You have no choice. My will is stronger than yours. You will do it . . . "

And out of that globular head, down near the tiny legs, suddenly a long wiry thin pole-like antenna sprung out. It was silver yet skin-like. It quivered and glittered, hung out there. The stewardess moved toward it. She lifted the whole apparatus upwards, then stuck the end of it into her mouth. Her ears quivered and the saliva ran down her jaws. She went to it as the Thing grabbed her hair with its tiny hands. The jet passed through a rain cloud. There was momentary darkness, then light as the Thing said, "Get it all, you bitch! Get it all!"

It was going to be another of those flights, another late arrival at LAX.

The Lady with the Legs

I first saw her in a bar on Alvarado Street. Lisa, that is. I was 24 years old, she about 35. She was sitting about bar center, and there was an empty stool on either side of her.

Compared to the average woman who came to that bar, she was a beauty. Her face was a bit round, and her hair didn't seem exceptional, but there was a quietness in the way she sat, and a sadness. I also sensed an eerie quality about her.

I left my stool to go to the men's room. I checked her twice, walking by, once from each side. She was small, a bit squat, but with shapely buttocks. But the most marvelous part of her was the legs: neat ankles, perfect calves, knees that ached to be squeezed, and also wondrous thighs.

It was as if *that* part of her body had maintained as the remainder had begun to lose out.

Her chin was too round, and her face was slightly puffy. She looked alcoholic.

Her high-heeled shoes were black and shiny, and she had three fake-gold bracelets on her left arm; also a dark mole just above the wrist. She was smoking a long cigarette and staring down into her drinking glass. She appeared to be drinking scotch along with a bottle of beer for a chaser.

I went back to my stool, finished my whiskey sour and nodded the bartender in for another. He trotted off. When he came back with my drink, I asked him about the lady with the legs.

"Oh," he said, "that's Lisa."

"She looks pretty good," I said. "How come none of the men sit near her?"

"That's easy," he answered. "She's crazy."

Then he walked off.

I picked up my drink and walked down to Lisa. I took the stool to her left, lit a cigarette and had a hit of my drink. I was fairly intoxicated.

I picked up my whiskey sour and drained it, nodded

the bartender in. "A refill for me and the lady. Also, two Heinekens for chasers."

Hearing that, Lisa knocked off her drink.

When the new ones arrived, she took a hit of hers, and I took a hit of mine.

Then we both just sat there, looking straight ahead.

Maybe a couple of minutes passed. Then she spoke: "I don't like people, do you?"

"No."

"You look like a mean son of a bitch. Are you?"

"No."

She knocked off her drink, took a good gulp of beer. I followed suit.

"I'm crazy," she said.

"Yeah?"

"Are you crazy?" she asked.

"Yes."

I waved the bartender in.

"I'll buy the next," Lisa said.

She ordered the refills like one who had done that any number of times. When the drinks arrived, I said, "Thank you, Lisa."

"You're welcome . . . .What's your name?"

"Hank."

"You're welcome, Hank."

Lisa took a sip, then glanced at me. "Are you crazy enough to break a bar mirror?"

"I think I already have."

"Where was it?"

"The Orchid Room."

"The Orchid Room is a stupid place."

"I don't go there anymore."

Lisa took a big drain of beer, set her bottle down, then sighed, "Well, I'm going to break *this* bar mirror."

"Go," I told her, "ahead."

Lisa drained her scotch, then stood up and grabbed her beer bottle.

I saw her raise it over her head. I leaped up to grab her

arm, but I was a bit late: I only slowed her overhand toss just a fraction.

The Heineken bottle looped in a slow, high arc toward the bar mirror as my mind quickly said, "No, no, no, NO!"

There was a sheer blasting sound as shards of glass came leaping out like giant icicles, and for some strange reason the lights went out.

It was frightening, glamorous and beautiful.

I drained my drink.

In the dark I saw much white rushing toward us. It was the bartender, most of him shirt and apron. He was moving fast.

"YOU CRAZY BITCH!" he screamed. "I'LL KILL YOU!"

I put Lisa behind me.

I found my beer bottle. I tried to time it as he came in. I was lucky. I caught him above the left temple. But he didn't fall. He just stood there in the dark in all his white. He was like a doorman waiting for a cab.

I switched the bottle to my left hand and cracked him on the right temple. He fell toward the bar, caught himself by grabbing the edge with both hands. He held there a moment, then began to tilt toward Alvarado Street.

When he hit the floor, the lights went on again.

For a second it was as if everybody were frozen in the light: the patrons, me, Lisa, the barkeep.

Then I yelled, "LET'S GO!"

I grabbed Lisa by the arm and pulled her toward the rear exit.

Then we were in the alley, and I yanked her along.

"COME ON! COME ON! HURRY!"

"I CAN'T RUN IN THESE GODDAMNED HIGH-HEELED SHOES!"

"TAKE THEM OFF!"

Lisa stopped and pulled them off, handed one to me. She took the other, and we ran down the alley.

When we got to the end, I looked back. We weren't being followed.

"All right, put your shoes back on."

She worked at it, slipping the first one on. Then holding to my shoulder, she got the other one on. Then she just stood there, swaying.

"Okay," I said, "come on!"

"Where we going?"

"To my place."

We were at the end of the alley near the corner. Then I saw a bus pull up to expel a fare. I waved at the bus and pulled Lisa toward it. The driver had closed the door, but he saw us. He was a nice sort and reopened the door. I pushed Lisa on and dropped in the fare. I tried to pull her to a seat, but she just grabbed onto the pole above the money meter and wobbled about there.

She glared at me through mad green eyes. "SHIT! I WANT A CAB! I'M A LADY! I DON'T RIDE A FUCKING BUS! I DON'T RIDE A FUCKING BUS!"

Lisa was like a beautiful drunken gazelle, her miraculous buttocks swaying to the rocking of the bus.

"I WANT A CAB! I'M A LADY! WHAT THE FUCK IS THIS?"

"Baby, it's only four blocks."

"SHIT! she screamed. "SHIT!"

The next stop was ours. I pulled the cord. The bus pulled up and stopped.

I pried Lisa's hands from the pole, got her about the waist and pulled her down the steps to the street.

The bus driver looked at me through the open door.

"Good luck, buddy. You're going to need it."

"You're jealous," I said.

He laughed, closed the door, and drove off into the night.

Lisa appeared to be getting drunker, and I wasn't too well off myself. I walked her along, one of my arms about her waist, the other pulling her right arm about my neck. She was rocking and staggering. Her beautiful legs were giving up.

"Doncha have a fucking car?"

"No."

"You're a bum!"

"Yes."

We were slowly and laboriously nearing my apartment.

"You got anything to drink up there? If you don't have anything to drink up there, I'm not coming!"

"Lots of bottles of wine . . . .The best . . . ."

"I'm sick," she said.

Lisa lurched to the left. I was too drunk to right her. We fell. Luckily, there was a large hedge on that side. We pummeled down into it.

I hit the greenery, rolled backward, and was upon my back on the sidewalk. I got myself up. Then I looked down.

And there in the moonlight was Lisa, half spread in the hedge and half upon the sidewalk. She was hanging from one side, dangling. Her skirt was pulled back, exposing the most beautiful legs on Earth. I stared in disbelief.

But I gathered myself, knowing that a possible prowl car was always any given moment away.

"Lisa," I said, "LISA! PLEASE WAKE UP!"

"Uh . . . ."

"THE COPS ARE COMING!"

It did something to her. As I yanked her out of the hedge, she made her legs behave. It was the act of a terrorized will . . .

I got her to the front doorway of the apartment, got her into the lobby, and moved her toward the elevator. I hit the button, the lift was there, and I worked her in. I hit the floor button and held Lisa upright, waiting.

"I miss my son," she said. "I want my baby."

"Sure you do," I said.

I got her out of there and down to my door. As I opened it, she leaned forward against me and we both fell forward into there . . . .

Lisa got up, straightened her nylons, picked up her purse, walked to a chair across the room, sat down, and fumbled in her purse for cigarettes. Outside in the night the mostly red neon of L.A. poured in.

I opened a bottle of wine for Lisa and poured her a water-glassful. To the slight sound of nylon rubbing, she crossed her magic legs.

On the couch across from her I had my own bottle, had poured my own glassful. I drained it, poured another.

Lisa looked at me. Her eyes got large and larger. She looked as if she were going nuts. Then she spoke: "You think you're *hot shit*! You think you're Mr. *Van Bilderasss*!"

I was down to my shorts and undershirt. They were soiled and ripped.

I got up.

I pranced.

I slapped my legs.

"Hey, baby, you think you got good legs? Look at *these*!"

Then I pushed my chest out and made a bicep out of my right arm. "Look at *that*, baby! I've decked many a slimy bastard with one punch!"

I walked back to the couch, sat down, drained half my glass. Lisa just continued to look at me. Her eyes still got larger and larger and larger.

"You think you're Mr. *Van Bilderass*!"

"RIGHT!"

She reached down and got her wine bottle, which she had corked. While looking at me, wild and wide-eyed she was, Lisa slowly lifted the bottle over her head, got her arm into the throw position as I yelled, HOLD IT!"

And she did.

I said, "NOW YOU CAN THROW THAT SON OF A BITCH, BUT IF YOU DO, BE SURE YOU KNOCK ME OUT! BECAUSE IF YOU DON'T, IT'S COMING RIGHT BACK AT YOU, AND I'M GOING TO KNOCK YOUR FUCKING HEAD OFF!"

While still looking wild-eyed, she slowly lowered the bottle to the floor.

I walked over, uncorked it, and filled her glass. Then I walked back to the couch and sat down. I was in a great positive state of mind.

"Now, whore," I said, "I want you to pull your skirt back a little more . . . ."

Positive or not, I was still a bit surprised when Lisa did.

The edge of her skirt was about two inches above her knees. I could see an inch of flesh above the edge of the nylons.

"Now," I said, "give me one more inch! No *more* than that!"

Lisa tugged her skirt up another inch.

I walked up and stood in front of her. Each valley and curve of her flesh was amazing. Her black high-heeled shoes glittered.

"TWIST YOUR ANKLE! KICK YOUR UPPER LEG A BIT!"

Lisa conceded.

"NOW STOP!"

She stopped.

"NOW GIVE ME ANOTHER HALF INCH!"

Lisa slipped her skirt up a bit more.

"YES! THERE!"

I was ape. I dropped to my knees, peering up her legs.

Lisa leered at me. "You're a fucking jerk; you're nuts!"

I reached out and grabbed a foot. I kissed that black high-heeled shoe on the side, just near the edge where the nylon was. Then I kissed her ankle.

"You're not a killer, are you?" she asked. "One of my friends, she went to this guy's room, and he tied her to his bed and took out this knife and carved his initials on her . . . . She screamed so loud, the police came and saved her . . . . You're not—"

"SHUT UP!"

I stood up and took it out.

I spit into my palm and started massaging myself.

"You fuckin' whore," I said.

I began rubbing with abandon.

"ANOTHER INCH! SHOW ME ANOTHER INCH!"

I flailed away.

"SHOW ME MORE! SHOW ME MORE!"

It was the secret and the trick and the entirety!

"THERE! OH, MY GOD!"

I came.

The greasy white substance spurted out, a buildup, a release of years of frustration and loneliness. As it gushed out, I ran up to Lisa and spilled the white glue of myself all over her nylons and upper legs. Still spurting, I held it there.

She screamed and leaped up. "YOU PIG! YOU FUCK-ING IDIOTIC PIG!"

I reached up, grabbed the end of my undershirt, and wiped off. Then I walked back to the couch, poured myself a glassful, and lit a cigarette.

Lisa came out, sat down in her chair and poured herself one. Then she lit a cigarette. She inhaled deeply, exhaled. And as she exhaled, her voice came out over the top of the smoke: "You poor miserable fuck."

"I love you, Lisa," I said.

She just looked away to her left.

Little did I know that that would be the beginning of two of the most miserable and invigorating years of my life.

When she looked back, she said, "Is this all you have to drink? This cheap fucking wine?"

"It's not so bad, Lisa. When I drink it, what I do is think of something pleasant as it runs down my throat—like waterfalls or a bank account of $500. Or sometimes I imagine myself in a castle with a moat. Or I imagine myself as the owner of a liquor store.

"You're crazy," she said.

And she was absolutely right.

Won't You Be My Valentine?

Norman clocked them doing 85 going north on the 405, a late model ivory Caddy, he switched on the red, they saw him and slowed. He waved them to the turn-off. They took it and he followed them down. It was 11:55 p.m. on a Wednesday night. But instead of stopping on the main boulevard the Caddy took a quick left and stopped at a residential street, flicked the lights off and sat there. Norman parked behind them, called in a check on the license. Then he got off the cycle and walked toward the driver's side with his ticket book.

The driver was a woman, about 32, with dyed red hair. She was smoking a cigarillo. Her only attire was a pair of brown, scratched boots and dirty pink panties. Her breasts were immense. On one of them were tattooed the words LOVE IS SHIT. That must have hurt.

Two fat men in their mid-forties were in the back seat. The back seat also contained a bar, a TV, and a telephone. The fat men looked very prosperous and relaxed.

"Your license, please, ma'am . . . "

"My license is up my ass," said the woman.

"That's Blanche, officer," said one of the men. "Now, Blanche, show the officer your license."

"It's up my ass," said Blanche.

"I'm going to have to cite you, ma'am, for indecent exposure, speeding, resisting arrest . . . "

Blanche turned her face full toward Norman. She spit out the cigarillo. Her large lipstick mouth snarled, showing broken yellow teeth.

"Shit, man, whattya mean? Under arrest? For fuckin' WHAT?"

"Your license, please."

"My *license*? *Here's* my fuckin' license! Take a good look at it!"

Blanche took two hands and lifted her huge left breast, which she plopped out over the edge of the window.

279

"Blanche," said the same fat man who had spoken before, "show the officer your license."

"Officer," said the other fat man, "we're sorry for all this. Blanche is very upset. Her sister died in Cleveland last night."

"Your license, please, ma'am . . . "

"Ah, kiss my pussy!"

Norman stepped back.

"All right, everybody out of the car!"

"Ah shit," said one of the fat men.

The other was on the telephone: "Hey, Bernie, we're being busted. Any instructions? Yeah? Really? O.K."

"Everybody out," Norman repeated, "NOW!"

He walked back to his cycle to radio in for a squad car.

"HEY!"

It was one of the fat men, the heaviest one. He ran up as well as he could. He was dressed in an expensive green suit. The suit was neatly fitted to mold about each of his curves of fat.

"Officer! Look! You dropped something! Lucky I saw it! Here!"

He placed six crisp new one hundred dollar bills into Norman's hand. Norman looked at the bills, hesitated a moment, then handed them back.

"For your sake, I'll pretend you never tried to bribe me."

The fat man rolled up the bills, jammed them into his pocket. He took out a cigar, lit it with a diamond-studded lighter. His eyes—what there were of them—narrowed.

"You know, you guys who always follow the book, you never get anywhere, it's all dead-end. And I mean, dead-end."

Meanwhile, back at the ivory Caddy, Blanche sat on the hood. She had lit a new cigarillo and was looking into the sky trying to locate the Milky Way.

The other fat man left the car and walked back toward the cycle. He was wearing an orange jump suit with kangaroo skin shoes. Around his neck was a huge silver cross, it was hollow inside but full, full of cocaine. An ugly film almost covered his entire left eye. But the right eye peered out, a specious but doom-filled green.

"Whatsa matter, Eddie, don't he take?"

"We got a cub Scout here, Marvin."

"That's sad."

"It's worse than sad. And it's too damned bad."

Norman picked up the mike to make his call.

Eddie pulled out the snub-nose.

"Put down the mike, officer. Please."

Norman did.

Marvin moved around behind him. Undid his holster. Took his gun. Then lifted his club.

Eddie motioned with the snub-nose.

"All right, officer, take the stroll back to the Caddy."

Norman walked back toward the car thinking, "Doesn't anybody see this?"

Where the hell is the citizenry when a cop really needs them?

For some reason he remembered the argument he had had with his wife before leaving for work. It had gotten pretty ugly. And had been over nothing. About where they would go on his vacation. She had wanted Hawaii. He had wanted Vegas.

"Hold it, Boy Scout."

They stopped while Marvin opened the rear trunk.

They moved on toward the Caddy. Blanche saw them and leaped off the hood. Her breasts almost pulled her to the asphalt as they landed.

She laughed.

"Hey, shit, what we got *there*? Can we wind it up?"

"We can do anything we want with it," said Eddie.

He pulled the rear door open, kneed Norman in the ass, shoved him in. Eddie got in on one side, Marvin the other. Blanche was at the wheel. The Caddy moved off.

Marvin whistled the opening bars of "God Bless America" and prepared himself a rum and soda from the bar.

"Care for a drink, officer?"

Norman didn't answer.

"What'll you have, Eddie?"

"Whiskey with just a splash of port."

"Blanche?"

"I'll have a sake. Hot."

"We make great hot sake, officer," said Marvin. "Sure you don't want one?"

Norman didn't answer.

"Hey, Eddie, ever noticed something?"

"Like what?"

"All traffic cops have asses shaped like Valentines."

"Yeah. Yeah. I think that's true. Wonder why that is?"

"God's ways are mysterious."

"Sure are."

Marvin passed the hot sake up to Blanche who swirled it off in one suck. She flipped the glass out the window.

"You people had better release me," Norman spoke.

"Oh, boy," said Eddie, "listen to that."

"It's sad," said Marvin.

"It's worse than sad," said Eddie.

"And too damned bad," said Blanche.

"Release me and you still have a chance," said Norman.

"You're the one whose chance is limited," said Marvin. "Officer, let me tell you something: you go by the book, you live poor and you die poor. And often, early."

Blanche turned her head.

"Ah, stop buggin' the poor creep! Guys like that, first time he jacked-off he ran to the confession box."

"Ah, said Marvin, "this guy's too dumb to even jack off."

"Shit, that's dumb . . . " said Blanche.

"Things get dumber and dumber in this Nuke age. It's sad," said Marvin.

"Worse than sad," said Eddie.

Then the ivory Caddy was back on the 405, winging through the night . . .

They pulled into a long circling drive, loomed in the silent darkness by trees with long branch arms like octopi; a bit of moon dripped through, but not much, and there were cages, some filled with birds, others with strange animals. All those—the birds, the animals were silent; they seemed contented in a kind of eternal waiting.

Then, there was a gate. Blanche touched a button in the car. The gate opened. It had long teeth, top and bottom. And as the car passed through there was a giant flash of light. The car and all its occupants were transferred to a Space Age security screen.

The flash made Norman sit upright suddenly.

"Relax, copper," said Eddie, "you are about to become part of the history of this place. Some dump. It's had many strange owners and visitors."

"Yeah," said Marvin, "like Winston Churchill paid a secret visit here, long ago, of course."

"And like," said Eddie, "they found out when Winston drank he never went to the bathroom. He just sat there and gulped down quarts of booze and just pissed and shit in his pants."

"Some stinking drunk," said Marvin.

"This fucking joint is many decades old," said Eddie. "Babe Ruth, one night he went on a binge and ripped out every toilet in the place, then gave one of the maids a thousand dollars just to suck the hair under his armpits. Some drinker, that Babe."

The car pulled up and stopped.

"Bogart once knocked out a butler who said he thought *Casablanca* was an ineffective film," said Marvin.

"They say Hitler came here after World War II," Eddie said, "and demanded rattlesnake meat for breakfast."

"Hitler died in the bunker," said Norman.

"That was a rigged scene," stated Eddie. "Hitler died in Argentina, April 3rd, 1972. Now, get out of the car!"

They all climbed out.

It was a warm night, a perfect night. As they moved toward the front door of the huge mansion, Marvin said, "You know, officer, it's too late now to take that 600. But I've got an idea that you damned well wish you had . . . right?"

"Right," said Norman, surprised that the words had come out of his mouth . . .

After they passed through a line of security guards, there he was: in front of the fireplace. With just a gentle burning of the logs. The fattest man of them all, Big Bernie.

Bernie was on the couch. Bernie almost never left the couch. He did all his business there, he fucked there, he got sucked there, he ate there, he dealt there (right off the phone), and he even slept there sometimes. There were 32 other rooms, 27 of which he hardly ever saw or wanted to see, many of them just stations of the security guards.

Big Bernie was 322, he had no children, no friends. He was on the meth and only interested in his work and income, of which most of said income was largely against the intent of the law. These resources were diverted and hidden in branches of legal business, covered and guided by some of the best lawyers and accountants in the world.

There was something almost Buddha-like about Big Bernie. And he was almost likeable. As great power sometimes makes men likeable. Because they tend to be so decently relaxed about matters major and minor.

Big Bernie watched from the couch as the group moved toward him, then stopped.

"Ah hah, what have we got here?"

"We got a cop, boss. The one we phoned in about."

Big Bernie sighed, "Damn, I hate this sort of thing! Well, I'm a fair man. Might as well send him to his grave happy. Never let it be said I had no compassion!"

Big Bernie looked over at Blanche.

"You give him a blow job now, Blanche."

"What? He's a COP! A cop killed my sister last night in that shootout in Cleveland!"

"My child, that saddened me just as much as it did you. But we must carry on. Now, unzip him and get to it!"

"Ah, shit! Do I *have* ta?"

"You do as I tell you, Blanche!"

Blanche got down on her knees and unzipped Norman.

"Shit, I hate this!"

"Half the world is run on hatred, the other half on fear. Proceed."

Blanche got going. She was a hard worker.

"Where were you born?" Big Bernie asked Norman.

Norman didn't answer.

"Answer me or you're dead with a stiff dick!"

"Pasadena, California."

"Well, you won't die there. You got any children?"

"No."

"That's good. That's real good."

Blanche kept working.

"Whatever made you want to become a cop?"

"The salary is good."

"Yeah? Compared to what? Being a dog catcher?"

"Oh," said Norman, "oh, oh, OH . . . !"

Blanche began bobbing wildly.

Norman ejaculated. Blanched zipped him up, spat on the rug, walked over to the bar, and mixed herself a whiskey sour.

Big Bernie rose from the couch and walked over to Norman. If Buddha ever walked then Big Bernie was Buddha. He looked at Marvin, shook his head sadly.

"Two things now. We've got to destroy the Caddy, even though the plates are fake. We don't take chances here. And we've got to destroy you. It's the only way. You have to realize that."

"We gotta do it," said Eddie.

"We gotta," said Marvin.

"I'm sorry," said Big Bernie.

"Fuck him!," said Blanche, gulping her drink, "he's just a cop."

"No Blanche," said Big Bernie, "cops have feelings, fears, desires, just like the rest of us."

"Fuck him!"

"Listen," said Norman, "let me go. I won't talk. I'll cover the whole thing."

"I'd like to, boy, but I can't chance it. You can ruin a 20-million-a-year business. I have 232 people working for me. You can destroy all their lives. They have families, sons and daughters in college, at Harvard, at Yale, at Stanford. I even have a man in the Senate and four in Congress. I control the mayor and the city council. I just can't chance your WORD, you understand that, don't you?"

"All right," said Norman, "but one thing I want to know. You're so smart, you're so in control of things, you know so much about what the hell you're doing, then how come you keep a dumb CUNT like Blanche around? I've met some bimbos but she's *tops*! Running around in public with bare breasts and dirty panties! And she can't even give decent head!"

"Blanche," said Big Bernie, "is my daughter."

"WHAT? And you had her give me head?"

"I know she gives lousy head, that's why I keep her practicing, so maybe one day she can give *me* better head."

"I can't believe you."

"It's straight."

"You're crazy!"

"You mean because I want better head?"

"You're some mad freak! What are you *on* anyhow?"

"Life," said Big Bernie.

Then he nodded toward Eddie and Marvin.

"All right, take care of him."

They grabbed Norman and pulled him through a doorway.

Big Bernie moved back to the couch, sat down. He turned his head a bit toward Blanche.

"Listen, baby, fix me a double whiskey."

"Whiskey and water, Dad?"

"Straight."

Big Bernie sat looking at the last burning of the logs in the fireplace. He was going to miss the ivory Caddy. But then he had four Rolls. Or was it five? It was just that the ivory Caddy made him feel like some kind of hot-shot pimp. He felt a bit tired. Running an empire was rewarding yet wearing. Each day for each man was filled with little problems that needed settling. Fail to attend to those and the walls came down. A monotonous attention to trivial detail was the secret of the grandest victories. Fail at small things, when the large ones arrived you'd lose your ass.

Blanche brought him his drink. He smiled, said, "Thank you."

A double whiskey was good for the soul.

He slammed it down and winter came to an end.

A Dirty Trick on God

Harry was in the bathtub and there was a bottle of beer on the ledge behind him. It was a bad place, an awkward place, but it was the only place to set it down. He reached around, grabbed the bottle, had a hit, and put it back down behind him.

Harry liked to drink beer in the tub. He never told anybody about it. Not that he knew too many people or even fucking wanted to. He saw enough people down at the factory every day. He was a packer. The crap came off the assembly line and he packed it. It came off the assembly line all day long and he packed it all day long. He guessed he could drink beer in the tub if he wanted to and it wasn't anybody's fucking business. He liked to get the water hot, quite hot, and then he got in and it burned a bit and he ran the cold beer down himself and it was really a relaxer—the factory dropped away and he felt almost real again.

Harry shared the apartment with Adolph, a very old man. Adolph just sat around talking about the WAR with this slight German accent. Fuck Adolph. But with the two of them paying rent Harry could have a nice apartment. Harry was tired of rooming houses. And the few times Harry picked up a woman, say in a bar, and brought her on in, Adolph understood: he vanished for a couple of hours. He'd met Adolph at a racetrack urinal. He'd pissed on one of Adolph's shoes. Adolph had been very gracious about it.

"Forget it," he had said, "it's nothing from what I've been through."

Harry had suggested a drink to make amends for his error and Adolph had accepted.

"I'm Harry Greb," he had said.

"Adolph Hitler," Adolph had said.

One drink led to another and then Adolph had mentioned the vacancy at his apartment. His buddy had died and he needed another to share the rent. And Harry had gone to see the apartment and it looked like a deal for his share of $195 and that had been it . . .

Harry washed under the armpits and under the balls, had another hit of beer. Adolph was in the other room watching cable TV. He always played it too loud. And he always watched the newscasts. The only other thing he liked was the Archie Bunker re-runs.

"HEY DOLPH! TURN THAT FUCKING THING DOWN!"

"Oh, ya, sorry . . . "

Adolph turned it down. Harry stretched out in the water. Maybe he'd get another fucking job. That fucking job was killing him. The next job would too but at least it would be a change.

Then Harry felt a fart coming on. He loved to fart in the bathtub. The bubbles would rise up and really stink. It gave him a great sense of accomplishment. Strange and good things sometimes happened in life. He remembered the morning after the big beer drunk he had shit a turd that seemed to be about two and one half feet long. Nothing like that ever. He had looked at it for some minutes. He had to take a butcher knife and cut it up so it would flush down.

The fart was too much. The bubbles shook and rattled. Harry reached around and took a good pull of beer to celebrate. Then a curious thing happened: the spot on the water where the fart had risen—that spot was becoming a brown-grey area.

"I've shit myself," thought Harry.

But it wasn't so. As Harry watched, the area began to rise slowly. It poked upward. It began to take form.

Harry was fascinated. Then fascination altered into fear—as out of the rising moil the forming became more definite. Harry's fear accelerated as a small head formed. Then arms. Little spindly arms. Then legs.

The thing bobbed up and down in the water looking at Harry. It was brown grey with tiny blue eyes and dirty blond hair.

Harry and the thing stared at each other. "I'm crazy," Harry thought. "Too many factory days, too many drunken nights. This thing isn't real. It's a spin-off from my mind. It's not real."

Harry reached his right hand out to push it through the vision. He got closer and closer to the thing with his hand. Then he extended his index finger and pushed it toward the face of the thing.

He felt a slash of pain.

The thing had bitten him!

Harry looked at his finger. The blood dripped into the water.

"You son of a bitch!" Harry yelled.

He didn't like being bitten by his own fart. He doubled his fist and swung. The thing saw it coming, leaped into the air, and Harry missed. Then the thing flipped into the water, swam around behind Harry and bit him on the ass.

Harry jumped out of the tub.

The thing was swimming about the tub on its back. Its little blue eyes seemed to be merry. Then it settled, relaxed in the center of the tub. It had a little cock and balls.

Suddenly it sent a thin spiral of water out of its mouth. It hit Harry in the face.

"ADOLPH!" Harry yelled.

"What is it?"

"Come in here!"

The door opened and Adolph was there.

"Look," said Harry, "My goddamned fart has turned on me! LOOK AT IT!"

Adolph dropped to his knees. He looked at the thing in the tub and began weeping a rather joyful weeping.

"Oh my God, mine gut . . . "

"What is it, Adolph?"

"It is . . . a little man . . . just as we planned . . . "

"As *who* planned? What the fuck you talking about?"

"Oh, my friend, we must celebrate . . . dis is dere beginning!"

"The beginning of what?"

"Come. Come, we celebrate!"

Adolph got off his knees and went into the other room.

Harry toweled off while watching that goddamned thing floating there. Then he got into his skivvies and went into the other room where Adolph had uncorked some champagne he had gotten from somewhere.

"My friend, this is one of the greatest moments of my life! Here's mud in your eye!"

Adolph lifted his drink in a toast. Henry lifted his. They clicked glasses.

They drank them down.

Then the bathroom door opened and the thing walked out. It looked like a sponge with tiny seaweed appendages. It walked across the floor and jumped into Adolph's lap.

Adolph cuddled whatever it was, then looked at Harry.

"My friend . . . you have seen here . . . one of the greatest inventions . . . greater than the atom . . . the hydrogen bomb . . . you have seen something to even make God Himself tremble, ya?"

"Hey, man, this thing came out of my ass! I can't give birth! I'm no woman!"

"Oh no, my friend, you are not a woman. But look . . . the blue eyes, the blond . . . Some baby, ya?"

The thing sat on Adolph's lap, looked steadily at Harry with those small blue eyes which seemed to loom just upon the edge of doom . . .

The next day at work, badly hungover, Harry wondered about the thing. The other workers just worked away, talking about sports, bragging about imagined exploits; others were silent, immersed in their work, beaten-down.

Harry had sat up most of the night drinking with Adolph as Adolph talked and raved about the creature.

What was that thing? Was it real? How could such a thing occur? If it were real it would seem to be a dirty trick against God.

Adolph had claimed that it was his "invention," that he and others had been working on the matter for decades . . . But how could anything be created out of a fart? A fart was a poison gas, an expelling of something bad. How could anything be created out of that? Maybe Adolph had worked some trick on him? Some illusion? He was a strange old guy, Adolph's eyes were mad, they glowed madly.

Stevenson, the foreman, walked up to Harry.

"Hey, Harry! You look like you're daydreaming! You're falling behind! Better pick it up! We got a basketful of phone numbers of guys who want your job! And maybe it's not much of a job but for a guy like you it's all there is! Now, get to it!"

"Sure. I'll pick up the pace. Don't worry."

Stevenson strolled off to see who else he could jump. The son of a bitch was right. Harry was 46. The line between Harry and skid row was a thin one, indeed. In deed and in fact. He forced himself to set a faster pace. The other packers had heard him get chewed. They loved it. With Harry as the target it made their own sorry jobs all that more secure.

But he couldn't help thinking about that "thing." What did Stevenson know? Had *he* seen that sponge thing with seaweed arms, blue eyes, blond hair? A greater invention than the atom bomb, Adolph had said . . . And now they had the hydrogen bomb and then all the nukes, nukes everywhere, stacked up and ready. Would the "thing" develop further? Harry had seen movies about "things" but this was the first one he'd ever seen in *real* life. And, it had come out of his goddamned ass!

He stopped packing a moment, reached around, touched his behind. It was rather a nervous reaction . . . all the confusion of everything.

Joe, the packer to his right, saw him.

"Got the old hemorrhoids, Harry? Go on, reach up and give them a good scratch! I won't tell anybody!"

"Kiss my ass," said Harry.

"Bend over, let me see what you got?"

"What you want, Joe, is hanging in front here! One big mouthful to rattle your tonsils!"

Stevenson came swinging back. "All right, you guys, knock off the shit! If you worked your hands like you did your mouths we'd get some goddamned PRODUCTION around here!"

I'll get both these guys some day, Harry thought. They

make each minute like an hour and each day like a week. I'll get their balls in a paper sack and take them over to the punch press.

Well, somehow the day went, it got done without too much further ugliness, just the standard grind ended as they went to their racks and got out their cards and rang out.

Ring out, thought Harry, ring out the old and the fucked and the weary again.

On the way back Harry stopped at a chain restaurant for dinner. He found a table alone. The waitress arrived. She was indifferent yet false, a bit fat and a bit unhappy. The fat and the unhappy fought each other for supremacy. She had no chance either way.

She took his order and walked off.

Then Harry began thinking about the thing again. It was surely alive. It moved. Blinked its eyes. And the teeth worked, he knew that.

He hoped Adolph knew how to housebreak the thing. What would it eat? Dog food? He hoped it wasn't cannibalistic.

Harry looked around at the people. They all looked ugly and tired. They were ugly and tired. They were losers. Where were the winners? Where were the beautiful people? All these around him: it seemed to be a crime to be alive. And he was one of them.

Harry sighed and looked down at his work-beaten hands. Hell, he was tired but it wasn't a good tiredness. It was like he had been gypped. Well, he had plenty of company: a world-full.

The waitress brought his plate. She slammed it down, smiled a horrible false smile, said "ENJOY!" with a rasping voice, began to walk off.

"Waitress," Harry said, "please don't forget the coffee."

She stopped, turned. "Oh yeah . . . Cream and sugar?"

"Straight," Harry answered.

"Like an arrow?" she forced a smile, thinking of her tip.

Harry answered, "Like an arrow."

The food was greasy and sad. The plate had a crack

which ran in from the edge and looked like a long hair. The coffee was bitter and doomed. Well, there was nothing to do but consume the mess. You couldn't live on air. Not that air out there. Harry worked away. All about him the people consumed their food in a dark surrender.

The waitress arrived to refill his coffee cup.

"Everything all right, sir?"

"Yeah," said Harry . . .

Then he was in the tub again, the water steaming hot, the beer cold. For Harry, that was as close as he could get to a peaceful mood. Stevenson was far away. These moments were his, entirely. Not that he really did anything with his moments. But at least somebody else wasn't using them. He took a great gulp of beer. Now we was equal to anybody, a president, a king, a movie star, a TV comedian.

Harry relaxed, noticed the cracks in the ceiling. He'd never noticed them before. The cracks formed a pattern. He could make it out. Quite strange and beautiful. Or maybe only nice: a great bull charging.

Then Harry felt like farting. He let it go. It was a good one. It boiled up out of the water. The bubbles almost rang.

As long as man could fart he stood a chance.

It really stank.

Harry reached around for a beer to celebrate. He got it, took a good hit.

Then he noticed the brown pool on the water. Then . . . the brown turned a brown-grey. Then . . . the area began to rise . . . slowly. It poked upwards . . . and began to take form.

A small head formed. Then arms. Little spindly arms. Then legs.

The hair was long and dark, the eyes green. The mouth formed a tiny smile and it began to swim around the tub.

Harry noticed the small breasts. It was a little woman, a woman-thing with the same sponge-like body and sea-weed arms. It swam about the tub.

"ADOLPH!" Harry yelled.

"What is it?"

"Come in here!"

The door opened and Adolph was there.

"Look," said Harry, "look what happened to my fart! It happened again! Why? What the hell's going on here? I can't even fart without this stupid thing happening!"

"Ah, my God in heaven, WE HAVE DONE IT!"

"Done what? Get that goddamned thing out of the tub!"

Adolph reached out his arms. "Come, my darling!"

The little bitch leaped out of the water and onto one of Adolph's arms and up that arm and then jumped up onto his shoulder.

"Listen, Adolph, what's going on here?"

"It's just a little bit of something I put in your beer."

"Listen, man, I want you to stop fucking with my beer!"

"Oh, no more now! These two are all we need now . . . "

He smiled at the little woman on his shoulder. "Come, my darling, I want you to meet a friend . . . "

And he walked away with the little woman . . .

At the factory the next day it was about the same. Harry felt like an experimental rat running on a treadmill. No matter how you kept going you go nowhere. All you could do, finally, was die. Meanwhile, you kept going, uselessly. Christ, didn't the others ever think about it? He looked over at Joe to his right. Joe was packing away. He had a cap on his head with the bill turned to the back. He was chewing gum.

Harry looked at the assembly line. All girls. And not a looker on the line. The girls moved deftly and with agility, keeping up with the line. They were good at that. And they showed no pain. The made little jokes. Sometimes they swore, other times they laughed. They went on, minute after minute, day after day. Food, shelter, and clothing. Transportation. Subsistence.

Stevenson came by. "How's it going, Harry?"

"Smooth, Mr. Stevenson, real smooth."

"O.K., keep it that way."

Stevenson walked on off . . .

Harry decided not to eat that night. He stopped at a bar near the apartment. It was a dreary place, full of dull and lonely people. The bartender's face was full of warts and there was a faint smell to him, an unkindly smell, something like the smell of piss.

"Yeh?" he asked Harry.

"Draft beer," Harry answered.

The bartender put the glass under the spigot, pulled the handle, and the beer came out, only it was mostly foam, a yellow curling foam, demented. As the foam spilled over the top of the glass the barkeeper took two fingers of his left hand and cut the excess off. He plopped the glass on the bar and the foam rand down the sides wetting the bar— highlighting the grains whereupon somebody had crudely carved in the word "SHIT."

"Nice night," the barkeeper said.

"Yeh," said Harry.

Harry worked at the beer, somehow got it down. Meanwhile, the conversations he heard about him were hardly endearing. It seemed almost as if people pretended to be stupid. So then, just to prove the fuckers couldn't run him out, Harry ordered another beer. It had more foam than the other. He worked at it. What an existence. You got fucked over at work and then when you came out to spend your money you got fucked over again. Everything possible was done to screw you up. No wonder the jails and the madhouses were overcrowded, no wonder skid row was packed.

Harry finished his beer. Nothing to do but go back to the apartment.

When Harry got there he had a long hot shower. To hell with that bathtub. He toweled off, got into some fresh clothes, and joined Adolph in the other room. Adolph was reading the *Wall Street Journal*. Harry sat down, picked up the daily paper from the coffee table. Same crap. Little wars everywhere. They were afraid to have the big one. Maybe some day it would come anyhow. All it took was one finger on one man to start it. Seemed like it was impossible not to happen. What a thing to think about after busting your ass in a factory all day and then drinking bad beer. He put the paper down.

"Hey, Adolph!"

"Yes, my friend . . . "

"Where are those two things?"

"In the bedroom."

"What are they doing there?"

"My friend, they are not sleeping . . . "

"Don't they need sleep?"

Adolph put the *Wall Street Journal* down. "These creatures . . . they don't need sleep. Or food. Or water."

"How do they get their energy?"

"Oh, that! That's a secret. I will tell you, though part of it is from the sun. Other sources, I cannot tell you . . . "

"Do they have to go to the bathroom?"

"No, they are not like us."

"Are they like us in any way?"

"They are like most of us in two ways, at least."

"Like?"

"They reproduce and they take orders. They reproduce and they obey."

"Listen, Adolph, I don't want those things running around the apartment."

Adolph picked up the *Wall Street Journal* and began reading again.

"Put that paper down, Adolph, I haven't finished talking to you!"

Adolph put the paper down and smiled. "Hard day at the office, Harry?"

"I don't want those two things running around the apartment!"

"Ah, I am so sorry, Harry, but there will be *more* than two. You see, these creatures reproduce in from 2 to 8 hours."

"What the fuck you telling me, Adolph?"

"That *this* is the greatest miracle yet, Harry, don't you REALIZE that? It's the greatest miracle since man walked the earth! Just allow yourself to THINK about it! A NEW LIFE FORM! And, you, yourself, helped evolve it! Can't you fathom the immensity of all this?"

"But what *good* are these things?"

"What good, indeed? These 'things' as you call them . . . they need no food, no water. They are loyal and obedient."

"They sound like slaves."

"Slaves, ha!" Suddenly Adolph's eyes blazed furiously. "THINK WHAT AN ARMY THEY'D MAKE!"

"Army?"

"Yes, and they could survive a nuclear attack for they have no needs. Isn't life finally strange?"

"What do you mean?"

"I mean because of the nuclear arms race most of us have felt that the world is doomed, or almost doomed, that there could be no alternative but total or near-total destruction. And now we have created these durable and self-sufficient creatures. There's hope now."

"But these aren't human. What about the humans?"

"There should be a few humans left to ally themselves with these new creatures. There will be hope and a rebuilding *and* a surviving nation."

"Which one?"

"That too, my friend, is a secret."

"Sounds like crap to me that those fucking sponges could do anything."

"Ah, my friend, if you could only know how carefully we have planned over all these decades."

"'We'? Who's 'we'?"

Adolph's eyes narrowed. For a moment he looked very dangerous. Then, he smiled. "Ah, Harry! I've just been JOKING with you! You see, I am just going to raise a few of these and then sell them to a circus. A freak show, you know. The Walking Sponges. The crowd will love them."

Adolph picked up the *Wall Street Journal*, glanced at Harry over the top of the page, then began reading again.

Harry got up and went to the refrigerator for a beer. When he came back Adolph was gone. Harry sat down with his beer and flipped on the Johnny Carson show . . .

He watched TV for some hours, drinking many beers. Between the factory and Adolph, life had become a little bit too much for him. After some time he passed out only to be aroused by something. The room was dark. He could make out the form of Adolph and then Adolph said, "NOW!" and five or six sponges rushed upon him. He knocked one off into space, catching it with a good right. It bounced right up and rushed him again. And the others were upon him. The things were powerful. He felt himself being lifted and he was being carried. He struggled but it was useless. The apartment door opened and he was carried down the hall. It was as if he were being flung along by a tornado.

Then they were outside. They were by his car. How did they know? He felt a seaweed hand go into his pants pocket for his keys. The thing had a sort of built-in prescience.

They unlocked the car doors, flung him into the front seat next to the driver. The driver started the car. The sponge knew how to drive.

Harry was driven down a street of night by sponges.

"God," he thought, "I am being taken for a ride! Just like a gangster movie."

"Hey, look," Harry said, "you're not going to get away with this! You're going to stop at a traffic light and somebody is going to see a *sponge* driving and all those other sponges sitting around. You'll be exposed!"

"Let us worry about that," said the driver.

"Hey, you guys can talk! Why haven't you spoken before this?"

"Speech is the last factor to develop in our make-up."

"But what do you know? You don't *know* anything!"

"We're programmed. Try us."

"Who sewed the 13 stars on the American flag?"

"Betsy Ross."

"Name a great American actress."

"Bette Davis."

"Name me a one-eyed black Jew."

"Sammy Davis Jr."

Harry leaned back. They were going to take him to some secluded spot and kill him, then return to Adolph and continue the master plan. History was riding along with him in his 8-year-old car.

Then they stopped at a traffic light. Another car pulled up along beside them.

"Make a sound," said one of the sponges, "and you're dead now."

Harry looked over at the other car. It was *Stevenson*, for Christ's sake! He was drunk and he was sitting in his car with a drunken floozie. Stevenson was smoking a cigar. Then Harry saw the floozie dive down to Stevenson's middle. Stevenson stared straight ahead. The floozie was giving him a blowjob right there at the traffic light.

The light changed and the sponge at the wheel dug out leaving Stevenson back there getting his. Harry knew he didn't have much time left. He had to think, and fast.

"Now look," he said to the sponges, "I am the FATHER of two of you and grandfather to the rest. Do you realize that? Do you want to kill your father?"

"Who doesn't want to kill the father?" asked the sponge driving the car.

"Dostoevski," said one of the sponges in the back seat.

"Yes, Ivan in *The Brothers Karamazov*," said another sponge.

Then they were on the freeway. It was a night more warm and splendid than most. Harry wished more than anything to be back at the factory again, to be dull and bored, to be useless, to be stupid, to be a slave. He wanted to drink more foamy and poisonous beer. He wanted to find a crass and unfeeling whore for his love.

"How can I get out of this?" he asked them.

"No way," one of them answered, "you know too much."

"Your goose is cooked," said another.

"You're up shit creek without a paddle," added another.

"We were created to re-create history," said the driver, "and you, my friend, are only a cipher in the totality."

"Thanks, motherfucker," said Harry.

They disgusted him. Their complete inhumanness. Farts out of his ass driving him to his very death. Sickening. Because he might spill the beans on the 2,000-year secret of the Reichstag. And Stevenson getting head at a traffic light. A wave of blackness passed over Harry.

They began to pass a gasoline tanker on the right and Harry grabbed the wheel and twisted it to the right and the car spun in a full circle in front of the tanker. The driver hit the brakes but it was useless.

There was the sound of the tanker groveling and grinding into the automobile.

There seemed a moment of nothing, then the auto advanced into a sheet of flame. With the tanker still pushing at it.

The driver finally halted his machine, then reversed it to back off from the fire as a Volks hit his rear, flipped, and went over the side of the freeway.

The tanker didn't ignite.

The driver edged his machine over to the freeway ledge, got out with road flares, and placed them around the tanker and then the flaming auto exploded. The tanker still lucked it but the driver was blown backwards. He got up, still all right except most of his eyelids were burned off.

When the squad car got there he told the cop, "I don't know what the hell happened. This guy just spun in front of me. That's all I know . . . "

Two days later in both of the major newspapers of that city an ad appeared:

WANTED; PARTNER TO SHARE EXPENSES IN A MODERN APARTMENT. ALL CONVENIENCES. CABLE TV, WALL TO WALL CARPETING. SOUNDPROOF. I AM A CONGENIAL AND UNDERSTANDING PERSONALITY THOUGH PRIVATE IN NATURE. REFERENCES REQUIRED. NO PETS. GENTLEMAN PREFERRED. $195 PER MONTH. NO FIRST OR LAST. CONTACT: A.H., 555-2729, 9 A.M. to 10 P.M.

The Bell Tolls for No One

When I got home from the auto parts warehouse—well, wait, it wasn't a home, it was a room, a room in a roominghouse—I opened the door and there were two men sitting there.

"Are you Henry Chinaski?" one of them asked.

Both men were dressed in grey suits and wore blue neckties and they really looked quite similar. Their faces were a bland, almost yellow color. They looked neither angry or unpleasant. But they did look proficient at whatever they wanted. And they wanted me.

"I'm Henry Chinaski."

"Do you want to put on a coat or something?" the other man asked.

"What for?"

"You're coming with us."

"For how long."

"For a long time, I think."

I didn't ask who they were. I felt it would please them too much. I walked to the closet and opened the door. They both stood watching me.

"Just reach for the COAT!"

I reached for the only coat I had.

"Put your hands behind your back."

I did and they snapped the handcuffs on. They seemed angry then. The man who applied the cuffs really snapped them on tight, digging the steel hard against the flesh.

I didn't say anything. They didn't tell me my rights like they did in the movies.

"O.K.," said one of them, "let's go . . . "

They pushed me through the door and down the stairway. Halfway down one of them shoved me and I rolled down the stairway. I cracked my head against the wall but what really hurt was rolling over the handcuffs.

I got up and waited for them.

They pushed me through the front door. Then at the top of the steps, leading to the street, each of them took me by the armpit and lifted me into the air and ran me down the steps, my legs dangling. I felt like some wooden and freaky toy.

There was a car down there, black. They stood me there, opened a back door and threw me in. I landed on the floor-boards. Then I was yanked up and placed between the two men in the back seat. The other two men got in the front, started the car and we drove off.

One of the men in the front, the one who wasn't driving, turned and spoke to the men in the back seat: "I've picked up a lot of men in my time but never one like this!"

"What ya mean?"

"I mean, he doesn't seem to give a damn."

"Yeah?"

"Yeah. He's got to be a prick, a real prick!"

Then the man in the front turned forward again.

The man to my left asked, "You a tough guy?"

"No."

The man to my right asked, "You think your shit doesn't stink?"

"My shit stinks."

We drove along in silence for a while.

Then the man in front turned again.

"See what I mean?"

"Yeah," said the man to my right, "he's too fucking cool."

"I don't like this guy," said the man to my left.

I watched the familiar buildings on the familiar streets go by.

"I could punch you out," said the guy to my right, "and nobody would ever know."

"That's true."

"Fuckin' wise-ass!"

He swung his fist in a short swift arc and it landed in my belly center. There was a flash of darkness, a flash of red, then it cleared. There was fire and whirling in my gut. I concentrated on the sound of the car motor as if it were my friend.

"Now," the man asked, "did I hit you?"

"No."

"Why are you so fuckin' cool?"

"I'm not cool. You guys are best."

"He's a fuckin' freak," said the man to my left, "he's a geek, he's a goddamned GEEK!"

Then he swung, again into my gut. It got to my breathing. I couldn't suck in air, my eyes began to water. Then I felt like puking. Something did rush up—blood or matter— I swallowed it back down. When I swallowed it, it seemed to soothe the pain.

"Now, did I hit you?"

"No."

"Why don't you ask us to stop?"

"Stop."

"You fuckin' geek!"

One of them slammed me across the face with an open palm. One of my teeth cut something inside of my mouth and I could taste the blood.

"Aren't ya gonna ask us why we're picking you up?"

"No."

"You prick. You PRICK!"

Something cracked across the back of my neck. Inside of my mind a huge yellow face looked at me and it had a red mouth which was half-grinning, half-smiling, just about to go into laughter. Then, I was into unconsciousness . . .

It was no longer evening. It was early night, a clear moonlit night. And I was being pushed through tall wet grass surrounded by trees. The grass was about knee-high and wet, it brushed along my legs and it was soothing. I was in a numb state. I could no longer feel the handcuffs against my wrists.

Then they stopped. They spun me about and stood there looking at me.

The men were all about the same size and weight. There seemed to be no leader.

"O.K., asshole," one of them said, "you know what this is all about, don't you?"

"No."

"Goddamn him! I really hate this fucker!"

Strangely then, I thought of myself in a bathtub, a bathtub full of very hot water and I was washing myself under
the arms while looking at the small cracks in the ceiling—
cracks shaped like lions and elephants, and there was one
large tiger, leaping.

"You got one last chance," one of them said, "say something . . . "

"Vacuum."

"That does it."

"Let's mutilate the son of a bitch!"

"Yeah, but first let's humiliate him!"

"Yeah."

In the night I could hear the sound of birds, crickets,
frogs . . . a dog barked and way off I could hear a train;
everything was graceful and full. I could smell the green
of the grass, I could even smell the tree trunks, and I could
smell the earth the way a dog smells the earth.

One of them grabbed me by the hair and threw me to
the ground, then yanked me up by the hair and I was on
my knees.

"Whatya got to say now, cool boy?

"Take the bracelets off and I'll whip your ass."

"Sure I will, cool boy, only first you gotta do this . . . "

He unzipped his pants and pulled out his penis. The
others laughed.

"You do a good job, no biting, just tongue it and suck
it and swallow it and then we'll take off the cuffs and see
what you can do."

"No."

"You're gonna do it *anyhow*, cool boy! Because I *said* so!"

"No."

I heard the safety go off.

"One last chance . . . ."

"No."

"*Shit*!"

The gun fired. There was a searing rip, and numbness.
Then a drip of blood. And more dripping of blood where
my left ear had been . . . .there were pieces and shards.

"Why didn't you kill him?"

"I don't know . . . ."

"You think we got the right guy?"

"I don't know. He doesn't act like the guy we want."

"What would he act like?"

"You know . . . ."

"Yeah."

I could still hear them. I could still hear. There was no
pain for the missing ear, just a feeling of coolness as if somebody had stuck a large piece of ice into the left side of my
head.

Then I saw them walking away. They just walked away
and then I was alone. And it was darker and colder.

I managed to stand up.

Curiously, I didn't feel bad at all. I began to walk along
not knowing where I was or where I could go.

Then in front of me there was an animal. It looked like
a large dog, a wild dog. The moon was to my back and it
shone into the beast's eyes. The eyes were red like burning
coal.

Then I had the urge to urinate. With the cuffs behind
me, I let it go. I could feel the warm piss running down my
front, down my right leg.

The beast began a long slow growl. It rose from his in-
nards and passed through the night . . . .

He bunched his body for the leap.

I knew that if I moved backwards that I was finished.

I ran forward, kicked out and missed, fell to my side,
rolled over just in time as the flash of fangs ripped the quiet
air, I got to my feet and faced the thing again, thinking, this
must happen all the time to everybody . . . one way or the
other . . . .

Bibliography

"A Kind, Understanding Face," unpublished, 1948

"Save the World," *Kauri* 15, July–August 1966

"The Way the Dead Love," *Congress* 1, 1967

"Notes of a Dirty Old Man," *Open City*, August 10–16, 1967

"Notes of a Dirty Old Man," *Open City*, November 1–7, 1968

"No Quickies, Remember," *Fling*, September 1971

"Notes of a Dirty Old Man," *NOLA Express*, September 9–23, 1971

"The Looney Ward," *Fling*, November, 1971

"Dancing Nina," *Fling*, January, 1972

"Notes of a Dirty Old Man," *NOLA Express*, January 27, 1972

"Notes of a Dirty Old Man," *L.A. Free Press*, February 25, 1972

"Notes of a Dirty Old Man," *L.A. Free Press*, May 12, 1972.

"Notes of a Dirty Old Man," *L.A. Free Press*, June 2, 1972

"Notes of a Dirty Old Man," *L.A. Free Press*, June 16, 1972

"Notes of a Dirty Old Man," *L.A. Free Press*, July 28, 1972

"A Piece of Cheese," *Fling*, March 1972

"Notes of a Dirty Old Man," *L.A. Free Press*, December 15, 1972

"Notes of a Dirty Old Man," *L.A. Free Press*, March 30, 1973.

"Notes of a Dirty Old Man," *L.A. Free Press*, April 20, 1973

"Notes of a Dirty Old Man," *L.A. Free Press*, May 11, 1973

"Notes of a Dirty Old Man," *L.A. Free Press*, June 8, 1973

"Notes of a Dirty Old Man: A Day in the Life of an Adult Book-
    store Clerk," *L.A. Free Press*, June 22, 1973

"Notes of a Dirty Old Man," *L.A. Free Press*, July 6, 1973

"Notes of a Dirty Old Man," *L.A. Free Press*, December 14, 1973.

"Notes of a Dirty Old Man," *L.A. Free Press*, March 29, 1974

"Notes of a Dirty Old Man," *L.A. Free Press*, June 14, 1974

"Notes of a Dirty Old Man," *L.A. Free Press*, August 9, 1974

"Notes of a Dirty Old Man," *L.A. Free Press*, September 27, 1974

"Notes of a Dirty Old Man," *L.A. Free Press*, December 20, 1974

"Notes of a Dirty Old Man," *L.A. Free Press*, December 27, 1974

"Notes of a Dirty Old Man," *L.A. Free Press*, January 3, 1975

"Notes of a Dirty Old Man," *L.A. Free Press*, February 21, 1975

"Notes of a Dirty Old Man," *L.A. Free Press*, February 28, 1975

"Notes of a Dirty Old Man," *L.A. Free Press*, August 8–14, 1975.

"Notes of a Dirty Old Man," *L.A. Free Press*, November 14–20, 1975

"Notes of a Dirty Old Man," *L.A. Free Press*, January 2–6, 1976.

"An Affair of Very Little Importance," *Hustler*, May, 1978

"Break-In," *Hustler*, March 1979

"Flying Is the Safest Way to Travel," unpublished, 1979

"Fly the Friendly Skies," *Oui*, January 1984

"The Lady with the Legs," *Hustler,* July 1985

"Won't You Be My Valentine?"*Oui*, June 1985

"A Dirty Trick on God," *Oui*, April 1985

"The Bell Tolls for No One," *Oui,* September 1985